His Yankee Bride

ROSE GORDON

HIS BROTHER'S BRIDE

Published by Parchment & Plume, LLC
www.parchmentandplume.com

Other Titles Available

SCANDALOUS SISTERS SERIES
Intentions of the Earl (Book 1)
Liberty for Paul (Book 2)
 To Win His Wayward Wife (Book 3)

GROOM SERIES
Her Sudden Groom (Book 1)
Her Reluctant Groom (Book 2)
Her Secondhand Groom (Book 3)
Her Imperfect Groom (Book 4)

BANKS BROTHERS BRIDES SERIES
His Contract Bride
His Yankee Bride
His Jilted Bride
His Brother's Bride

OFFICER SERIES (AMERICAN SET)
The Officer and the Bostoner
The Officer and the Southerner
The Officer and the Traveler

Coming Soon!
GENTLEMEN OF HONOR
Secrets of the Viscount
Desires of the Baron
Passions of the Gentleman

~Chapter One~

May 1787
England

John Banks shut his Bible and heaved a heavy sigh. It was days like today when being the youngest son of a baron was not nearly as appealing as being the oldest.

But that was John's lot in life. He wasn't the oldest; therefore, he had only three options: he could become a barrister, which he detested the thought of; an officer in the military, which made him shudder to think of; or a vicar. Even common born men had more options than he did. He nearly snorted. Even some *criminals* had more options than John did. At least they could be transported far away, then... Well, that's the end of their advantage over John. Truly, once they arrived at wherever they were transported, it could not be a good experience.

"Is something the matter, John?" Edward, Lord Watson, and John's eldest brother asked, coming into the room where John spent no less than eight hours a day reading his Bible in solitude; Edward's wife, Regina, and their three-year-old son, Alex, coming in right behind him.

"No. I'm just memorizing Psalms 119."

Regina's brown eyebrows furrowed. "Didn't you say that was the longest chapter in the Bible?"

"Yes."

Edward lifted Alex onto his shoulders and walked to the bookshelves, telling him to pick any book he'd like. While Alex studied the red, green, blue and black spines with gold lettering, Edward said, "Well, I wish you the best of luck with that."

Regina cleared her throat. Then, lacking the desired result, she cleared it again.

Edward sighed. "All right, Alex, it appears your mama will be the one reading to you. We'd better go look at the storybooks so she doesn't fall asleep reading you one of these vastly interesting science tomes you love so much."

Regina smiled and shook her head. She was a good sort; quiet, amiable, humorous at times, and always understanding. She'd make an excellent wife for a vicar. How unfortunate Edward married her first. Not that there was really anything unfortunate about it. Their marriage was arranged, and John was only fourteen at the time of the wedding, far too young to know to be jealous. But ever since he'd gotten to know her, he knew he desired his wife to have the same temperament.

Alex closed his fingers around the spine of the book he wanted and gave it a hearty jerk, leading it to fall from the shelf and smack his father right in the nose. John grinned. The times had been countless when John had wished *he* could have gotten away with hitting his brother that way.

As if he'd read his mind, Edward shot him a pointed glance.

John threw his hands into the air. "Don't look at me. I didn't tell him to drop the book on your face."

"No, but I'm sure you'll reward him with a biscuit for his excellent aim later."

"Can't blame an uncle for spoiling his favorite nephew, can you?" John asked.

Edward shook his head and lowered Alex to the ground before picking up the fallen book. Regina took it from him and John looked away. Those two had been married almost five years and still looked at each other as if they'd married only a week ago. That was another thing he admired about Regina: she confined her affections for her husband to the bedroom. Not that other ladies didn't, but that was because most ladies he knew didn't actually love their husbands. And the few who did had a hard time keeping their hands—and lips—to themselves. He shuddered at the memory of Lord and Lady Craven, who were rumored to have a love match, sharing a close embrace when they thought nobody else was around.

But John had been around, and he'd forever be plagued with the memories of the couple engaging in intimacies better suited for the bedchamber.

"Come along, Alex," Regina called to her son, holding her hand out for him to hold.

"Is something troubling you, Trouble?" Edward asked, falling into the chair opposite him. "Are you struggling with what to preach about after dinner tonight?"

"No, Edward," he said with a sigh and a slight smile at his brother's nickname for him based on all the "trouble" he'd been accused of causing when he was younger. "With all *your* deplorable habits, I doubt I'll ever run out of things to preach about."

"Good. I should hate for it to be said that I'm the kind of older brother who neglects the needs of his younger brother—even his need to practice putting everyone to sleep with his preaching each night."

John smiled weakly at his jest. Truly, that's all it was. Edward didn't say it to be cruel or because he was annoyed with him and his past behavior. But, it didn't make it any less true. In the time since he'd concluded his studies at Eton—and for as much of his life as he could remember before then, if the truth had to be exposed—he'd been memorizing Bible passages, giving Biblically based advice, and delivering impromptu sermons as part of his ministry training. And why shouldn't he? Edward always knew he'd grow up to one day be a baron and spent his life looking after others and learning the skills he'd need to be a baron. So why shouldn't John have spent his life preparing for his future? Because it was maddening; that's why!

Not to imply that the Lord's work was maddening, mind you. But the always being honest, always thinking before acting, and the overwhelming pressure that every word you say or action you take could one day be used against you and ruin your entire future was more than any gentleman at the ripe young age of nineteen should be concerned about. But John was, and the pressure was threatening to surround him until the last atom of oxygen in his lungs was squeezed out.

"John, have you considered that a life in the ministry isn't for you?" Edward's softly spoken words startled him straight from his woolgathering.

"There isn't another option." He glanced out the window. "At least not one I care to pursue."

Edward nodded. "I can accept that. An officer's life isn't for everyone."

"And neither is a barrister's," John added.

"No, it's not." Edward ran his hand through his hair. "Have you considered going on a Grand Tour?"

"No. It's too late for that now anyway. The archbishop said he'd have placement for me in June. That's not enough time."

Edward waved him off. "Then go on Tour and have the archbishop assign you to another mentor when you return. There will always be lost souls in need of saving, John. The profession is not on the verge of extinction. It won't hurt you to delay your life's work by a few months or even a year."

John exhaled. Edward didn't understand.

"I understand more than you might think," Edward said softly. He grinned. "I seem to remember a conversation we had a few years ago when I reminded you that I, too, was once fourteen. Fortunately, the circumstances of this conversation are vastly different; but I can also tell you that I, too, was once nineteen and felt the weight of the rest of my life and the future of all of you boys pressing down on me. Father had just died, and I didn't have a choice but to step up and fulfill my role as baron. I'm not saying that your role in life is any less important, but your need to begin is not immediate. Go and have a bit of fun now while you still can."

John sat motionless as his brother left the room. Then, he picked up his Bible and flipped it open, resigning himself to the fact that living in a metaphorical glass box where he could be observed and made an example of for the rest of his life was what his life was to be. The words blurred in front of him. This couldn't be it. He was only nineteen! Far too young to live out the rest of his days in a small country village, precisely what would happen as soon as the archbishop found placement for him. He shut his Bible again and set it down on the table in front of him. Perhaps Edward understood better than John thought he did. What would it hurt to spend a little time seeing the world? Then, when he was done, he could return and settle in to a calm serene life as a country vicar and find a meek and mild lady to be his wife.

~ Chapter Two ~

July 1788
Charleston, South Carolina

"The only thing that could salvage this ball would be if everyone stopped dancing and played charades," Carolina Ellis whispered to her friend and neighbor Marjorie Reynolds, who was standing in the back corner of the ballroom with her.

"I thought you liked to dance."

Carolina tucked a tendril of her long curly, brown hair behind her ear. "It's not the dancing I don't like. It's the talking to all the dimwitted gentlemen I find annoying. At least with charades, everyone has to keep quiet unless guessing the act."

The corners of Marjorie's lips twitched in what seemed to be the only open expression of humor or amusement she had shown since the end of the war. Not that Marjorie actually had a reason to smile. She didn't. The war had taken so much from her, from her family's home and wealth to Marjorie's own fiancé. "Surely, it's not that bad."

"Surely it is," Carolina countered, tamping down her jealousy for her friend never being asked to dance. "The worst is when they try to infuse a history lesson about the formation of the city during their dance."

"And you don't like that?" Though her facial expression was bland, Marjorie's gray eyes danced with amusement.

"No," Carolina confirmed, scowling. "Truly, I don't know which is worse: when they try to educate me on the wisdom of how old Charles Towne came to be; or when they think it's oh-so-fascinating to tell me about when what's-his-name advised they build the streets wide in the city, so as the city expanded, houses and land wouldn't have to be compromised."

"Perhaps you'd do well to have a retelling of that one," Marjorie teased.

"No, thank you. I might not remember his name, but I certainly remember the rest." She'd never be so rude as to voice this to Marjorie, who seemed never to have a dance partner; but in her mind, she'd always try to guess which historical fact her current dance partner would use in his attempt to impress her.

"Oh, look who just walked in."

Carolina wasn't sure she wanted to look, but did so anyway. "Willard Boyles."

"You don't sound very excited," Marjorie murmured.

"That's because I'm not. Of course, Mother thinks he'd be a good match, but— Oh dear, he's coming this way." Carolina bit her lip and looked to Marjorie. "May I take your glass?"

Marjorie started. "No, I'm not finished drinking it. Besides, I know what you're about, and it won't work. You'll just have to dance with him yourself."

Carolina thought to protest, but before she could, Mr. Boyles walked up.

"Miss Ellis," he said.

Carolina stared at him but didn't respond.

"Miss Reynolds," he said reluctantly.

"Mr. Boyles," Marjorie said.

"Would you care to dance, Miss Ellis?" Mr. Boyles asked.

Though she'd like to, she couldn't very well make a scene and refuse him until he treated her friend better. Marjorie couldn't help that her family had gone from being one of the wealthiest in the lowlands to the absolute poorest in the span of a night. But whether *she* could help it or not, it had changed how people treated her. With the same reluctance Mr. Boyles had shown with his muttered greeting to Marjorie, Carolina accepted his offer.

"How are you finding the city?" Mr. Boyles asked once they

were on the dance floor.

"Very well," she said without thought, the same way she answered all the others who asked her the same question.

"Good," he said with a curt nod. "When I first came here fifteen years ago to start my upholstery shop, I found it to be quite lacking in comparison to where I grew up in Philadelphia. But I've grown fond of old Charles Towne since then."

Carolina involuntarily jerked in his hold. Whether due to his indirect reminder of how much older he was than she, or the fact he'd referred to Charleston as Charles Towne, which admittedly was the original name but not used since the colonies had formed a union and gained their independence, she'd never know.

The wistful smile on his face made her uneasy. While he was a prominent citizen who'd never be confused for a loyalist or falsely accused of being one due to his slip, the fact that he appeared to be transported back in time to when he'd first arrived was unnerving —but not unheard of. Many of the gentlemen she'd met who were past thirty had a habit of doing this.

"Did you know when Charleston was first being settled, it was suggested that the streets..."

Carolina pressed her lips together to suppress the small giggle that was threatening to burst forth from her lips. She *knew* it! Sadly, this game of guessing which historical fact her dance partner would choose to bore her with was the only interesting thing she'd found to entertain herself with since coming to Charleston. It was also the reason she'd likely remain single until her dying day if she didn't depart this life early due to death by tedium. Or marry Charlie. Not that *that* was even a viable option as far as she was concerned.

"Say," Mr. Boyles said, breaking into her thoughts when the music reached a softer part, "did you know that according to Poor Richard's Almanac, it's supposed to be a harsh winter this year?"

"Is that so?" Carolina murmured, inwardly cringing. She hated discussing the weather and what it'd mean for next year's planting season almost as much as being bombarded with historical facts.

"Sure is," he said with a nod. "Is your father worried about what that'll do to his land before next planting season?"

Carolina nearly groaned. "I don't know." And that was the truth. She didn't know, nor did she care. Other than the fact that her family grew indigo on a thousand acre plantation located on the westward outskirts of Charleston, she didn't know—or care—much about what they did. Sure, it was her family's livelihood and the legacy they'd pass down through the generations. But that mattered naught to Carolina. The family's plantation and the wealth that went along with it would pass to her cousin Robert if she didn't marry a man who wanted it—not that she minded Robert inheriting it. She didn't. She'd spent her entire life on the plantation, playing with the field hands' and house workers' children when her brother or the closest neighbor children weren't around. Plantations and all that went with them were not for her.

That's why she'd hoped she'd make a match during her time in Charleston. But with each Charleston gentleman she met, she was swiftly becoming convinced that gentlemen born of sophistication were no more entertaining than the pigs her brother had once kept.

And Willard Boyles with his talk of crops was just as dull as all the others she'd met.

Blessedly the reel ended before Mr. Boyles could bore her into a state of unconsciousness.

"Wait here and I'll get you a new glass of punch."

The only way Carolina would wait there was if thousand pound weights suddenly attached themselves to her ankles. It wasn't that Mr. Boyles was a bad sort. He was just tedious; and if she were made to endure his company much longer, she might blurt something unkind.

She made her way back across the room to where Marjorie stood alone in the corner.

She so desperately wished some gentleman would see fit to ask Marjorie to dance; then, the others might do the same. Carolina knew better than to ask any of her dance partners to ask Marjorie to dance though. Marjorie might not enjoy coming to this particular assembly each year, but she hated pity even more; and while Carolina's motives were inspired by anything but pity, Marjorie might not see them that way.

"You didn't have to come back," Marjorie said.

"Nonsense. I wanted to."

"You're a good friend, Carolina." Her whispered words made Carolina's heart squeeze.

"And so are you." No matter what others thought of Marjorie and her unfortunate situation, Carolina would always be her friend. Mounds of wealth and the nicest things money could buy wouldn't alter that. She craned her neck to see around the man right in front of her. "I think your mother is looking for you."

"It's probably time for us to go," Marjorie said, setting her empty glass on the window sill. "Our crops are ready to harvest, so we have to get back to the plantation early tomorrow."

Carolina didn't know whether the part about the crops being ready was true or not, but she had no intention of embarrassing Marjorie by questioning the truth of her statement. "Very well; I hope you have a safe journey. Would it be all right if I came to see you when I return to the country?"

Marjorie bit her lip and a pale blush stole over her cheeks. "I'd love to see you, but..."

"Then it's settled," Carolina said with a quick clap of her hands; grinning. "I'll come by to see you after I return."

Marjorie shook her head. "You're impossible."

"No, I'm a friend who cares about *you*. Not what you do and don't have, but you."

"Very well. Come whenever you please then. I must be going."

A somber feeling came over Carolina as she watched her friend's retreating back. Marjorie had pride, she knew that, but sometimes pride was a very damnable thing.

"The next reel is about to start." said the familiar voice of Myron Cale.

Carolina turned to him and forced a thin smile. "Are you asking me to partner you?"

Myron chuckled and flashed his best grin. "Always so direct; that's what I love most about you!" He held his hand out to her. "Come, let's line up."

Reluctantly, Carolina took her spot in the middle of the floor. Though Myron Cale, with his painfully firm grasp, wooden feet, and the ability to ramble for half an hour about absolutely nothing, was one of her least favorite dance partners, this reel was one of her absolute favorites, mainly because it moved too fast to allow an abundance of talking!

An assembly of house servants sat in the back corner. One was positioned at a black piano, two held crudely fashioned banjars, and one had a tambourine, ready to keep time.

For a brief moment, Carolina's heart lifted. Those four men were actually having fun. That was quite extraordinary considering the hard labor the field hands were subjected to on her father's plantation.

Two quick strums of the banjars rang out, followed by a series of fast notes on the piano and Carolina grasped the middle of her red satin and velvet skirt with her gloved hands and dipped.

One and two and three and four. She moved her foot back, then kicked to the right, took a step left and slid to the back. In front of her, Myron mirrored her actions, a grin the size of a cotton bushel splitting his sun-beaten face.

The music sped up, and it was now time to be led around the room by the gentlemen. Enjoying the music and losing herself in the steps, she barely winced when Myron's callused hands took hold of her hand and waist. He marched her around the perimeter of the room, then through the aisle of parted couples, and then released her so they could take their respective places.

All around them, women wearing beautifully crafted

ballgowns and men dressed in the tattered blue and red uniforms that had become the Colonial Militia official uniform in 1779 danced. But no one said a thing about the difference in dress, as only a fool would believe those beautiful gowns would have been possible without the sacrifice of those dressed in the filthy and torn blue jackets with the red lining that covered the stiff, tan field shirts General George Washington declared would be fitting for proper military uniforms for the Continental Army.

This event had become a tradition when one July night eleven years ago, Mr. and Mrs. Jeffery Brown had decided to host a ball to raise money for the militia group which had formed in South Carolina and subsequently joined the Colonial Militia to fight against the Redcoats for the Colonies' independence. Each July that followed, Mr. and Mrs. Brown opened their home—either their townhouse or their plantation home when the English had occupied Charleston—again to raise money and garner more support for the war effort.

It had been five years since the war ended, and yet each year, the tradition continued. But instead of raising money or recruiting men to fight, the event was now held to celebrate the returned and fallen heroes of South Carolina. Thus, the men who'd fought wore whatever articles of clothing they'd worn home from the war, and the ladies dressed in their finest to "welcome" them.

Of course, not all the gentlemen in attendance had fought, and neither had all the ladies been old enough to welcome their sweethearts back. But that mattered very little. It was a tradition— one that, as far as Carolina was concerned, would never fade. It was because of this unfailing tradition and Mr. Reynolds' prominent role in the war that Marjorie and her family had even bothered to venture away from their plantation and face the whispers.

The piano player quieted and the banjars got louder as the men once again partnered their ladies and danced them the other direction around the perimeter of the room. Carolina loved this part of the reel and hummed right along with the music.

"Yer lookin' mighty pretty tonight, Lina," Myron said breathlessly. He released her waist in order to do the next move which was to lean back and allow her to spin, then he pulled her tightly to him again. "I want to talk to you about something really important."

Carolina's feet moved to the steps in time, which was a miracle considering the chills skating down her spine at those words, and she continued to hum to cover up her sudden discomfort that had little to do with being held so tightly. The last time Myron—or anyone for that matter—had voiced those exact words, they were soon followed by an offer of marriage. "Not now, Myron," she said between hums and then resumed as he led her down the aisle created by the other couples.

"We'll talk later," he said, relinquishing her hand.

Their spot was in the middle of the two lines, and at least eight other couples had to pass between them to form the lines before they'd have to clutch hands and finish the reel. It wasn't much time, but it would be long enough to form a plan of escape for when the dance ended.

Holding her red skirt between her fingers and mindlessly doing the steps, Carolina searched the ballroom for a gentleman who'd be able to save her from having to deflect another proposal.

Ernie Michaels and Barry Truitt stood by the door. She scowled. Neither of them would work. Ernie hedged on the side of simpleminded. Myron wouldn't believe Carolina had an interest in speaking to him, and Barry was set to marry Myron's sister Lucy in a month. A couple passed in front of her, and Carolina shifted her gaze to the far wall where a cluster of seven eligible bachelors stood together drinking punch.

Drunkard.

Old enough to be her father.

Seemed to still think the country was at war due to his never-ending talk of Valley Forge.

Handsome, but she'd once seen him go off into the bushes with Martha Palmer. Three weeks later, Martha decided to go stay a while on her cousin's plantation...

Dullard.

Charming, but smelled horribly of tobacco from his habit of continuously overindulging in the product while in public, which he felt was appropriate due to his ancestors having been tobacco farmers from Virginia.

Had attempted two proposals—both of which she'd dodged in the same manner she was attempting now.

She sighed and turned her attention to the back corner of the room. There were only two more couples to come through the line, so she'd better make a decision and quick.

Shorter than her—which was astonishing since she was only five foot two—balding, and had the strangest fascination with discussing everything he ate along with the aftertaste it left in his mouth following the meal.

Handsome, but was extremely condescending and cruel toward those he felt were inferior.

Ah, Donald O'Leary. He had unusual speaking patterns and, like most gentlemen she'd met, talked overmuch about the plantation he one day longed to own; but compared to her other choices, he'd do just fine.

The last couple passed in front of them, and with no warning whatsoever, Myron's strong hands found her again and started leading her in the final steps. He pulled her closer than was proper, crushing her breasts against his chest.

A slow sense of unease washed over Carolina. She hated it when her partners did this. Did they think she didn't know they did it on purpose?

Yes, awkward Donald O'Leary would certainly suffice as her next dancing companion if it meant getting away from Myron and his unwanted attentions.

"Lina, would you care to join me on the balcony?" Myron

asked as soon as the music stopped.

Carolina flashed him her best attempt at a smile, considering that he was still holding her in a way that pressed her breasts against his equally soft chest and had her looking straight up into his red-tipped nose when she tried to meet his eyes. "How about another time? I need to ask Mr. O'Leary a question, and I'd like to speak to him before all the other young ladies flock over to him."

Myron snorted. "Surely, whatever it is you have to say to the Irishman can wait. This will only take a moment."

Maybe a moment to him, but to her it would seem like a lifetime as he praised her brown hair and matching eyes, then went on to say how lovely her daughters would be with her delicate features and perfect smile. Then, he'd take her hands into his and squeeze them until she'd think her fingers might break while he'd compliment her flawless manners and would blush and tell her that she was far more intelligent than he, which would be a point in the favor of any child she bore. And then, just as the uncomfortable pressure surrounding her was about to choke the air from her lungs, he'd ask if she thought...that is...if she could accept a lumbering oaf like him as a husband. Then those beautiful, intelligent children could be theirs together.

At least that's what would happen if history repeated itself. After having two proposals by three other men, she was quite convinced history did, in fact, repeat itself; but only if allowed. And Carolina, for all the charm and manners a young lady of her station was thought to have, did not want a repeat of that particular history lesson.

"No, Myron, I really need to ask him something now. It's important."

He raised a brow.

"It's about my brother," she continued, inwardly congratulating herself for her quick thinking. "I wanted to ask if Mr. O'Leary has seen any letters from him." Though she doubted he had. Her brother had left to join the war seven years ago and that was the last time her family had seen or heard of him.

"Wouldn't he have delivered them to your house?" Myron hedged.

Carolina shook her head wildly. "Oh no, not at all. The post is still being delivered out to the plantation where my father is staying."

He nodded once then sighed. "Oh, all right." He released her and wagged his finger in her face. "Just don't you be forgettin' I have somethin' I want to talk to you about."

"I won't," she murmured, walking as quickly as she could to get away from him without it looking obvious.

He really wasn't a bad sort; he just wasn't *her* sort.

"Mr. O'Leary," Carolina greeted with her best smile as she approached Donald O'Leary.

He stood with his arms crossed and his shoulders leaning against the wall. Upon her arrival, his green eyes lit and a small smile tugged at his lips. "Aye?"

"I was wondering if you'd seen any letters from my brother come through the post."

"Nay. Me's not seen nothin' of the sort, Miss Lina."

Carolina bit her lip and nodded.

He reached out and clucked her on the chin with his thick callused fingers. "Ye donna be worrin' now, ye hear. He'll be back soon 'nuff, I spect."

"Thank you, Mr. O'Leary." She glanced over her shoulder and saw Myron's keen eyes on her. Carolina turned back to Mr. O'Leary and cut her eyes at him.

Nothing.

She batted her lashes at him, praying he'd understand her silent plea and ask her to dance the next reel with him to save her from a trip to the balcony with Myron.

Nothing.

The idle strums of the banjars started, indicating the beginning of the next dance. If Mr. O'Leary didn't do something fast, she'd have to resort to bold tactics and lead him onto the dance floor herself.

Just then, the soft ring of a plucked banjar string grew silent, as did the rest of the room.

"Are you *British*?" Hubert Brown, the son of the host and hostess of the ball, demanded loudly in a voice that dripped with disdain.

All eyes in the room flew to the stranger who'd just walked in. He was tall and blond with a small patch of reddish-brown whiskers. His clothes were just as unkempt as his hair with various shades and sizes of stains covering the torn garments he wore.

Though several of the men present wore shabby garments that rivaled this fellow's, not a one of them had the same confident air about him that, in the span of a second, had captivated Carolina's full attention.

"'Fraid so," the stranger said in the thickest English accent Carolina had ever heard.

Around the room, low grumbles, muttered curses, and even *spitting* could be heard.

"And just what do you think you're doing at a ball held in celebration for the men who served our country to defeat yours?" Hubert asked with a snarl.

The uninvited stranger, who actually looked rather dashing in a rugged and mysterious sort of way, tipped his left shoulder up in a casual shrug. "I thought I'd come tonight to represent what the Redcoats looked like after getting our arses whipped by you Yankees."

~ *Chapter Three* ~

The tension drained from John's body as the hostile crowd around him evaporated into loud, unbridled laughter at his half-hearted jest.

Thank goodness.

Had the arrogant man to his left not mentioned something about a celebration to the Colonial Militia, he wouldn't have had a clue what he'd have said to divert the attention from himself. After more than a year in the northeast, he'd learned hostilities toward the English were still common. He'd also heard southerners were far more outspoken about such, which didn't speak much for John's common sense when he agreed to travel with his friend Gabriel to South Carolina to experience a different type of American culture.

The arrogant man with the oversized nose standing next to him slapped him on the back. "Very good, then. Enjoy your night."

John nodded. "Thank you, sir."

In a moment or two, the crowd went back to talking and the musicians played the beginning notes of another reel. Heedless to the odd looks he was receiving, John made his way to the corner to search for his friend Gabriel, who had said he'd be here tonight.

Around him, the music grew louder and the gentlemen, who were dressed little better than he, twirled the beautifully dressed ladies around the floor. Odd. Not odd that they were dancing, that was normal enough, he supposed. But, of the few local assemblies he'd attended in England before coming here—and even the handful of balls he'd been to in Boston and Philadelphia—no gentlemen would dress in such a way. He shook his head. His brother Edward with his unbridled love for biological science would love to visit, because there was no doubt about it, this was a whole different breed of humans who inhabited these parts.

"Ooh, excuse me," murmured a petite young lady wearing a crimson gown.

John stepped back to let her pass. "Pardon me, miss."

She didn't move, just stood right there no more than half a step away. She looked at him with the darkest brown eyes he'd ever seen. But for the life of him, he couldn't understand why she just stood there staring.

"Am I keeping you from something?" he inquired, taking another step back so she could get through without touching his dirty breeches with the skirt of her pretty gown.

"Someone," she said with a slight smile, her eyes shone with all sorts of mischief—the very thing he wanted no part of. She tucked a tendril of hair behind her ear and gave her head a slight shake to the left.

John's eyes traveled in the direction she'd indicated. A decent looking gentleman with a blue shirt and buff trousers stood against the wall with his arms crossed and what appeared to be a scowl on his face. "Are you telling me you'd prefer a Redcoat's company to his?" he asked, lifting his brows.

His new companion licked her pink lips and whispered, "He wants to propose to me."

"And you don't want him to?"

"Would you want him to?" she retorted.

"No. But that might be because I'm not a lady."

She sighed. "Believe me, even to a lady, he holds no real appeal."

"Why not?" John forced an overdone frown. "He doesn't seem so bad. A bit gruff, perhaps."

"A bit gruff doesn't begin to describe it. Every time we dance, I end up with two hand-shaped bruises and a limp for a week."

"Have you danced with him already tonight?"

"Yes," she said, scowling.

"Pity, I thought to ask for your next dance. But now that I know you're bruised—" he shrugged— "I'll have to find another young lady to dance the next set with me."

She flushed the brightest red he'd ever seen. "I'm sure I can put on a brave face for you," she said, peeking up at him from under her lashes.

He shook his head. It didn't take a gentleman who'd survived a decade—or even two weeks—on the Marriage Mart in London to see she was hedging for an invitation to dance. Perhaps after he gave her a spin around the floor, she'd go find another gentleman to use in her mission to avoid the lovesick fool in the corner and leave him be.

Together, the pair waited for this song to end and the next to start. This brazen creature stood closer to him than most would consider proper, John noted as he began scanning the room for Gabriel again.

"Oh, they're starting the next reel. Let's go," she said, grabbing his hand.

John's gaze shot to their entwined hands. Hers was small and delicate, covered with a long, white lacy glove, while his was cut up and dirty from a hard day of work at the mill. He tried not to scowl at her or pull his hand from hers, but inwardly he cringed. It was ladies like her, the ones who were too forward and played loose with their affections, who made fools of their husbands.

He sent up a silent prayer of thanksgiving that after this dance, he'd be free of her and her scandalous behavior.

John made his way to the center of the floor with her and nearly groaned when he recognized the piece as a slower song, one that didn't allow for changing partners or even a temporary separation from the dancer's original partner.

The piano player began with a slow minuet, and instinctively, John moved his feet to those familiar steps he'd been made to practice as a boy.

"Why were you exiled?"

John snapped his eyes down toward the boldness-in-a-skirt who was his dance partner. "I wasn't," he said slowly. He twirled her and then brought her back against him. "Why would you think that?"

She flashed him a smile that nearly stole his breath away. She might be bold, but she was certainly beautiful, too. "I just assumed, that's all. I haven't seen too many English around since the end of the war. I didn't think any would come here, unless they found themselves in a condition at home which was worse than the hatred they'd find here."

"Indeed," he agreed. Fortunately, in the northern cities he'd visited, nobody had questioned his loyalties or where he'd come from and why. He'd assumed that was because his accent was similar to theirs, thus they hadn't noticed the difference in his speech as the folks of Charleston had. "But, no, I am not living out the rest of my days in exile."

"Then why did you come?"

He shrugged. She couldn't possibly begin to understand the heavy weight he'd felt concerning his life and having had it all planned out since the day he was born. Nor did he really wish to tell her. "My brother suggested I come."

"Has he been here?"

"Not the one who suggested I come. But two of my other brothers have, and both of them returned dressed identically to how I look tonight," he said with a quick grin.

Her cheery laughter filled the air and an uninvited tendril of desire coiled in his gut. "Did they fight in the Revolution?"

"You mean the Rebellion?" He winked at her when she misstepped. "Yes."

"I'm sorry," she murmured.

He heaved an exaggerated sighed. "I suppose I'll have to forgive you. But just don't shoot Jarred in the backside again, please."

Her brown eyes grew to the size of his sister-in-law's favorite tea saucers, just as he'd hoped they would. If she thought to play the role of cosmopolite by boldly pressing him for an invitation to dance and going so far as to stand close and touch his person, then he'd play right along with her and adopt Edward's tendency to say whatever scandalous thing came to mind for the sole purpose of shocking her.

"Wh-what?" she stammered.

"Two of my brothers, Thomas and Jarred, came to fight in your revolution," he said, hating the way that word tasted bitter on his tongue. At least his brothers had returned home, he reminded himself. Beaten and weary, they may be, but at least they'd returned. "They returned, but not without their share of injuries. One was the result of Jarred taking a musket ball in the derriere."

She choked on her laughter. "You cannot be serious."

"I am," he said flatly. Did she truly find that humorous? There went his attempt to scandalize her into leaving him alone. Not that he should have actually expected it to work. His words were evidently too mild for a forward young lady like this one. "Still there, too," he continued. "The physician who came to Watson Estate said it was in there so deep that it'd be best to leave it."

Her face shone with laughter—or perhaps that was the candles' reflection off her damp cheeks, where tears, presumably borne of laughter, had streamed down her face. She blinked her eyes and sniffled once. "Watson Estate? Is that the name of your...your...whatever you call it back in England."

"My home?"

She made a show of rolling her eyes. "Yes, I assumed that; but here our large pieces of land are called plantations because we grow crops on them. I didn't know what you called them there."

"Ah, nothing so fancy, I'm afraid," he said with a casual shrug. "Watson Estate is just the house and land that's positioned at the seat of my brother's barony."

Her eyes widened again as he knew they would. "Your brother is a land baron?"

He nodded slowly. "Yes, he's a baron. But you're too late; he's already married."

She knit her brows as if she didn't understand his jest and then forced a thin smile.

"You do know what a baron is, don't you?" he asked.

"Of course," she said, blushing.

John shook his head. She very clearly didn't know a thing about English titles. Not that it mattered. Most people his age who he'd met here didn't. A few did, but mostly only those who had immigrated here as children. It would seem in their hurry to form a new world, things such as class and peerage were abandoned and not missed.

"What are your reasons?"

She blinked at him. "Pardon me?"

"Since my dancing with you is keeping you from Goliath's proposal, I think I should at least get to know your reasons for wishing to evade it."

"Other than him being as tall as a tree and as rough as its bark?"

He nodded.

"It's not him, necessarily..." She shrugged. "The problem is more that I've told him no before. He just keeps asking, and I hate to see that sad look come over his face and know I caused it."

"I see," John said, though he didn't see at all. Why would a gentleman ask the same lady more than once to marry him? She was attractive, to be sure, but who wished to subject himself to rejection twice?

A soft humming that went in time with the music floated to his ears. Without even needing to look to confirm it, he knew whence the merry sound was coming. At least it was better than her talking or flashing him her smile, he told himself. This way, he could force himself to stare at something—*anything*—other than her in order to keep himself distracted and not seem rude.

He danced her around the room in companionable silence until the music came to an end with a grand ringing crescendo.

Relief washed over him like a seaquake. This young lady was extraordinarily beautiful to behold, but she was not for him, and the sooner he could get away from her, the better off he'd be. He offered her his arm like the proper gentleman he'd been brought up to be, then led her to where a little cluster of older women had congregated.

"You're a wonderful dancer," his former dance partner said without showing a sign of releasing his arm.

He stared at her. What was her game? Did she think if she held onto him and complimented his dancing that he'd agree to keep her company for the rest of the evening so she could escape her lovesick suitor? If so, she was about to be sorely disappointed. He had no desire to be used tonight. He just wanted to find his friend then go back to his rented room and sleep. Dancing with an attractive but shameless young lady was not a priority.

Apparently, according to both this young lady and fate, his plans were unimportant at the moment.

"Thank you," he said stiffly, trying to remove her hand from his arm without being too obvious.

Her grip tightened and she flashed him a smile. "Don't worry; I shan't expect you to dance again so soon. How about I introduce you to everyone?"

He didn't want her to show him around. He'd scanned the crowds as they'd danced. Gabriel wasn't here. He needed to leave so he could find the man, not chat it up with a room of southern aristocrats who hated him on principle alone.

"Come, I'll introduce you to my mother."

John bit his tongue so he didn't say something unkind. "Miss —" He frowned. He didn't even know her name! A slow smile spread his lips. "Lead the way."

She eyed him askance, and he averted his eyes. While he had no strong urge to meet her mother, he was rather curious how this quick to action, but not so quick to thinking, miss would introduce him to her mother given that they hadn't even been properly introduced.

Suddenly, something hard and forceful landed on John's shoulder.

John spun around and met the large green eyes of the man from the corner.

"I believe 'tis my turn with the lady," he sneered; his distaste for an Englishman escorting his desired lady evident.

John glanced at the lady in question and watched her visibly swallow. A kernel of pity took root somewhere within him, and he instinctively reached for her hand again and mindlessly placed it back on his arm, then covered it with his free hand. "I believe she's still spending time with me," he said smoothly.

The other man twisted his lips then he ran his purple tongue over his stained teeth. "Is that so?" He moved his eyes to the young lady standing next to John. "Have you forgotten we was supposed to talk after you spoke to O'Leary?"

The young lady's fingers tightened their hold on John's arm as if it were some sort of lifeline she'd been thrown while drowning in the Atlantic. "I'm sorry, Myron, I cannot marry you," she whispered.

The other man's face fell. "But, why not? I own my own business. It's not too fancy now, but it'll be enough to keep you in town, I think," he asked; his lower lip holding the slightest quiver.

"I know," she said, licking her lips. "I just don't think I'd make you a good wife."

Myron didn't look convinced. "That's not true. You'd be a great wife."

She smiled. "Thank you, but what I said was that I don't think I'd make *you* a good wife."

The other man folded his arms and gave a curt nod to her. Next, he turned his attention to John and let his gaze travel from John's mussed hair to his worn shoes then shook his head.

Frankly, if John were him, he'd be confused, too; there was

nothing wrong with that gentleman. She was a fool to let him go.

"What are you doing?" John asked without ceremony as soon as the man was out of earshot. "He may not have a gentle grasp and might lack a few manners, but otherwise, he's quite a catch."

The addled woman looked at him, shrugged and said, "Just as I'll make a fine wife for someone else, he'll make a find husband for another woman. Besides, I've set my sights on someone else."

John didn't even pretend to misunderstand her. He couldn't. There was absolutely no way that could possibly be misunderstood, from her blushing cheeks to her not-so-discreet smile to her subtle-as-a-hippopotamus-pulling-a-carriage-down-the-streets-of-London statement. She'd set her cap on him, and God only knew why.

He lifted his free hand and idly scratched his temple. It was merely irritating when he'd thought she was using him to escape the company of another gentleman. But, for her to have formed some sort of attachment to him after only twenty minutes was pure lunacy.

John cleared his throat uncomfortably. "I think we need to discuss something," he said as calmly as he dared.

"No, I don't believe there is anything left for the two of you to discuss," a waspish woman with shrewd brown eyes and a deep scowl said, coming up to them.

The raven-haired young lady blushed. "Mother, I'd like you to meet—"

"Do not finish that sentence," her mother snapped. "I have no desire to make the acquaintance of any vagrant."

John didn't even try to hide his grin. Her mother had good taste. If he were she, he wouldn't wish to make his acquaintance, either. However, her easy dismissal and obvious disapproval of him provided him the perfect means to escape the clutches of this misguided miss. He removed her hand from his arm and gave her a final nod.

One thing was for certain: she'd been correct when she'd said she'd make someone a good wife. But like Mr. Cale, it wouldn't be John.

~ Chapter Four ~

Carolina stood paralyzed as the man who just might forever hold her heart walked from the room.

"Stop gawking, Lina," Mother said in a tone hard as steel.

Despite her mother's edict, Carolina didn't stop staring, as in her mind, the memory of them dancing played over and over.

"Oh look, Lina," her mother said in a voice dripping with false charm and an overdone smile taking her lips. "Speak of the devil, there is Liam Farnsworth!"

Liam Farnsworth, who was no less than ten years older than her father but wealthy enough for Mother to see him as a young, virile twenty-five, lumbered over. "Good evening, Miss Lina, Mrs. Ellis."

With a none-too-gentle reminder of her manners by way of a sudden vice-like grip on her arm just above her elbow, Carolina murmured her greetings and agreed to dance with him.

Fortunately, the reel started out more upbeat than the last one had, and Liam wasn't afforded much opportunity to engage her in conversation for the first half of the dance. Not that she'd have been able to pay attention anyway. Her mind was far too occupied with thoughts of her former dance partner to be able to bother with trivial matters such as Liam Farnsworth would like to discuss.

He led her to the dance floor and, like all the other gentlemen she'd met this summer, followed the first half of the dance routine exactly. The music slowed down, indicating it was now time to slow their steps and dance closer together.

"I hope you're enjoying your stay in the city. Did you know it was named Charles Towne because in..."

Carolina was overwhelmed with the urge to pull all of her own hair out. There was no doubting it now; she *had* to find a way to manage another meeting with her English stranger. Then, when she found him, she'd have to hold onto his arm and never let go.

As if those who influence fate were smiling down on Carolina Ellis and her scandalous dream of being swept away by an Englishman, such an opportunity was afforded her not twenty-four hours later when she saw him while trying to avoid anyone who might recognize her on this side of town.

"What are you doing here?" the handsome stranger asked as if that were a perfectly acceptable way to greet someone.

Carolina mindlessly swept a stray hank of hair behind her ear. "It's wonderful to see you again so soon."

He grunted and shifted the small pile of logs in his arms, presumably to make them easier to carry. He must have worn his nicest clothes last night, for the ones he wore today were far more stained and ill-fitting than the ones he'd worn to the ball. His tattered, blue trousers had two large holes in the knees, and around the holes, the fabric was fraying. What she could see of his shirt was covered with large brown stains; and as the large muscles in his arms and shoulders flexed to hold the wood, she noticed a split in the arm that looked to be on the verge of tearing more. Oh how she'd like to feel those muscles. Her eyes grew wide at the scandalous thought!

"How did you find me?"

Carolina shrugged and flashed him her best smile, ignoring the jar of butterflies that seemed to be let loose in her stomach every time he spoke to her. "'Twas fate."

He scoffed and shook his head. "No, it was you stalking me."

"Stalking you?" she gasped. "And how do you propose I did that? Waited for you to leave the ballroom last night and then walked a safe distance behind you? Oh, then I'd have had to sleep somewhere—on your front stoop, perhaps? Only to wake before dawn to stand in the shadows until you emerged from your home, then crept like a cat behind you and waited in the foreman's quarters until just now to present myself to you? Not only does that *sound* ridiculous, you've forgotten that I've changed my gown since then."

His eyes narrowed. "Lady, you know far too much about what would be involved in stalking a man for your own good. It's rather unnerving." He shifted the logs in his arms. "But just so you know, I'm not dimwitted enough to believe *you* actually did the stalking. I assumed you'd hired someone."

Carolina waved her hand in front of her face. "Not at all. As I said, it was fate that led me to you—both times."

The handsome but terribly disheveled man in front of her muttered something she couldn't understand other than something about something being unbelievable.

"It's not unbelievable. I actually have a good reason to be here."

He shot her a dubious expression. "And what is that?"

"Silas."

"Silas?" he repeated. "What business does a young lady like you have with him?"

"None," she acknowledged. "But Bethel seems to like him quite a bit."

"Bethel?" he asked, frowning.

"She's...uh..." she swallowed her unease. "She works in our house." Carolina glanced over John's left shoulder to where Bethel and Silas were engaged in conversation. Silas had to be the luckiest man Carolina had ever met. Not only had their neighbor Jacob Reynolds granted Silas his freedom at the end of the Revolutionary War, but he'd somehow managed to win Bethel's heart.

Trips to their Charleston townhouse were rare; so when they came to town, Carolina tried to think up reasons to go to the mercantile as often as she could to give Bethel a chance to see Silas while she took the long way to the store. It was the only relationship the two would ever have. He lived in town. She didn't. He was free. She wasn't. They could never really be more or have more than a passing relationship.

Carolina pushed away her thoughts. There was nothing she could do to change Bethel's fate and wishing she could only led to more sadness. "I'm glad I found you though," she said. "I've been meaning to talk to you— what is that about?" she demanded when he started shaking his head.

"Do you realize you don't even know my name?"

Carolina started. He was absolutely right. "I'm sorry. Usually —never mind. I shall break custom of a proper introduction and tell you my name is Carolina. Like the state."

He shook his head again as if annoyed by her mere presence.

"Aren't you going to tell me yours?"

"John. Like the saint."

"A state and a saint, we're quite a match, wouldn't you say?"

He didn't look quite as amused as she was. "I must be getting back to work now."

She sobered. "Do you not have but a minute to talk?"

"No. I have to have this wood delivered to Mr. Sawyer before the hour if I want to get paid," he explained, lifting his arms full of wood to emphasize his point.

Carolina's face burned with shame. Being born to a family of wealth, she'd never wanted for monetary things. He'd said yesterday his brother was a land baron. But, she knew from watching the struggles of other planters in the region that just because you have land, doesn't mean the whole family prospers from it. "Of course."

He made a move to walk past her.

Carolina bit her lip. This was her last chance, for if she didn't say something now, she might not get a chance again. She reached out and placed a staying hand on his hard, muscled shoulder. "Wait, would you care to join my family for supper tonight?"

"Absolutely not," Mother's shrill voice trilled, sending shivers up Carolina's spine. How had she found Carolina? "Remove your hand from this filthy vagabond at once!"

Slowly Carolina removed her gloved hand from his strong shoulder and dropped it to her side, fisting it into a tight ball to keep from making a scene by pulling her mother's hand away from where she was holding Bethel by the ear. Swallowing uncomfortably, she met John's clear blue eyes once more and saw a calm in them she hadn't noticed before.

He glanced to her mother and then turned his impassive face back to meet Carolina's eyes one final time before walking away to the little wagon nearby.

"What is wrong with you, Lina?" Mother demanded in a low, sharp tone. "What is it about that—that—rogue that fascinates you so? He's dirty, poor, and *English*. Decidedly not worthy of you."

Carolina bit her tongue so not to remind her mother that she, too, was of English descent. But it would do no good. Ever since the Revolution, it was as if their heritage had been forgotten in favor of just being considered American—free from English rule.

Mother's exaggerated, yet typical, sigh pulled Carolina from her thoughts. "Well, Lina, you have just received your wish."

"My wish?" she echoed, climbing into the back of the buggy her family used around the city.

Mother waited for Dalton to set the horses to pace before she spoke again. "Your behavior is unbecoming and deplorable for a young lady of your station. Several times you've expressed your wish not to marry any of the gentlemen you've met here so far, and I do believe once word gets out that you've been throwing yourself at that no-good vagrant you'll not have to worry about gentlemen callers again."

Carolina pursed her lips. Just as well. As long as that particular no-good vagrant wished to marry her, she saw no problem with her mother's complaint.

***

John dropped his armful of heavy logs into the back of the wagon then dusted his hands off on his trousers. What were the odds he'd have run into her again? Of course, nothing had changed.

He still wanted a meek, quiet wife, and she was just as forward in the daylight as she'd been at the ball last night. He shook his head and readjusted his left suspender strap then stalked back inside to grab another heavy load of logs.

The house where he was to deliver the logs was only a mile away—on a normal day. But just to make certain he didn't cross paths with his breathtaking stalker and her vulturous mother, he steered the horses in the opposite direction they'd taken to leave.

The soft, familiar sound of horse hooves on the ground filled the air, serving as a pleasant reminder of how close he was to returning to England. After today, he'd have enough money to return home to his family.

From the corner of his eye, a lady with large hoops under her skirt struggling to exit a carriage caught his attention, and he whipped his head to the side to make sure it wasn't that intolerable chit who had a habit of appearing when he least expected it. He shook his head to clear her from his thoughts. A wife like her would only lead to a life of misery as her carefree—or perhaps care*less*—attitude and impulsiveness would quite possibly lead to her husband's ruin.

"Whoa," he called to the horses, pulling back on the reins. Whistling, he jumped from the wagon and unloaded the wood for Mr. and Mrs. Sawyer before riding back to the mill.

"You're a stubborn man, Banks," Mr. Morrison, the foreman of the mill, called to John as he steered the horses toward the back of the main building. "But it's what I admire about you."

"Thank you, sir," John said quietly as he dismounted the wagon and then moved to unhook the horses. The Sawyers were the last delivery of the day which meant it was up to him to put the wagon away and take care of the horses for the night.

Morrison sighed. "If you're ever in need of a job, you'll always have one here."

"Thank you," John murmured. He'd have to find himself desperate indeed to accept a job here. As it was, working here the past three weeks to earn enough to fund his travel back home had been quite enough. Of course, if it had truly been *that* bad, he could have swallowed his pride and accepted money from his brother. But he didn't want to do that. He might not have had a problem doing just that before he'd come across the ocean. But seeing how everyone here worked for his own wage, he'd decided to step out from his brother's protection and support himself. Getting that first handful of coins as payment for work he'd done, only spurred him to harden his resolve and refuse to accept his brother's generosity.

"Do you plan to return to England?" Morrison asked, presumably just to make conversation.

John removed the bridle from the second horse and nodded once. "Yes. It's time."

"You can't mean to tell me that no pretty young lasses have caught your eye in the weeks you've been here."

An image of the hoyden he'd seen earlier flashed in his mind. "None that I'd like to marry," he said, unable to meet the other man's eyes.

A slow smile spread across Morrison's lips, and he cocked his head to the side in interest. When John didn't say anything else, the older man pursed his lips and made an unusual face. "Very well," he said, reaching into his pocket. He withdrew a handful of coins, picked out a few of the larger ones, and then dropped them into the gaping pocket in the front of John's shirt. "There's yer pay."

~ Chapter Five ~

Three Days Later

Carolina swung open the door to the traveling coach, heedless to whom or what might be standing right outside. Her mother was driving her to insanity! For the past three days, Mother had spoken of little else except how Carolina was making a display of herself and a mockery of her family.

Then it came.

Last night, a letter from Father came. The note, only four words in length, had turned Mother into a lunatic—raging in hysteria that Carolina's loose behavior had found its way back to Lowland Cross, thus the reason for the note that read: *Come home at once!*

But even as harsh and unyielding as Father had been when she was a child in need of punishment, his displeasure toward her would be a welcome escape from her mother's madness.

"I shall take a walk around the street," Mother chirped, brushing out her thick skirt.

Carolina nodded slowly as a wave of sadness washed over her. "Must you?"

"Yes. This is your behavior to answer for, not mine."

Carolina didn't give a thousand cakes of indigo about that. Her conversation with Father would probably be far more enjoyable than what was to come of Mother's walk down the street, which was comprised of the crudely built log cabins near the edge of the plantation where the field hands and other skilled workers slept. Mother had no respect for anyone's privacy and would randomly walk around their quarters, reprimanding them for things out of place, or worse, ordering them punished if something was broken or missing. A lead weight settled in Carolina's chest. On more than one occasion, she'd tried to talk her mother into being less severe, but it did no good. Mother felt taking charge this way helped to remind them who their master was.

Following the war that turned her father into an invalid and claimed the life of her older brother, it was left to Mother to run the plantation. And that meant she could treat her "hands" any way she wanted. The taste in Carolina's mouth turned bitter. Nobody deserved to be treated the way her mother treated them.

"Go on," Mother said with a stiff shooing motion.

Fighting the urge to run to the street as fast as her slippers could carry her and warn whoever she could of Mother's impending visit, Carolina took Bethel by the hand and dragged her heavy feet in the direction of the house.

"It's good to be home," Carolina mused as they walked inside.

"It sho' is, chile," Bethel agreed, running her open palms down the white apron she wore over her black dress. "I's jus goes sees what's needin' ta be done in da kit'en."

"You be sure to do that, Bethel," Carolina's father said with a hint of a smile.

"Yessa." Bethel bobbed a quick nod toward Father then hurried off.

"'Tis good to see you, Lina," Father wheezed as he slowly rolled his invalid's chair into the entryway.

Despite her distaste for her nickname, she offered him a smile. He was the only person who could call her that without making her cringe. Carolina bent forward and threw her arms around him. "I've missed you."

"I'm sure you have," he whispered, patting her back with his one remaining arm. "That long alone with your mother and I'd be in need of saving, too."

A slow smile took her lips. "You have no idea." She wet her lips. "Is that why you wrote to us? To save me from Mother?"

He chuckled and for a brief moment Carolina glimpsed the man she remembered him being before the war. "Well, no. That's not the entire reason I wrote. Here, let's go to the parlor."

Carolina followed her father down to the hall and to the beautifully decorated formal parlor. The familiar sound of labored breathing filled the air as Father used his only arm, by turning his right wheel, then reaching across to give a turn of his left, to wheel himself across the room, positioning himself to the left of the window. When Father had first returned home without his left arm and the use of his legs, Carolina had tried to help him as best she could, only to be barked at to leave him alone, he could do it. It might take him thrice as long as it would take her to get him to his destination, but his pride was too strong to accept any more help than was absolutely necessary.

Sighing at what was to come, she sat down on the dark green settee and waited for what he had to say. Not that it would change anything. She still planned to find and charm her Englishman. She might have to wait a few weeks for her parents' ire to settle before returning to Charleston, but she *would* find him again, and perhaps one day even marry him.

"Lina," he said with a ragged breath.

"Yes."

"Is there a certain young gentleman of your acquaintance that you'd like to see again?"

Carolina shifted in her seat. "Perhaps," she said airily, smoothing her hands over her lavender skirt.

Father showed no sign of emotion, a talent at which he was most skilled. "Oh?"

Heat crept up her face. Why didn't he just scold her for her inappropriate behavior and get it over with? His calm tone and imploring eyes were unnerving! "Yes, there is a young gentleman with whom I'd like to become better acquainted."

"What does your mother think?"

Carolina scowled. "She doesn't approve."

"I see," Father said, nodding slowly.

She had no doubt that he did. Father always was an observant one.

"And is this why you've taken a fancy to him?"

"No." She wouldn't lie. Her mother's dislike might have spurred her to like him more, but it wasn't the reason she'd liked him in the first place.

Father chuckled as if he could read her mind. "I hate to disappoint you, Lina, but there is nothing I can do at the moment to reunite you with your suitor; however—" he grimaced and repositioned himself in his chair— "I can arrange a reunion between you and another gentleman."

Images of a skinny boy with black hair, chipped teeth, and a permanently blank face formed in her mind. Charlie Fields was the son of a neighboring plantation owner whose father had always pushed for a marriage between him and Carolina. Panic settled in Carolina's stomach. Was her punishment for flirting with the Englishman marriage to Charlie? If so, she'd climb out her window tonight just to escape. "Must I meet with him?"

"He asked for you specifically."

She doubted that. He seemed no more interested in marrying her than she was in marrying him. His parents had likely told him to say that. Though she'd never been cruel enough to express her disinterest for him to his face, it should have been as obvious as the sun rising in the sky each morning to her parents that they didn't suit. "Please, don't make me marry Charlie, Father. I'll..." She'd what? Pursue John with a little more dignity? That didn't sound right.

Her father cut her off with a quick hand gesture. "No need to do anything except go out the back door, then go to the right, and greet the first lad you see wearing a white shirt and blue trousers."

Carolina stared at her father. Had something fallen from a shelf and hit him on his head during her stay in Charleston?

"Go on, now," he barked.

With what she hoped looked like a smile, but was certainly more likely to resemble a grimace, Carolina stood. Her father had never been known to make such odd requests as this, but if all she had to do was greet the neighbor's son, she could do that. And if he tried to propose to her, she'd just distract him by changing the subject. "Very well."

"Good. Now go before your mother returns."

Carolina eyed him curiously one last time before leaving the parlor and making her way to the back door of the house.

She lifted her hand to block the bright sunlight that was in her eyes and walked down the wooden steps. Taking one more calming breath, she turned her squinting eyes to the right, and immediately, her breath caught and her heart beat out of control. *"Gabriel!"* she squealed, dashing in his direction as if a ravenous mountain lion were nipping at her heels.

Running too fast to slow down, she barreled directly into her older brother, who wrapped one arm tightly around her and clung tightly to a large wooden walking stick in his left hand.

"Lina," he whispered, tightening his hold on her and then letting her go.

She stepped back and gazed up at his face. Seven years might have passed, but she'd have recognized him anywhere. He'd certainly aged while away, much like she expected she had, too. His soft brown eyes were now harder than she remembered. Faint lines in the skin around his eyes and lips were now visible. Then, of course, there was the large scar that divided his left cheek. He twitched and Carolina's eyes narrowed on where his hand clutched his walking stick then slowly drifted to his legs. Her eyes widened as they fell to the left cuff of his trousers.

Immediately, she brought her gaze to his.

He nodded once, a silent confirmation that he did indeed now walk with a wooden leg.

She swallowed hard. This must be why he'd stayed away so long. She opened her mouth to assure him that his wounds and scars didn't change anything. Under it all, he was still her brother, and she was just glad he'd finally returned; but she was cut off when Gabriel jerked his gaze away, then called, "Banks, come here. There's someone I'd like you to meet."

***

John lowered his axe and jerked his head in his friend's direction.

Then slowly, every ounce of blood in his body drained straight to his toes. Ever since he'd run into Carolina that day at the mill, he'd been seeing and hearing her everywhere. Well, not really, because that same evening he and Gabriel had left Charleston to travel to his family's plantation. So, those women they'd seen riding in buggies headed the other way down the country roads weren't really Carolina—and once he'd blinked rapidly for ten seconds and had cleared his vision, it had been easier to see that. Same with the excited high-pitched squeals he'd been hearing since he'd arrived. At first, he'd whip his head around every time he'd hear one, thinking she'd found him, only to realize it was just one of the many children who lived on the plantation having fun.

That's why, when he heard that high-pitched squeal a few moments ago, he forced himself to ignore the way it made the hair on the back of his neck stand up and reminded himself it was just a gleeful child.

But, he could no longer attempt to convince himself of such. Seeing only the petite form, complete with the gentle curves of the chit, who stood next to Gabriel there was no denying it: she'd found him again.

His axe slipped from his numb fingers and made a soft thud as it hit the ground.

"I've got work to do," he shouted, snatching up his axe with a scowl. He didn't know—nor did he care—what her game was, but as far as he was concerned, she could use her wiles on Gabriel. He wanted no part of it.

"That can wait," Gabriel called. "I want you to meet my

sister."

Any amount of blood which had begun circulating back through John's body drained again, and this time, when he dropped his axe, he had to swallow the cannonball sized lump that had recently formed in his throat. "Sister?" he croaked.

Gabriel nodded. "Yes, Lina. The one I told you about."

John closed his eyes. In the six months they'd been acquainted, Gabriel had spoken of "Lina" many times. Each time, John quickly found a way to abandon that topic for one less uncomfortable. John had come to America for a chance to escape his pressing duties and responsibilities, not gain more.

Commanding his heavier-than-lead feet to carry him forward, he made his way over to the siblings. "It's a pleasure to make your acquaintance, Lina," he said, avoiding her eyes.

"And it's a pleasure to see you again, too, John," she said, touching the back of his callused hand with her dainty one. The action sent a jolt of desire directly to his groin and a grimace to his lips. This was exactly what he didn't need.

"Do you two already know each other?" Gabriel asked; his curious brown eyes challenging John to deny the charge.

"Yes," he bit off.

"Is she the one you told me about?"

John nodded. "Yes." He bent his head and ran a hand through his hair, trying in vain to ignore the way his face was heating. Considering just what he'd told Gabriel about her, it was hard to meet his friend's eyes at the moment.

"I see," Gabriel drawled.

Beside him, Carolina—or Lina—whichever she was going by these days, tittered and grinned, presumably at the knowledge that John had spoken to her brother about her. Little did she know exactly what John had said, and he prayed for her sake, Gabriel didn't decide to tell her. Not that it was cruel or decidedly unflattering; it wasn't, but it sure wasn't the words of love and admiration she might have hoped he'd said.

"Shall we all go inside and have some refreshments?" the object of his thoughts asked.

John wanted to protest but was spared when Gabriel shook his head and said, "And be subjected to being in close quarters with a vulture, no thank you."

Carolina's merry laughter filled the air. "You have no idea just how beastly Mother's become since you've been gone."

John did, though, he thought with a cringe. "I'd best be getting back to work."

"Work?" Carolina asked, her large brown eyes widening.

He nodded as, not for the first time since Mr. Morrison had given him his pay, he wished he'd counted the money before signing the ledger. He'd thought that'd be insulting to the man. But now, he wished he'd been insulting—for at least that way, he'd be on his way home, not working on a plantation. Particularly one that had his blasted female stalker in residence.

"Banks here is— Lina, is something wrong?" Gabriel asked.

Carolina's face had lost all color. A strangled sound escaped her lips, then just like the odd chit he remembered her to be, she ran off.

Both he and Gabriel shrugged. Perhaps now that she knew he was working at her father's plantation—even if it was only temporary—she'd lose whatever interest it was she had in him.

~ *Chapter Six* ~

Carolina could not get back to the big house fast enough.

And, she had no desire to embarrass herself by casting up her accounts in the grass.

Which is exactly what would happen if she didn't get inside and find a chamberpot quickly.

He was working here?

That couldn't be. She could accept that he was visiting, but not working here.

Mother already held him in disdain. Now she'd have no reason to treat him better, and everyone on the plantation knew how she treated those she didn't like.

Bile rose in her throat, and her shaky hands poured the water from the floral pitcher in her room into the matching basin. She splashed water on her flushed face. *Why?* Why had he come here seeking work? Did he truly need it or was this an attempt to become better acquainted with her?

She wrung her hands together and shook her head. No, that didn't make any sense. Father was so tight with his money he wouldn't willingly pay anyone for what the hands could do without a good reason—and likely some convincing from Gabriel. Besides, he'd seemed just as surprised to see her here as she was to see him. Which presented the question: how did he and Gabriel know each other?

Not that it mattered. None of it really mattered except that he was here now, and she'd have to convince him he didn't have to work here in order to win her favor.

The thought dissolved in an instant, aided by Mother's ear-piercing shriek.

Carolina flew out of her room and down the oak staircase.

"This is still my home, and this bounder will not be sharing it," Mother said with enough venom to rival a rattlesnake.

Carolina peeked around the corner to see what was going on in the room, because just hearing it didn't seem adequate.

"It's good to see you, too, Mother," Gabriel said, folding his arms across his chest.

"Don't lie to me," Mother snapped. "If you truly had an interest in seeing me, you'd have at least had the courtesy to come see me during your stay in Charleston. But I guess even that would have been an imposition on a son who's been away from his family for seven years."

"As if you'd have wanted me to ruin your plans for an afternoon."

"Of course not," Mother said airily. "But you could have sent a note and arranged a time to come visit me when I had nothing planned."

Gabriel stared at her; a muscle in his jaw ticking. It was no secret that Gabriel's feelings toward Mother rivaled Carolina's. In fact, it would seem that no one who bore the Ellis surname held Mother in any esteem. Instead, their love and respect went to Bethel. She'd always been the one who'd cleaned a scraped knee and kissed a wound. She'd offered the love and motherly affection her real mother had denied her and Gabriel. Given the choice between the two, she'd choose Bethel, and she was certain Gabriel would, too.

"Your disdain for your own mother is not what we're discussing. Your utter disrespect for your family by bringing a filthy wanderer here is," Mother said.

"I don't see what the problem is," Father intoned. "And I certainly don't see how his presence is a disrespect to this family."

Mother pursed her lips. "I will not be made a mockery of, Calvin. If we are in need of more field hands, I'll go to the auction next month and find one. But *he*—" she said, pointing an accusing finger at John— "will not be staying on my plantation."

Father's gray eyes narrowed. "I have no idea why you have such a strong dislike for the man—"

Carolina bit her lip so not to give herself away by blurting out the answer to that.

"—but he is staying. This is still my plantation, Hazel, and I will run it how I see fit."

Mother sucked in a sharp breath and stomped from the room.

Carolina ducked into the dining room to avoid her mother's gaze. Then, when she was certain Mother had passed, she stepped into the parlor.

"Good afternoon again, fellows," she greeted with a bright smile, lingering for a few seconds in John's direction.

Was it her or had his cheeks just turned a bit pink?

"Come sit, Lina," Father invited.

"I need to go repair the eastern fence," John said abruptly.

Carolina frowned. Did he not wish to be in her presence in front of her family? Surely, he wasn't embarrassed for her family to know of the feelings they shared for one another. His fidgeting and red face suggested otherwise. "You don't have to leave," she whispered to him.

"Yes, I do." He cleared his throat. "I'm not being paid to sit in the parlor for afternoon tea."

"Just so," Father agreed. "Those fences need mending before dinnertime if you want to earn your wages; so you boys need to get after it while Lina tells me all about her favorite suitor from Charleston."

A sound akin to a strangled grunt erupted from John's throat.

"Yes, well, we'll be out repairing that fence," Gabriel said, clapping John on the shoulder then casting a quick wink in Carolina's direction.

She blushed. He knew! Exactly what he knew, she had yet to determine, but he most certainly knew *something*. She'd have to ask him later, right after she asked why he stayed away for so long.

"Lina, what do you think of Mr. Banks?"

Carolina's face burned, and she couldn't meet her father's eyes. "I like him well enough."

Father chuckled. "I'm a cripple, Lina, not blind."

"I know," Carolina said, taking a seat on the green settee he had invited her to sit on earlier. "You don't think less of him because he's in your employ, do you?" She had to ask. She had to know. She might not care about her mother's opinion of her choice in suitors, but she did care about her father's.

"That's only temporary." The softness in his tone and the gentleness she glimpsed in his gray eyes gave her pause. There was something he wasn't saying, but what?

"Do you not think it's temporary?"

He twisted his lips and turned his head to the side a fraction. "No. I'm fairly certain that it's temporary. When he arrived the other day, he explained that he needed only enough funds for passage back to England."

Carolina's heart sped up. England. She'd never been to England. It was thousands of miles away. She'd never see her family again if they went there. Not that she minded his desire to return to his homeland, but she wouldn't deny she was a bit displeased he hadn't seen fit to ask her opinion on where they'd live.

"Well, I suppose it's not the literal end of the world," Carolina said a moment later.

Father blinked at her. "What's that?"

"Moving to England."

"Moving to England," he repeated slowly.

"After we marry."

"Marry? That boy asked you to marry him?" Father asked, jerking his thumb in the direction of the window.

"Well, no," she said cautiously. It had been a long time since she'd seen her father's face quite so dark, she thought as she chose her next words with extra care. "But he will."

Father stared at her for a minute. A long minute. "I'm not sure I want to know the answer to this, but I feel compelled to ask: have the two of you done something to ensure that there will be a marriage?"

Carolina stared at her father, dumbfounded; then blinked; then shrieked in surprise. "No! Nothing of the sort," she rushed to assure him. "See, we met at the Brown's annual ball—where he stole everyone's attention by coming dressed as a 'defeated Englishman'—and we danced. Then he stuck by my side until he was ready to leave," never mind that his departure that night was a result of Mother driving him off, "then the next day, we spent part of the afternoon together."

"You did?"

"As a matter of speaking, yes."

He sighed. "Lina, I don't intend to upset you, but talking to the man on two occasions does not mean he plans to ask you to marry him. You're an intelligent girl; you should know that."

Carolina sucked in a harsh breath. "When stated that way, it does sound ridiculous. But I'm not wrong." She cleared her throat. "You have to believe me. In those first moments we spoke—I knew."

"Knew what?"

"That he'd be my husband," she said easily. "And if that is not enough to convince you. We ran into each other the next day, and now he's working here. See, it's fate's plan that we're to marry."

"And does he know of fate's destiny for his life?"

He should. It seemed pretty obvious, it should be to him, too. "I think so, yes."

Father looked doubtful. "Then perhaps you'd do well to remind him."

~ Chapter Seven ~

"John?"

The muscles in John's arm tensed. Slowly, he turned his head around to meet Carolina's soft brown eyes. "Yesh?" he asked around the two nails he was holding between his teeth.

"I was hoping to talk to you."

He turned his attention back to the fence post and board in front of him, then took one of the nails from between his teeth and put it into position. "It'll have to wait," he said, driving a nail into the board he was holding.

She didn't leave. "Why can't we talk now?"

Why did she always ask him questions when he was working? Wait. He knew the answer to that. Because, other than the night of the ball, that was the only time she'd ever seen him. He took the other nail from his lips. "How about if we talk later?" he suggested.

"No," she said, stepping closer to him. "I need to talk to you now. It's important."

He cast her a sidelong glance. What could she possibly have to say to him that was that important? He shook off the thought. Females, he'd learned, thought *everything* was of the utmost importance. He lifted the nail to the board and tightened his grip on his hammer, ready to swing. "And you're sure it cannot wait until a more opportune time?"

She shook her head so vehemently that two tendrils of her curly hair came loose. "It's about our wedding," she said just as he gave his hammer a hearty swing.

John's hammer collided with his nail.

Unfortunately, not the metal one that would attach the two boards; no, his hammer hit *his* nail, his thumbnail to be exact.

"Confound it all!" he burst out, tucking his thumb against his palm and curling his fingers around it.

"Are you all right?" she asked, her small hands reaching for his.

He pulled his hand away. "I'm fine," he replied, but only if fine meant being in severe pain from hitting oneself with two pounds of solid metal.

She didn't seem a bit put off by his reaction and reached for his hand again. "Let me see."

"No," he bit off. "I think you've done enough."

"I don't recall hitting you with the hammer."

"You might as well have," he muttered to himself, squeezing his thumb as tightly as he could.

"What's that to mean?"

He gritted his teeth. "Nothing; just go, so I can get back to work."

"But I need to talk to you."

He stared at her and suddenly the discomfort in his thumb was quickly being replaced with another sort of discomfort, the one that had caused him to hit himself with the hammer in the first place.

"When did you plan to return to England?"

"As soon as possible."

Her cheeks grew pink, and the smile that spread her lips was enough to make a man's heart stop. "Well, not too soon. Weddings take time to plan, don't you know?"

There she went again talking about a wedding. "What wedding?" he burst out, his stomach knotting in anticipation of her answer.

"Ours."

"Yes, I heard that the first time." He sighed and leaned back against the fence post. "Carolina," he started. For some reason he couldn't name or place, he preferred to use her full name. And it had nothing to do with her preferring it; at least, that's what he told himself. "I don't know what I might have said or done to make you think there would be a wedding taking place where I would be your bridegroom, but I'm returning to England—alone—as soon as I earn enough for my passage." To be quite blunt, she'd have better luck waiting for her mother to grow a heart than for him to exchange vows with her.

It wasn't that he didn't like her; he did, well, in a way. She was as annoying as his older brothers used to claim him to be. But still, there was something about her... Something fresh and unique; something intriguing and intoxicating; something he didn't want—nay, didn't *need*—to discover.

"Mmmmhmmm," she hummed in a sing-song tone, stealing his attention. "That's what I thought."

He scowled. "What's what you thought?"

She gave a sigh worthy of an actress who'd spent her whole life on Drury Lane. "Your pride and your heart are at war, John."

He knit his brow. What was she talking about? Nonsense, if he had to describe it. "Listen to me, please. I have no intention of marrying you."

She looked unmoved.

Praying she wouldn't ask him to elaborate further than what he planned to tell her, he said, "Carolina, for the majority of my life, I've been practicing what my brother Edward calls near honesty and haven't knowingly told a lie for nearly ten years."

She grinned at him. "See, you haven't *knowingly* told a lie, which is why you're lying to me now; you just don't know it's a lie."

John groaned. "No. I'm not. Carolina, we're from two entirely different worlds. We cannot marry."

"Then just put aside your pride about accepting work from my father and then we'll get married."

John's jaw dropped. "What, pray tell, has transpired between us in the last four days that has made you certain I planned to ask you to marry me?" he asked, matching her blunt tone.

She shrugged. "It's your eyes."

"Pardon? My eyes?" he asked, blinking.

"They told me so," she said simply.

"I wasn't aware eyes could speak."

"Normally, they don't. But yours do." She grinned at the blank look he must have on his face. "See, I'm not one who puts a lot of credit in someone's words. To me, their facial expressions—including eyes—say far more. It's a gift, really. And your eyes, John Banks, say you want to marry me."

"Really? And why have I never before heard of this—this—" he made a rolling gesture with his hand in hopes he'd think of a better word than preposterous— "unusual phenomenon of my eyes telling a young lady of my feelings for her?"

"Because you've never been in love before," she said matter-of-factly.

John took a deep breath and closed his eyes, lest they tell her of the annoyance he felt toward her at the moment. He pinched the bridge of his nose then rubbed his closed eyelids. He hated the thought of saying something cruel to her; she might be an annoyance, but she didn't deserve cruelty. Unfortunately, he didn't know how he could explain what he was thinking without being cruel. "Carolina," he said uneasily, forcing himself to meet her eyes again. "I think you're a fine young lady, but I'm not ready to get married."

"That's all right," she said airily. "Mother would never agree to a short engagement anyway."

"No, your mother doesn't seem the sort who would agree to *any* engagement between the two of us." He sighed. "But that's not the point." Swallowing hard, he took her hands in his. "Do you remember when you told Mr. Cale you'd make a fine wife for someone, just not him? The same could be said for me."

She recoiled as if he'd slapped her.

His eyes widened. "Wait, that's not how I meant it," he said with a ragged breath. "I think you'll be a wonderful wife, but I'm not the husband you need. You need someone who—" He racked his brain for a positive adjective that didn't fit him, but couldn't be considered an insult to her—sadly, no such adjective came to mind. He sighed in frustration at his lack of finding the right words. Her brown eyes were still penetrating his and he shifted his weight from one foot to the other. "Right now you think you're attracted to me because I'm somewhat of a curiosity. But that will pass. In a week or two, you'll wake up and realize that I was nothing more to you than a passing fascination."

She didn't respond, and that bothered him more than if she had. The workings of her mind were a puzzle he doubted even Edward could solve. He nearly snorted. That wasn't much of a stretch. Edward had the hardest time determining his own wife's feelings and desires. In fact, it was John who had to help him. But, as easy as it was to recognize what did and didn't interest Regina, where Carolina was concerned, he was at a loss. The only thing he knew for certain was that while she was the most beautiful creature he'd ever laid eyes on, she was also the most willful and brazen. How fortunate for him she had somehow taken into that unusual mind of hers the notion that one day, presumably in the not-so-distant future, they would be wed.

Her hands squeezed his a fraction tighter. "Very well. I'll let you get back to that fence."

Then, before he could have a chance to question her motives and talk her out of trying anything foolish, she fled.

~ Chapter Eight ~

Carolina had often been termed willful, bold, brazen, or even shameless, but anyone who'd called her that, hadn't seen what she was truly capable of yet!

A passing infatuation gone in two weeks, is that really how he'd termed their feelings?

At nineteen, she may not know a lot about life, but she did know her own feelings. Her heart told her this was love. If she needed any more confirmation, she only had to look at the workings of fate that had brought him to her once again. Now, she just had to prove it to him.

Unfortunately, while she didn't need to do anything more than merely exist for the gentlemen in Charleston to flock to her, she had no idea what to do in a situation where the gentleman in question was resisting her.

"Bethel," she said, flinging the back door wide open.

Bethel's head snapped in her direction. "Yes, chile?"

"I need some help."

Bethel's black eyes widened, likely because the last time Carolina had spoken that exact sentence to her, the two of them had to spend the afternoon in the dye house dying one of Mother's dresses a dark blue to cover up the blood Carolina had gotten all over the front, when she'd cleaned the gash one of the hands' children had gotten in his head. She wiped her hands on the front of her white apron. "Wot hab yous done now?"

"Nothing." Yet. Carolina cleared her throat and waved her hand through the air. "It's nothing like last time. I just need you to help me court John."

"Wot you say?" Bethel asked, her dark brows puckering.

Carolina sighed. "John is being as stubborn as Father's mule, and I've decided to court him, but I need your help."

Bethel didn't look very convinced. "Yous does know 'tis da boy who should be doin' da courtin', don't yous?"

"I know," Carolina said through clenched teeth. "He's just reluctant to do so." She sat down at the little table where Bethel and the other house workers took their meals, picked up a wooden mixing spoon, and idly ran her fingers over the handle. "I think he's afraid to admit his interest in me because he works for Father."

Bethel's eyes softened. "An' yo' sho e's da one yo' wan'?"

Carolina nodded. "I'm sure."

"Wot Mrs. Ellis tink?"

"She doesn't approve," Carolina said, tossing the wooden spoon back onto the table with a hard *thwack*.

"Uh huh." Bethel readjusted her apron and sat down at the table. "An' does yous hav' a plan?"

Carolina bit her lip and shook her head. "No. I just know that I need to court him. I just don't know how."

A slow smile spread across Bethel's lips. "I's gots an idea. Yous come back har 'morrow a hour 'fore yous an' Mrs. Ellis take dinner."

"All right and what do I do before then?"

Bethel's eyes narrowed on her. "Yous ta be doin' nothin', hear?"

"Yes, Bethel," she said, standing.

Bethel's large, callused hand reached out and closed around her arm just above the elbow. "You's not 'bout ta do somethin' stupid, is you?"

Heat burned Carolina's face. Bethel knew her too well. "No, Bethel."

Bethel shook her head. "I's knows be'er dan dat, Miss Lina. An' I tellin' yous, let Bethel hep if yous wan' dat boy."

"But I don't see—"

"No, yous don' see. Listen, chile, if yous wan' him, yous gots to make him knows e canna live witout yous. Jus' do what I say an' in a week that boy won't be able to ask yous to marry him fas' 'nuff."

For some reason, she doubted that, but knew better than to argue with Bethel. "Fine," Carolina said on a sigh. "I'll try it your way."

"Dat's all I's askin'."

"But in a week if it doesn't work—"

"Den yous is ta be doin' yous own thin'. I know," Bethel said with a rueful shake of her head and a wide gap-toothed grin.

"Well, as long as we're clear on that."

"We's clear." Bethel released her hand. "Now, yous be runnin' alon' an' goes sees yous fr'end Marjorie like yous pro'mised an' leab everythin' ta Bethel."

***

Marjorie lived just to the west of Lowland Cross. Despite being four years Carolina's senior, when they were younger, Marjorie would come to Lowland Cross to play with Carolina and Gabriel and any of the field hands' children who wanted to join their games nearly every day before the war began.

After the war ended, everything had changed. Gabriel hadn't returned and Marjorie's life had transformed from the daughter to the wealthiest planter around to the daughter of the poorest.

Carolina ducked between the planks of wood that made up the border between Lowland Cross and Reynolds Ridge and paused a moment. Leading up to the war, Jacob Reynolds had been one of the strongest voices for independence and because of it, the Redcoats had made sure to burn his house and fields to set an example. Though six years had passed since that terrible night, to a stranger it might seem like it had only happened yesterday.

Their once glorious two story brick home that was the envy of everyone around lay in a heap of char and bricks. A smaller structure no larger than the barn back at Lowland Cross was now where they made their home. As promised, Mr. Reynolds had freed every man of color who'd fought alongside him for America's independence, Silas included. The others who'd chosen to stay behind had either run off or been taken captive the night of the fire.

All around Carolina was dry grass and hard dirt where indigo plants as far as the eye could see once grew. She started forward. Having no house nor workers had been hard for the Reynolds as they struggled to rebuild. But they had pride, and they had heart. And combined, they weren't yet ready to give up on their beloved plantation.

"Good afternoon, Marjorie."

"Carolina," Marjorie greeted from where she sat on the hard ground, pulling weeds.

Carolina sank to the ground next to her and looked away so she wouldn't see the grimace she was sure had to be on Marjorie's face. Marjorie may be seen as an outcast to some due to her family's financial ruin, but they were still friends and Carolina cherished her friendships far more than other people's opinions.

"Please don't," Marjorie said quietly as she continued to pluck the weeds that surrounded the Indigofera tinctoria plant.

Carolina gave an exaggerated sigh. "And is it a punishable offense to come sit by my dearest friend in the middle of the afternoon?"

Marjorie cast her a dubious look then turned back to her task. "It should be," she muttered.

Carolina harrumphed while simultaneously plucking the weeds closest to her. "And what is that to mean?" she demanded in mock irritation as she continued to pluck weeds.

"You know exactly what I meant."

Carolina did, indeed. "I did tell you I'd, be coming by," Carolina reminded her. Truly, she didn't know who these visits were harder for. Carolina who felt she was fighting a battle with an army of ten versus one thousand, trying to let Marjorie know that despite all that had happened, she'd always be her friend. Or perhaps it was harder for Marjorie who'd once been the envy of so many to be reduced to doing the work of a field hand. Though Marjorie had never once been the kind to think of anyone as inferior or talk down to anyone, it still had to be hard for her to be seen this way. And then of course there was the rumor regarding her fiance and his throwing her over.

"I know," Marjorie said, breaking into her thoughts. "And I didn't think for one minute that you'd forget."

"Actually, if you find my presence unwanted, you should blame Bethel. I'd planned to come see you tomorrow, but she insisted I needed to come see you right now."

Marjorie made a sound similar to that of a soft snort. It was almost as if she was trying her hardest not to laugh. "How is she?"

"Bethel?"

Marjorie nodded.

"She's all right. She misses Silas something awful."

"We all do." The sadness in her voice was unmistakeable. Though Silas was what Carolina thought some might find scary or intimidating due to his sheer size, he was a very gentle, compassionate man who wouldn't harm a mosquito unless he thought it carried malaria and was about to bite one of the Reynolds', particularly Marjorie.

Carolina reached over and patted her friend's hand. "Do you remember when they first met?"

"Yes," Marjorie said with a wistful smile. "It was at my father's spring barbecue. Silas had only been with us about a month and as soon as Bethel came into view juggling two bowls of cooked vegetables, a pan of fried tomatoes and a loaf of fresh baked bread, Silas ran to help her. And that's when—"

"*She knew*," they both finished in unison.

Carolina shook her head and laughed. "I'll never forget that story and how Bethel knew immediately she was in love for as long as I live."

"Would that be because Bethel retells it all the time?"

"No." Carolina glanced away from where her fingers were wrapped around a cluster of weeds. "Not anymore. She quit telling it when Silas was freed. But I heard it often enough before then."

"Has she seen him since he moved to Charleston?" The concern and longing in her voice was unmistakable.

"I try to make up reasons for her to see him." She sighed and pulled more weeds. "But I think she's given up on him."

"Hmm," was all she'd say.

Carolina's hand stilled over the clump of weeds she'd just gripped and she turned to face her friend. "Marjorie?"

"Hmm?" she said, not stopping in her work.

Carolina twisted her lips. Other than Gabriel, who was her true sibling, she'd considered Marjorie as the sister she'd never had and while she loved them both, they both had this irritating habit of refusing to tell her things. With anyone else this wouldn't be a problem, she'd just find another way to ask until they divulged all the secrets they kept, but for some reason, she had yet to discover a technique that could work on either of them and knew better than to push as it only made them more determined not to say anything. She sighed. "Why do you tease me with your secrets so?"

Marjorie's lips twitched. "Because if I told you, it'd no longer be a secret."

~ *Chapter Nine* ~

Carolina's jaw dropped, "A jar of water?"

"Mmmhmmm," Bethel said, carefully pouring a ladleful of water straight from a metal water pail into one of Mother's canning jars. "A hot day like taday, a man's be needin' some wata."

"But won't he already have a canteen with him?"

"I sho e does. But tis is fresh wata an' it been sittin' in da ice hous' all morn'n so it coo, too." Bethel put down the jar she'd filled and picked up another.

"Why are you filling up two?"

"If Mr. Gabriel is workin' wit him, yous need ta give him a glass, too. O else Mr. John migh' not take his." She finished filling that jar and set the ladle back into the bucket. "But, if e alone, yous can stan' thar while e drink his glass, then leave the other one wit him."

Carolina wrapped her arms as far around Bethel as they'd go and gave her a tight squeeze. "Thank you."

"You's wec'um, chile. Now, take these out thar 'fore theys get warm."

"Oh, right." Carolina released Bethel and picked up the tray with the two jars of water.

Bethel walked to the door with her and opened it, winking to her as she passed.

Carolina willed herself to stay calm as she walked over to where John was working on the roof of the carriage house. It wouldn't do to let her excitement get the better of her and spill the water.

John's tall, broad form came into view, and Carolina halted beneath a shade tree to watch him for a minute as he straightened and pulled his shirt over his head. The sun glistened off the sweat that covered his muscled abdomen and chest. She swallowed. Hard. He was very well formed with hard planes and thick muscles; he looked like he'd been chiseled from marble. He balled up his shirt and ran it across his face and shoulders.

He could certainly use some water, she thought, resuming her steps. "John," she called.

John's body jerked in surprise at her shout, and he lost his footing. With what Carolina thought might be an Englishman's curse—something about Zeus—or was it deuce?—John slid down the steep incline of the roof and over the edge. He was spared an untimely, and quite possibly painful, meeting with the rock-covered ground when his hands found purchase with the edge of the roof just as he went over.

"Did you require something, Carolina?" he asked as cool as can be while dangling from the edge of the roof.

"T-to give you water," she stammered; still in shock.

"I already had water," he pointed out, taking a deep breath. He let go of the roof and jumped down to the ground.

"I know, but I thought you could use some fresh water," she said, walking over to him.

John nodded once then took one of the glass jars of water, not once meeting her eyes. He took a swig. "Thank you."

"You're most welcome. Would you like to go stand in the shade while you drink that?"

"No," he said, taking a large gulp.

Carolina frowned and set the tray with the remaining glass on the ground. "Are you sure? Your skin is going to blister and burn if you continue to stand in the sun."

John's blue eyes went wide as if he'd just remembered he wasn't wearing a shirt. Lacking all sense of grace whatsoever, he quickly lifted the jar of water to his lips and gulped it down as fast as he could, heedless of the two rivulets of water that were streaming out either side of his mouth. If her mother were here, she'd gloat about being right about him being no gentlemen. He finished his glass and wiped the back of his forearm across his wet lips then handed her his empty glass. "I need to—"

"Be getting back to work," she finished for him. "It seems that's what you always say to me."

"That's because you always seem to find me when I'm working."

She cocked her head to the side. "Does that mean, if I sought you out when you weren't working, you'd talk to me?"

"No."

If she didn't want to marry him so badly, she'd shake him silly for his belligerent tone and foolish stubbornness. Employing every ounce of self-control she possessed so not to break her agreement with Bethel, she simply nodded. "All right, then. Get back to work. But here, take this with you." She reached down and grabbed the other glass jar of water and shoved it in his direction.

"Take it with me?"

"Yes, so you can drink it later."

He rolled his eyes. "And just where do you think I'll keep it until it's time to drink it, Carolina, in my pocket?"

"No, just take it up there with you and set it down close to where you're working."

He pushed her hand away from him. "Did you not see me slide down the roof? If I put that jar of water down on the roof, it'll slip right off."

She shrugged. "Then stand here and drink it. I don't mind."

"I'm sure you wouldn't," he muttered under his breath. "Carolina, truly, I thank you for bringing me the water. It was a very nice thing for you to do, but I cannot continue to stand here and drink water when I should be working. It's not fair to your father. He's paying me to do a job, and I'm not doing it."

"Oh, don't worry about that," she said with a dismissive flick of her hand. "Once we mar—" She bit her lip to stop herself. She cleared her throat. "You could pour it into your canteen."

"I already have water in my canteen," he said with a hint of annoyance.

His annoyance with her only served to make her more annoyed with him. "Then give it to one of the other men. I'm sure that unlike you they'd be more than appreciative to have some fresh water."

He ground his teeth. "Do you see anyone else up there working with me?"

Carolina glanced to the carriage house and blinked. She hadn't even noticed he was the only one who'd been working up there. Of course, when she'd walked up, she'd only been looking for him, so hadn't noticed he'd been alone. She shrugged. "All right, how about if I just leave it for you under the tree over there?"

"Fine," he all but growled.

Irritation bubbled in her blood. "There is no reason for you to be treating me this way. Everyone else out here has to drink hot water from a dirty, old canteen or go to the well. One would think you'd be a little more grateful. Not only did I bring you a cool drink now, but I'm offering to leave you another glass. Yet, you act annoyed that I called you down to take a break for a little refreshment."

"I was busy," he said through gritted teeth. "Unlike you, I work for my keep, and I don't have time to take frequent refreshment breaks."

Carolina sucked in a sharp breath at his cold words, and before she could think better of it, she splashed the contents of the jar in John's handsome face. "There. I do believe the dilemma of what to do with this second jar of water has been solved."

~Chapter Ten~

Carolina dropped her head into her hands. "I *cannot* bring him another glass of water," she said to a grinning Bethel.

"Yes, yous can. An' you is."

Carolina dropped her hands and balled them into fists at her sides. "Did I not tell you what happened last time I brought him a drink?"

Bethel nodded. "You did, but I don't think that'll happen again this time."

No, it wouldn't, because there wasn't going to be a "this time". "Isn't there anything else I can do to get his attention?"

Bethel's eyes narrowed at her. "Yous ta do 'xactly wot I says ta do an' I says ta take dis here wata out ta Mr. John, now."

"But he doesn't want it," Carolina protested.

"Yes, e do. He jus' want yous ta think e don't."

"What makes you so sure of that?"

Bethel shrugged and snatched up a white rag from the table. "I's jus knows," she said, reaching into the large black cook stove and removing a pan of baked treats. "Yous better hurra 'fore e goes to de well."

"Yes, ma'am," Carolina said, picking up the tray with the two glasses on it. Since Mother wouldn't let him sleep or eat in the big house, this would be her last chance to see him today. If he didn't respond any better to this glass of water than he had to the last, today would be a total waste.

"Is that for me?" Gabriel asked her as soon as she stepped out the back door and onto the top step.

Carolina wet her lips and pulled the tray closer to her. "No. I'm bringing them to the workers." Had he been over by John, she'd

63

have gladly let him have one of the glasses, but she couldn't show up with only one.

"Uh huh, and would the worker you had in mind happen to answer to the name of John?" he asked with a wide smile and a sparkle in his brown eyes she hadn't glimpsed since his return.

"You know very well that he does." She changed her grip on the tray and glanced over her shoulder through the window to make sure Bethel was still working by the stove and not standing by the window listening to their conversation. "Do you know why he pretends not to like me?" she blurted.

"What makes you certain he's pretending?" he asked, not unkindly, but not in the teasing tone he'd used so many times when they were younger. Despite the wooden leg, the scar that bisected his cheek, and the decidedly harder look to his face, he was still a good-looking man, if not a little more serious.

Carolina shook her head. "You know as well as I do that he is."

Gabriel forced a shrug and leaned against the side of the house. "He hasn't discussed you at all since you've arrived, so I don't know if he returns your interest or if it's you who has enough romantic interest for the both of you."

"Oh, and what did he say before I arrived?"

Gabriel pursed his lips. "Not quite the same thing you're telling me."

She scowled. "Just because he hasn't told you how he feels about me, doesn't mean I'm imagining it. I'm not. Just forget I asked you anything."

"All right." He sent her a fleeting glance then went back to work repairing the ramp that had been put in place to help Father enter and exit the house without help.

A small measure of sadness settled over her. Gabriel was six years older than she was and, despite their age difference, they'd played together almost every day when they were younger. Back then, he'd gotten into just as much trouble as she had. She nearly snorted. That wasn't entirely true. He'd gotten into more. It was Gabriel who'd taught her if she wanted something, it was up to her to fight to get it. More times than she could possibly remember, they'd schemed up plans to avoid doing their chores so they could ride horses all day instead. Perhaps if he hadn't been injured in the war, he'd be interested in scheming up a plan to make John admit his feelings for her.

She swallowed the lump that had formed in her throat at the realization of Gabriel's lost innocence and the cynic he had clearly become. Last night after Mother had gone to bed, she'd tried to ask him why he'd stayed away so long, but his face had grown hard and he'd refused to answer.

Pushing the thought from her mind, she walked in the direction of the carriage house. She took a deep breath and called John's name—a little more delicately this time.

"Yes?" his loud voice called back.

Carolina took a deep breath. She could do this. He clearly didn't appreciate her efforts, and they seemed not to be working; but if she wanted Bethel's approval of her plan to snag John however she saw fit, she *had* to do what Bethel asked first. "Would you like to come down and have another glass of water?"

A loud grunt was his only reply.

Now, *that* was a pleasant response. Carolina felt like grunting in aggravation herself. Instead, she walked over to the side of the carriage house she was sure the grunt had emanated and tilted her head up toward the roof where he must be working out of view. "Would you quit acting like a mule and come drink some water?"

"I'll drink it as soon as you give it to me," a soft, deep voice said behind her.

Carolina spun around so fast the jars almost tipped. "John."

"That's what they call me." He flashed a smile. "May I?"

"Of course. Oh, would you take them both, please?" He frowned at her, but before he could argue, she said, "I'll drink the second one. I just need you to take it off the tray so I can set the tray down."

He gave her a queer look but took the two glasses of water, so she could set down the heavy tray. "Thank you for bringing me water," he said, handing her glass to her.

"You're welcome." She took a sip, relishing the way the cool water felt going down her throat. She could only imagine how much John must crave cold water. Lowering her glass, she allowed her eyes to drift down to his broad chest. She might have seen it earlier, but that didn't mean she couldn't look at it again. She cringed on his behalf. Just as she'd warned him, his skin that was once as white as a cloud had a distinctively pink hue to it now, the start of a painful South Carolina sunburn.

John cleared his throat, stealing her attention from his chest. He lifted his brows at her when she met his eyes. "I wanted to talk to you about earlier—"

"It's of no account," she said, flicking her wrist and remembering her promise to Bethel that she wouldn't mention the words marriage or wedding to John again until after he'd proposed to her. Frankly, if not for that promise, she might have demanded he make amends by putting aside his stupid pride and admitting he wanted to marry her.

A strange look came over John's face, and he dropped his gaze to where his dirty and worn leather boots were kicking at the rocks beneath his feet. "No, Carolina, it is of account," he said, lifting his head and taking a keen interest in the jar in his hand. "I was frustrated and spoke to you in a way that was most inappropriate. You were kind enough to bring me a drink, and I should have been more thankful. It was most kind of you to bring me another glass this afternoon, but if you don't bring me another, I'd certainly understand."

Carolina stared at him as he turned to the side and struggled through a coughing fit that had suddenly developed. Was this an attempt to get her to stop? Since he refused to look at her, she couldn't be sure; but if that *was* his plan, he was about to learn the definition of persistence. She'd bring him a glass of water every hour with the intent of getting him fired if that's what it'd take for him to stop this nonsense.

She took a long drink of her water then forced a smile. "As I said, it's of no account."

He nodded once then drank what was left in his jar. He handed it back to her and wiped his mouth with the back of his dirty hand. "I must be—" He shrugged. "Well, you already know what I was about to say."

Yes, she did already know. She also knew she was one day closer to being done with Bethel's nonsense.

***

Sadly, the second day of Bethel's plan consisted of doing exactly the same thing: bringing John two glasses of water. At first, he'd acted surprised to see her. But the second time, he looked as if he were expecting to see her.

So, it was with great reluctance that she entered the kitchen on the third day.

"Please tell me I am not supposed to bring him water again today, because I fear that plan is not working."

"No, no wata taday," Bethel said, offering her a wide smile. "Come back har a hour 'fore Mrs. Ellis take her dinner an' I'll have everythin' ready."

Resisting the urge to protest, Carolina went away to amuse herself with a novel for a few hours. Not that she read any of it. She didn't. She just sat in the shade and pretended to read it while she watched John from the distance as he and Cain, an older field hand, replaced some of the boards around the storage shed.

Bethel's shout from the kitchen brought Carolina from her fog. She scrambled to her feet and ran into the kitchen.

"What's that?"

"A pic-a-nic ham'er. Wot it look like?"

"I know it's a picnic hamper. But why are you putting food into it?"

Bethel dropped two apples into the hamper and closed the lid. "Because yous and Mr. John be goin' on a picnic."

"Are you sure this is a good idea?"

"Yes, it is," Bethel said, pursing her lips. "Miss Lina, a boy who work so har be needin' nour'men' an' dat food de han's make ain't good 'nuff. E's be wan'ing foo a good meal."

Carolina nodded. That made sense. "But are you sure I shouldn't just invite him to join us for supper?"

Bethel's hands shot to her hips. "No. You's ta brin' him the pic-a-nic ham'er like I tells ya ta."

Carolina stared at the picnic basket. What if he didn't want to eat with her? He didn't seem to be enjoying her lingering for the five minutes it took for him to drink his water twice a day. Why would he agree to go on a picnic with her?

Bethel's callused fingertips touched her chin and tipped Carolina's face up until she was looking into Bethel's dark eyes.

"You stop worrin' an' take dis ou' there 'fore e runs off wit the ot'ers ta eat."

Carolina swallowed her nerves as she walked toward the shed. "John," she called as she approached.

No answer.

"John."

No answer again.

She sighed and walked to the building to see if he was working on the roof or one of the sides now. He wasn't there. She frowned and peered inside to see if he was hiding from her. No, not in there, either.

Where could he be? She lifted her hand to block the sun and walked back in the direction of the western border. Perhaps a board had come loose or something. She frowned when she reached the other side of the cluster of buildings only to find nobody near the fence.

Transferring the basket to her other hand, she spun around and walked toward the indigo fields. Surely, he hadn't been told to go work over there. But then again, there were only so many repairs that needed to be made around the plantation. Her stomach knotted at the idea of him working in the indigo fields.

The knots tightened when the field came into view and she caught sight of Mr. Haney as he walked around the field with his large whip coiled in his hand.

Nausea threatened to overtake her and she turned away. So many times she'd wished she could run away, never to witness another day of slavery again. Of course, to voice her dislike for the practice would get her ridiculed and scorned as it was the natural way of life here. But it wasn't *her* way, and she longed to be free of the plantation that seemed to enslave her just as much as it did those who worked on it.

Taking deep breaths, she walked as fast as she could away from the fields. She suspected everyone knew of her compassion for those who worked on the plantation—they just either didn't care or couldn't do anything about it. If the plantation were hers, she'd free them all. But the plantation wasn't hers.

"Is something wrong, Lina?" Gabriel asked.

She blinked in surprise. She'd been so caught up in her thoughts she hadn't realized where she was walking. "No. Not at all. I was just looking for John. I brought him lunch." She lifted the hamper to emphasize her point.

"Check the pasture."

"The pasture?"

He nodded. "I gave him the afternoon off while Dalton rides back to town to pick up more boards."

"Thank you," she said.

Gabriel looked as if he were about to say something more, but then decided against it and shut his mouth. Odd.

The pastures were on the opposite end of the plantation, and by the time she reached them, she had most certainly worked up an appetite.

Unfortunately, John was nowhere in sight.

Irritation swelled in her breast; irritation for John and his annoying pride and irritation for Bethel for making her act like some trained dog by waiting on John. This method of bringing him things several times a day might work for some, but it clearly wasn't for Carolina, and it only made her look like a fool, besides.

Too hungry and annoyed to bother to go back to the big house or search for John any longer, she decided to take the hamper to the little pond that was hidden behind the trees and have a picnic alone. Any other day, she'd have preferred to picnic at the larger pond. It wasn't surrounded by as many trees, but the picturesque view was far more impressive.

Shifting the hamper back to the opposite hand, Carolina made her way toward the little pond and froze when she heard a noise. Her eyes narrowed as she looked through the thicket of trees. Then they widened when they landed on the creator of the noise she'd heard.

There, just through the trees, in the pond swimming, was John —shirtless.

~ *Chapter Eleven* ~

John's skin prickled with awareness. Someone was out there watching him.

He sank lower in the water until all that could be seen was his head.

"Who's there?" he shouted.

Nothing.

He kicked his feet and moved to the middle of the pond to get a better view of the trees that encircled the pond. A soft sound of twigs breaking under someone's foot stole his attention.

"Show yourself."

His command went unheeded and he continued to scan the thicket of trees.

Mrs. Ellis seemed to have a severe distaste for him, but surely even she wouldn't be so coarse as to approach him while he was bathing.

A flash of pink caught his eye.

He groaned. "Come on out, Carolina," he called.

He thought she might ignore his request and was quite relieved when she stepped out from behind her hiding spot in the trees and walked toward the pond.

"What are you doing?" he demanded.

She shrugged. "I came over here to have a picnic and..."

If he was one who placed wagers, he'd guess she'd been looking for him so he could be her picnic companion. "Well, if you've satisfied your curiosity, I'd appreciate it if you'd find something else to amuse yourself with this afternoon." He sorely hoped she'd take his meaning and leave. There were only two possible outcomes if someone were to find them like this. One was marriage, the other was death. One of those—he wouldn't say which—was slightly more preferable than the other. But only slightly.

"There's another pond, one far more private, just over that way." She pointed to the left; her eyes still trained on where he was treading water in the middle of the pond. Had she no shame? He already knew she lacked the manners all the other females of his acquaintance possessed, but did she have to stand there and stare at him?

"Thank you. I'll keep that in mind."

She took a seat on the plush green grass that lined the edge of the pond. "Would you like to come out and have lunch with me? I'm sure Bethel packed enough for both of us."

He'd just bet she had. "No, I think I'd like to swim a little longer."

"Oh, well, that's all right. You keep swimming. I'm famished. I have to eat."

"Is there nowhere else you can picnic?" *Perhaps somewhere that wasn't within a stone's throw of a naked man in a pond?*

"No." She opened the picnic hamper and began removing some of the items. "I rather like it here."

She wouldn't like it if he stepped out of the water. Actually, *she* probably would. He suppressed that thought immediately. "Carolina, do you think your stomach can manage not to eat itself for just a moment, so you may leave while I get out of the water?"

Carolina seemed not to hear him and continued to pull items out of the basket. "You need not worry. I've seen a man's chest before."

"Perhaps so, but have you seen a man's pego?" The words were out before he could think to stop himself from saying them.

"Pardon me, what?"

In for a penny, in for a pound, he supposed. "A man's pego, rudder, snake, rod, bauble, tallywag, member. Have you seen one before?"

Her cheeks turned bright red, as he'd hoped they would. "N-no."

"Very well, and if you plan to keep it that way, then you'd better leave, so I can get out of the water and put my clothes back on."

Carolina's eyes shot to where his clothes were in a pile by the shore, but she made no move to get up. "How about if I turn around? Then, when you're dressed, we can have lunch together."

John wanted to groan. "Does anything scandalize you?"

"No." She tucked a long, curly tendril of hair behind her ear. "At least not where you're concerned."

"Why the devil not?" he burst out.

She brought her hands to her lap and looked at him. "Because I know you're only saying those things to put me off. But I have news for you, John Banks. It's not working."

"And I have news for you, Carolina Ellis. Your news isn't news at all. Furthermore, if I didn't think it was possible for your brother or someone else to happen upon us at any moment, I wouldn't hesitate to get out of this water."

"Then go ahead."

"No," he bit off. "I'd rather not get married with the barrel of your father's gun pressing into my back."

"Ah, so you do wish to marry me."

He ground his teeth. "I never said that."

She shook her head and sighed. "I don't understand why you're being so stubborn."

"And I don't understand why you think I want to offer you marriage."

Carolina's face fell. "I already told you. It's the way you look at me."

"Yes, well, perhaps I think you're beautiful. But that's as far as my attraction for you goes." He tore his eyes away and coughed, silently praying she didn't challenge the validity of his words.

Silence filled the air between them and he dared not venture a look in her direction. "Are you practicing your near honesty now?" she asked airily, emphasizing the word near.

He ground his teeth. "No. That was a perfectly honest statement."

"All of it?"

"Yes," he bit off.

"Say what you wish." She gestured to the food she'd laid out. "Wouldn't you like to join me? I'm sure you're hungry after working so hard this morning."

"No, I'm quite content, thank you. I had a large bowl of slop before I came out here. I should be able to tread water for at least another four hours before requiring anything else."

"Suit yourself," she called back, taking a bite of a roasted chicken leg. "You do realize if you tread water for four hours straight, you'll likely get a blistering sunburn?"

It wouldn't take that long. He'd been so hot the last few days he'd taken his shirt off several times before feeling his skin burn and remembering to put it back on. That's actually why he came to the pond: to soothe the blisters he already had. Unfortunately, they might only get worse if he didn't get out of the sun soon. "Then perhaps, if you don't wish such a fate as blistered skin upon your darling, you should leave so he may dress."

Carolina nearly lost her grip on her chicken leg. "Now, I'm certainly not leaving."

"Why, so you might torture me longer?"

"No, because you just admitted to being my darling."

"You know that wasn't what I meant." He brought his cupped hand up to the surface of the water and moved it in a sweeping semi-circle, creating a large spray of water. "Why are you here?"

"To enjoy a picnic."

"And it's just a coincidence you decided to have your picnic forty feet from a naked man?"

"Actually, it is. I didn't know you were here when I came to the pond."

A few minutes went by with John treading water and Carolina happily eating her lunch.

"Why are you really here, Carolina," he burst out at last.

"I told you. I came to the pond to have a picnic."

"No, not that. Why are you always finding reasons to turn up where I am?"

"So we can talk."

"Why do you want to talk to me so much?"

She flipped her long thick braid over her shoulder. "Because I want you to know there's nothing to be ashamed of. I don't care that you don't have as much money as the men in Charleston. Your lack of wealth doesn't matter to me and won't influence my decision to marry you."

"So you think by plaguing me, one day you'll break down my defenses and I'll ask you to marry me," he said bluntly.

"Yes. No." She blinked at him. "When worded like that, it sounds most unkind."

"Ah, then it came out how I meant it." He'd tried humoring her, ignoring her, scandalizing her, and nicely telling her he had no desire to marry her; and nothing had worked to deter her. Perhaps the only way she'd understand would be if he abandoned all the tact and decorum his tutors had tried to instill in him and gave her the blunt truth. "Carolina, listen to me. I cannot fathom why you enjoy my company so much. Nor, do I pretend to know why you think I plan to offer you marriage. But I don't. The look you think you see in my eyes is lust—not love."

"You're wrong," she fired back, matching his fierce tone. "I know you're wrong. You're just scared to admit your feelings for me. But I hope for your sake that you don't tread water and play this game too long. I might be sitting on the shore waiting for you now, but I won't always be here." Then, either to prove her point or save herself from embarrassing herself further, she took to her feet and walked away.

John watched her retreating form as she made her way through the trees and felt torn. Likely, he'd gotten rid of her permanently. Unfortunately, it was at the expense of her feelings. And blast it all; now that he'd done it, he wasn't so sure it was what he wanted after all.

Before someone showed up to collect the picnic hamper Carolina had abandoned on the shore, he got out of the water and pulled his clothes on.

"What are you doing here?"

John snapped his head up and met Gabriel's brown eyes. "I was swimming."

Gabriel dropped his gaze to the picnic hamper at John's feet. "Ironic, because I just passed Lina on the other side of the trees, and she said she'd been here having a picnic."

Tension fisted in John's gut. "She did," he confirmed. The proof was there. There was no use lying about it.

"And you were swimming," Gabriel's words a statement, not a question.

"Yes."

Gabriel's eyes traveled from John's wet hair to his dry trousers. "Would you care to offer me any type of explanation?"

"No, I don't believe I would."

Gabriel didn't crack the slightest hint of a smile. "You do realize, though this is considered the 'new world' and we've abandoned most of the same customs you still honor, we have not abandoned the one regarding unwed ladies being alone with gentlemen—especially one who's just confessed to having been undressed in her presence—and I am within my rights to demand you marry her."

John crossed his arms. "You can demand it. And I'll even honor it if you do so. But as a brother who clearly loves his sister, I don't think you'll make such a demand because you wouldn't wish to condemn her to a life of misery with an unhappy groom."

"Do you find her disagreeable, then?"

"Not disagreeable, exactly; she seems to have a very nice

personality when she's not angry or running after me with glasses of water while trying to convince me that I'm being ridiculous for not putting aside some pride she's imagined I carry around with me in order for me to marry her." He grimaced. "I hate to tell you this, Gabriel, but your sister is too forward by half."

Gabriel sighed. "I can't blame her. Mother's never bothered to teach Lina to be a lady. She's too absorbed in her own doings. But don't worry; I'll take care of this."

"You're not going to hurt her feelings, are you?" John asked, finding a sudden fascination with the bark on a nearby tree.

Though John couldn't see them, he felt Gabriel's eyes boring into him. "No," Gabriel said slowly. "Though why you should care whether I hurt her feelings or not does seem a bit odd."

John bristled. "Yes, well, I think it's odd that after you came back outside from the kitchen earlier, you informed me that we didn't have enough boards to continue working for the day and suggested I go to the pastures. However, I know I saw at least twenty-four boards behind the big house, and you don't hear me musing about the coincidence, do you?"

Gabriel threw his hands into the air. "Point taken."

~ *Chapter Twelve* ~

John winced as the rough fabric of his shirt rubbed against his skin. Just as Carolina had predicted, he'd blistered and burned. While it had hurt mildly yesterday, it was quite intense today— almost as intense as the headache he'd had since he'd woken up this morning.

"Banks," Mr. Ellis called from the open window in the big house. "I'd like to talk to you."

John froze. He needed to talk to Mr. Ellis, too. But the look on the older man's face made it fairly clear they did not wish to discuss the same thing. Carolina seemed convinced the two of them were to be married and had likely thought it prudent to discuss the matter of John working here with her father. He let out a deep breath and walked inside the big house. "Sir?"

Mr. Ellis gestured to the settee closest to him. John hesitated. Mrs. Ellis had made it quite clear he was unwelcome in the house. She might expire on the spot if she walked in to find him sitting on her satin settee in her formal parlor.

"Sit," Mr. Ellis encouraged.

John gingerly sat as close to the edge of the settee as he could.

"Don't mind her," Mr. Ellis said with a scowl. "Sometimes I think she'd have preferred it if I'd not come back from the war at all."

The bitter disappointment in his voice was unmistakable even to John. "Surely she doesn't think that. She's just unhappy that I'm here."

Mr. Ellis shook his head and frowned. "No. She was this way before you arrived. I thought she might be forlorn because Gabriel hadn't returned." He twisted his lips. "I didn't believe Lina when she tried to convince me that wasn't the reason. But after spending the last six years inside the house with her and then witnessing her lack of excitement at Gabriel's return, I'm more inclined to believe Lina." He shook his head, a rueful expression on his face this time. "Damnable girl, she is," he muttered, a pained expression on his face. "When she was younger, she used to tell me she might not always understand words, but she could decipher actions and facial expressions. I guess she was right even then, but I was too doubtful to see it."

Unease settled in John's stomach. Was Mr. Ellis telling him this because he truly believed it, or because he, too, was trying to convince John that he and Carolina should make a match? Either way, the entire conversation was making him unsettled. Try to fight it as much as he might, he *did* find himself attracted to Carolina and desperately hoped the whole "it's in your eyes" claim was just a ploy.

Otherwise, he was in trouble indeed.

"Is something troubling you, son?" Mr. Ellis asked, startling John.

He swallowed. "No."

Mr. Ellis didn't look very convinced but didn't say anything further. "I've been meaning to talk to you about something." He grimaced and shifted in his invalid's chair as best he could then used his hand to roll himself backward and away from where the sun was flooding the room through the large window to his left. "How would you like to stay on here at Lowland Cross?"

"I thank you very much for the offer, but soon I'll have all I need." He found a sudden fascination with the laces on his boot and mumbled, "It's time I go home." How strange that a small wave of sadness washed over him at putting voice to those words. He dismissed the unwelcome emotion easily enough. He had been on this side of the ocean for more than a year now; it was natural that he'd feel a little sad about leaving.

"You don't have to," Mr. Ellis said. "We won't hold it against you that you're an Englishman."

John ran his hand through his blond hair the way he'd witnessed Edward doing so many times. Carolina had to be behind this conversation. He shifted in his seat, but not so much that he rubbed any dirt from his trousers onto the green settee. "Mr. Ellis," he began unevenly. "My interest in...er....what I mean is..." He shifted again as something akin to nausea settled into his stomach. How exactly did one tell a lady's father, who just so happened to be his employer, he had no interest in marriage to her without both losing his job and angering said man for hurting his daughter? What a coil; one that was making him feel like he was about to lose his breakfast. "Mr. Ellis, my interest here at Lowland Cross is to earn an honest wage. I'm not here to pursue your daughter."

Mr. Ellis blinked. "I never said you were." His eyes narrowed. "Is there something I need to know about, Banks?"

"No, sir," John rushed to say, heat creeping up his face. "I just thought..." He cleared his throat and patted his chest with his hand, then flinched at the added pain of touching himself.

"Lina's been relentlessly pursuing John," Gabriel said, limping into the room.

"I wouldn't say she's been relentless," John said with a frown. He didn't require Gabriel's assistance with this, and for some reason, his involvement was swiftly becoming more annoying than anything Carolina had ever said or done. "She's just a bit—" he waved his right hand in a circle through the air— "I can't think of a good word to describe it other than to say she keeps showing up."

"And it annoys him," Gabriel added.

John scowled at his friend.

"Well, doesn't it?" Gabriel asked.

John swallowed. "Yes," he said, curling his fingers into the fabric of his trousers, so he wouldn't pat his chest and hurt himself again. It wasn't Carolina, in general, that annoyed him, but the thoughts that ran through his head while she was present.

She was a very beautiful woman, and as much as he'd like to deny it, he certainly desired her. But as much as he desired her and spent his nights dreaming of removing one of her fancy dresses, he couldn't do that without offering her marriage. That was the crux of it: he couldn't offer her marriage. They might be content with each other for a while, but eventually her scandalous behavior would lead to his destruction. And unlike his father, who'd fallen in love with and married a lady whose affections lay elsewhere, he had no desire for either of them to be publicly embarrassed.

Across the room, Mr. Ellis sat quietly with his head cocked to the side, staring at him. "So you have no interest in marrying my daughter?" he asked at last.

John sent up a silent prayer of thanks that he'd specifically asked about marriage and not an interest in his daughter in general. For he knew he wouldn't have been able to lie to him had he asked the latter. He met the older man's eyes. "No."

Mr. Ellis lowered his gaze and nodded his head once. "I'll be sure to speak to my daughter."

"Speak to me about what?" Carolina said, walking into the room as if she were floating on air.

She wore a lavender dress with white lacy accents that clung to her full bosom in a way certain to drive any man mad with desire. He jerked his gaze away and refused to look in her father's direction.

"You're plaguing John," Gabriel said, seemingly oblivious to John's discomfort. "He doesn't like you coming out to speak to him while he's working."

Carolina blanched as if her brother had struck her, and John had the strangest urge to refute Gabriel's words and comfort her. But that wouldn't do anybody any good. She'd just take that as encouragement and that'd only lead to more trouble. Better to just wound her pride a little today than devastate her when it was time to leave.

"I brought him water," she explained to their father, who was staring at her intently.

"You find being brought a glass of water to be an annoyance?" Mr. Ellis asked, piercing John with his steely gaze.

John pursed his lips together. When stated like that, he was the one who seemed to be unreasonable. He shot a pointed look to Gabriel. Why did he have to bring this up today? John was perfectly content he'd handled the situation with Carolina yesterday. Now, she thought he went around telling everyone she was an annoyance and even got her father involved. He sighed. "I don't wish to cause any trouble. I didn't ask her to bring me the water, and I should hate for her to think she has to in order to be hospitable."

All three of the other occupants in the room stared at him.

"Son, were you trained in the art of wartime diplomacy?"

John grinned. "No. If I told you what I'd been trained to be, you probably wouldn't believe me." With his dirty, haggard appearance and understanding of manual labor, nobody would believe he was the younger son of a wealthy baron who'd always imagined he'd grow up to become a quiet country vicar, whose only cuts on his fingers would be gained by flipping pages of his Bible.

"Well, nobody here cares what you came from, just that you do an excellent job—which you clearly do. Now that Lina won't be interrupting you, I can't wait to see what you accomplish around here. Let's go," Gabriel said, giving John a hearty slap on the back.

John jerked—and though he was embarrassed to admit as much, he yelped—at the pain of Gabriel's palm colliding with his sunburned back.

He immediately straightened and tried to ignore the inquisitive stares of Mr. Ellis and Gabriel.

"I'd be happy to bring you some tea leaves for your sunburn, but I'd hate to be an annoyance," Carolina said with a triumphant smile; then, before he could form a response, she swept from the room as if she were the fairest in the land. Which, undoubtedly she was.

~ *Chapter Thirteen* ~

Carolina was angry. And mortified. Oh, and decidedly unsympathetic toward John as she stood in the hall just outside the parlor and watched him remove his shirt, exposing a burn worse than any she'd ever seen. His skin was a dark red that rivaled the color of an apple's peel.

If she were anything like her mother, she'd prance back in there and remind him had he listened to her and come out of the water, he wouldn't resemble a boiled lobster. But she wasn't like that. Nor was she the type who could idly stand by when somebody was in pain—no matter how much she thought he might deserve it.

Tearing her eyes away from the painful sight, she went up to her room where she'd hidden a jar of salve made from honey mixed with aloe and tea leaves. She swallowed a hard lump in her throat at the sight of the little jar. She'd first made the ointment to soothe the broken flesh of one of the field hands when Forrester, their previous overseer, had used the whip on him. After that night, she'd mixed together a small jar and kept it in her room for whenever it might be needed.

She gripped the jar tightly and descended the stairs.

"Do you know where Bethel is?" Gabriel asked, poking his head out of the parlor. "I rang but nobody came."

"Mother asked Bethel to air out the attics, and both Mary and Cherrie were sent to the sewing house to make Mother another dress for the supper she's hosting later this week."

Gabriel scowled. "Why does she need another dress? Does she not think she has enough already?" He shook his head. "Never mind; could you find someone to bring us some water and cloth, please? I'd do it myself, but..."

"I know," she said quietly. Gabriel's use of a cane would make it impossible to juggle a basin of water and bandages. "Here, have him put this on while I go get the water."

Her brother took the jar of salve from her and went back into the parlor while Carolina went downstairs and gathered a basin of water and a white sheet they could tear.

She draped the sheet over her arm and held onto the outer edge of the basin with both hands, walking slowly so it wouldn't spill.

"Where do you want me—"

Her words were cut off with the most awful, wretched sound she'd ever heard as John cast up his breakfast in one of Mother's potted plants.

"Well, if she didn't hate me already, she will now," he said, closing his eyes and leaning backward. He winced when his bare back hit the back of the settee.

"You need to be in bed," Father said matter-of-factly.

John gave his head a single shake. "No. I'm sure I'll be fine now that I've ridded my body of the unidentifiable slop I was served for breakfast."

Silence enveloped the room. Carolina knew his words were meant as a lighthearted jest, but to her they were anything but. She'd argued with her mother mercilessly over the years to allow the field hands the supplies necessary to make better meals for themselves. But just like every other time she'd spoken to her mother, she'd been sent away with a sharp word and a smarting cheek.

"Nevertheless," Father began in a voice that sounded as if there was a pound of gravel in his throat, "you need to lie down."

Although she thought he might, John didn't offer another weak protest. Instead, his eyes were almost closed and his face was completely relaxed.

"Lina, go find Lamar and tell him we need his help," Gabriel said.

Carolina's skin prickled.

"Lamar's not here," Father said. "Your mother sent him to Charleston with Dalton."

"You'll have to help me get him down the hall, Lina," Gabriel said. He walked over to where John appeared to be nearing sleep on the far end of the settee and set his cane down.

Carolina put her basin and sheet down on the end table and joined her brother. Careful not to hurt him too badly with her touch, she helped Gabriel pull John to his feet. Gabriel put one arm around John's waist and pulled John's arm around his shoulders for support, then grabbed his cane again. Carolina tried to mirror the stance then nodded to Gabriel when she was ready to start walking.

Gabriel took a wobbly step first, then Carolina. John, it would seem, was so nearly passed out, his feet slipped from under him when he tried to walk.

"Keep going," Gabriel said; his face contorted with pain.

Carolina continued to walk, heedless of John's inability to walk himself. His heavy arm wrapped around her shoulders, only made heavier by his deadweight, made it impossible to walk very quickly. She could only imagine how much Gabriel must be hurting.

Since he'd returned home, Gabriel had been staying with Father in what used to be the less formal parlor. Neither could navigate the stairs in their condition, and with no bedrooms on the first floor, the only option had been to convert a common room into a bedroom. Unfortunately, there wasn't another such room that could easily be compromised, so until something else could be arranged, the two had to share. And if Carolina didn't know any better, she was certain those two would be sharing that room with someone else tonight.

"Let's put him on my bed," Gabriel said with a grunt.

Carolina nodded her response.

With another series of grunts and a few vile curses Carolina would have never thought Gabriel capable of uttering, they managed to get John into the bed, lying on his stomach.

"His back is burned far worse than his chest," Gabriel explained.

Carolina righted her gown and went back to the parlor to get the water, salve and sheet. As she neared the door, another series of vile curses floated to her ear. She walked back into the room. "What has come over you?" she insisted.

Gabriel at least had the manners to look shamefaced for his foul words. He gestured to John. "Could you just see to him, please?"

"Of course," she set the basin of water down on Gabriel's nightstand. "Can you tear this cloth for me?"

Gabriel took the fabric and sat down on the bed while Carolina uncorked the jar of salve. Dipping three fingers into the large mouth of the jar, she took a large scoop of the ointment then brought her hand to John's shoulders where the burns were the worst.

A small sigh of relief escaped John's parted lips, and despite her irritation with the insufferable man, she smiled.

"Does that really help anything?" Gabriel asked, not looking up from where he was shredding the sheet.

"The salve?"

A grunt was his only response.

"I believe so, yes."

A hush fell over the room and Carolina continued to apply the salve. When it appeared she had covered the worst of his burns with the ointment, she recorked the jar and reached for the fabric Gabriel had separated. It was still in rather large pieces, so she doubled it over then dunked it in the water basin at her side. She gently squeezed it to get out some of the extra water, but not too much, and then placed the strip of wet fabric on John's back.

He groaned in response. She picked up another section of cloth and did the same thing. From beneath his heavy eyelids, John made eye contact with her then lost the battle of keeping them open.

She blushed when she caught sight of Gabriel watching her stare at John.

"He's a good man," Gabriel said softly when a series of low snores filled the room.

Carolina lowered her lashes. "Just not good enough for me?"

"I never said that."

"Then are you trying to insinuate that I'm not good enough for him?"

"No."

"Then what's the problem?" she blurted. "What have you against us marrying?"

"I never said that I didn't approve of the two of you marrying." He hiked his right trouser leg up, exposing the wooden leg underneath.

She jerked her eyes away so not to embarrass him by looking at his leg and turned her attention back to where John's tan, chiseled face rested on the white pillow. "You didn't have to say anything. Your interference this morning was quite enough."

Gabriel sighed. "Lina, you cannot throw yourself at the man and expect him to take notice of you. At least not in the way you'd like."

Carolina cast a scowl in her brother's direction, praying the man in question couldn't hear them. "I wasn't throwing myself at him; I was bringing him water like Bethel said."

"And the picnic?"

Carolina blushed. "That was Bethel's idea, too."

Gabriel unbuckled the straps that held his wooden leg in place just above his knee. Carolina sucked in a quick breath. His skin was a red color that rivaled John's sunburn. Immediately, Carolina handed him her salve to rub on his raw skin.

"Since when did you start asking Bethel advice regarding gentlemen?" he asked as he applied the salve.

"Since I don't know how to get him to put aside his pride and admit he wants to marry me. That's when."

Gabriel stared blankly at her. "Well, if that was your plan, then you were certainly going about it the wrong way." His face contorted in pain.

"Well, it's not like you or anyone else around here was inclined to give me advice. Besides, she did get Silas' attention, didn't she?"

"John's a gentleman, not a field hand, Lina. You have to be more subtle."

She bit her lip. "So then what should I do?"

"Be more subtle," he said, as if that explained everything. He touched what must have been a particularly painful spot on his thigh and grimaced. "You can bring him the water but don't stay to talk to him. Just hand it to him then leave."

Leave? That was the stupidest thing she'd ever heard. "I can't just leave. He'll try to give the water back if I do that."

"Yes, but he'll have to chase after you to do so, won't he?"

"Yes," she admitted.

"And that's what you want, Lina. You need to create a situation where he's the one pursuing you."

"How do I do that?"

"I already told you," he grumbled, buckling the straps again. "When you see him, only give him a little sampling of what he can have. Then leave and make him chase after you."

Carolina idly chewed her lip. "I think I can do that."

Gabriel pushed to his feet with a grimace. "I'd never doubt a clever girl like you could."

~Chapter Fourteen~

John needed to retch.

And just his luck, there was no proper receptacle nearby.

With a groan, he reached under the edge of the bed and felt for the chamberpot. His fingers brushed against something hard and cold. He used the last of his strength to slide it out from under the bed then emptied the remaining contents of his stomach into it.

He groaned again. He *hated* being sick. Had he remembered this particular aftereffect of spending too much time in the sun, he just might have taken his chances and come out of that water to get dressed sooner. He buried his face in his pillow. He owed Carolina an apology, and not just for this morning, for yesterday, too. He'd been most unkind to her. He might not understand her fascination with him, and he certainly didn't welcome it, but that was no cause to speak to her that way.

"Would you like some water?" a familiar voice said from the door.

John turned his head to the side. "Please."

The fabric of Carolina's thick skirts swished as she walked across the room to him.

Grimacing, John turned onto his side. "Thank you."

She handed him the water. "You're welcome."

"Carolina, I've been meaning to talk to you about yesterday."

Her face reddened. "Please, don't speak of it. I should have left when I saw that you were swimming. I'm sorry for not doing so."

"Don't apologize. I'm the one who called you to the shore." He set the glass of water down on the nightstand. "I was wrong for what I said yesterday."

She nodded once. "So then you don't lust after me?"

Despite the flames that seemed to have begun licking his face in the last second, he held her gaze and swallowed. "No, that part is true. I certainly have a physical attraction to you. I cannot deny that. But what I meant was that I was wrong for telling you that. I should have chosen my words more carefully."

"Ah, that's the thing about words, isn't it? They have this unnatural ability to cut deeper than a knife." She shrugged and walked to the door. "Not to worry, you didn't hurt my feelings yesterday," she said softly, then left.

John didn't believe her but was too tired to call her back to argue with her. With a silent vow that he'd apologize again and make it right later, he lay back down and closed his eyes.

A few hours later, he was awakened by the touch of delicate fingers sweeping the hair from his forehead.

"Carolina," he grumbled, opening one eye.

"Hmm?" She wasn't looking at him but at where her hands were on the cloth by the basin. She pulled a large white piece of cotton from the water and began to fold it.

"What are you doing with that?"

She didn't answer him, or if she did, he didn't hear her answer. A minute later she pressed something cold and wet to his forehead and cheek. "You have a fever," she said quietly. "Do you still feel nauseous?"

"No; just tired."

"Rest, then," she murmured, gently scratching his head with her nails.

He closed his eyes and sighed.

"You like this?" she asked.

A half-grunt, half-groan was the best answer he could form.

He heard her lips form a smile. "Then I should send Bethel in. She does it far better than I do."

If he had another ounce of energy, he would have shaken his head in protest. He didn't want Bethel to scratch his head. He wanted her. Carolina.

What felt like only minutes later, he was being awakened again.

"Drink," she said, handing him a glass.

He took a sip then handed it back before falling against the pillows again, hoping she'd scratch his head the way she'd done last time.

Carolina didn't say anything as she resumed her seat on the edge of his bed and gently ran her fingernails across his scalp in the most relaxing and enjoyable way imaginable.

"Don't stop," he said into his pillow a few minutes later when Carolina's hand had stilled. Or perhaps he only dreamt he said it because she did stop and quietly quit the room. Afterward, he slowly drifted back to sleep.

A little while later, he gradually awakened to soft footfalls in the hallway: Carolina.

An uncontrollable sense of ease and pleasure came over him knowing she was close. "What have you brought with you this time?" John asked without opening his eyes.

"A bedpan," said a deep voice.

John snapped his eyes open to find a grinning Gabriel standing right in front of him, holding a bedpan. "I don't need it," he grumbled, closing his eyes again.

"I'll just leave it here in case you do." Gabriel set it down by the basin of water then walked to the door. "Oh, just so you know, I'll not be allowing Lina to come back in here to see you until you've used that. Either you use it now, or Bethel can help you later. I'd hate for Lina to be subjected to a life of misery with an unhappy groom because she sees something she shouldn't while trying to help you."

"You're enjoying this far too much," John grumbled against his pillow. Gabriel had lost a leg in the war; surely he knew how enjoyable it was to have a lady take care of him. Gabriel was just doing this to torture John—and worst of all, it was working.

Gabriel cleared his throat. "Is there something you require?"

"Yes, I believe I require you to help me empty my bladder."

"Is that necessary?" Gabriel asked, the color in his cheeks heightening.

"You're the one who insisted I use it. I would have been more than content to wait for you to leave to use the chamberpot." John grinned at him the best he could, considering how much he hurt and how sick he felt.

"Then see that you do," Gabriel said, taking a seat on his father's bed. "You two deserve each other. You do know that, don't you?"

John's grin faded. "I already told you, Gabriel. It's not that I find her personality disagreeable. It's just that I can't marry her."

"Because she chased after you, you can't marry her?"

John closed his eyes. "No. It's complicated."

Gabriel shrugged and stretched his legs out in front of himself. "I haven't got anything else to do this afternoon."

If he were anyone else, John would test him on that. He'd just ignore his guest and lie there until he fell asleep. But like John, Gabriel was a persistent sort and would likely be there waiting for his answer when he awoke later. "I can't take her to England with me."

"Do you think she won't go?"

John snorted. "No, she'd go. She'd probably even offer to swim beside the boat if she thought the only reason I wouldn't take her was lack of funds for her passage." He scrubbed his face with his hands. "I can't take her because she wouldn't fit in."

"You mean because she's an American?"

"Partially; see, ladies there are quiet and reserved. They speak when spoken to and would never dream of plopping down and eating a picnic while watching a man tread water wearing nary a stitch of clothing. They sleep until noon then spend the rest of their day in the drawing room sewing or taking calls. If they have a charitable pursuit, they'll do whatever is necessary to keep up with that and the rest of the time they keep to themselves."

"And all the ladies in England are like this?"

"Well, not all," John said with a scowl. "Some aren't, but those are very rare, and they usually remain unmarried or are packed off to live in a country estate where they cannot be an embarrassment to their husbands."

Gabriel shook his head. "That sounds very tedious to me." The pity in his voice was unmistakable.

"No, it's the way it is. But now you know why I couldn't take Carolina with me."

"She does have a tendency to make sure everyone knows she exists, doesn't she?" Gabriel said with a rueful grin. "I'll let you rest now," he said, standing. He walked to the door and paused. "Next time I see Lina, I'll tell her it's fine for her to come to see you—but only if she wants to."

***

"Don't go in that room again for the rest of the day."

Carolina looked up. "I hadn't planned to. He needs to rest if he wants to get better soon."

Gabriel didn't look convinced. "I know you, Lina. But I'm telling you, if you want to keep his interest, you won't go in there for the rest of the day."

Keep his interest? She wasn't even sure she had it.

"Lina? Are you listening to me?"

"Yes," she murmured, barely looking up at him. "You told me not to go in there. But it seems you didn't hear me when I told you that I hadn't planned to."

"And what are you planning?"

Carolina pressed her lips together. She couldn't very well tell him she had nothing planned to get his attention once he was well again, even if it was the truth. Suddenly an image of their neighbor Marjorie Reynolds formed in her mind. Of course! Having snared not one, but two gentlemen, Marjorie would know exactly what Carolina should do now.

"Lina?"

She shrugged and forced herself to look impassive. "Nothing so profound yet; I'm just taking your advice of not being overly friendly with him."

"Just see that it remains that way."

~Chapter Fifteen~

"It's rather warm out today, isn't it?"

Marjorie started. "Carolina."

"You seem surprised to see me," Carolina said, walking down the center row of the little patch of indigo they'd been cultivating the last five years toward her friend and stopped at the plant three down from her. Unlike most crops, indigo wasn't planted, harvested and immediately ready for sale. The purple leaves of the *Indigofera tinctoria* plant were plucked, then soaked in a foul smelling liquid until the leaves had lost their color and the liquid turned blue. Then the leaves were removed and lye was added to the mixture, then pressed into cakes and dried. Sometimes, they'd add special powders to the mixture if they wanted the cake to be a lighter shade. But a family as poor as the Reynolds likely wouldn't have money to waste in this way.

"I'm not surprised you came," Marjorie said. "You're the only real friend I've ever had and despite my not being able to offer you refreshments and lighthearted chitchat like I once did, you always come back. That wasn't the surprise. It was just how soon. You do know you came here to see me just three days ago, don't you?"

"I know." Carolina didn't care that Marjorie couldn't offer her snacks and inane conversation, she just wanted to be her friend. But because she didn't want to push her or make her too uncomfortable, she'd tried to keep her visits to only once a week. Not only did she wish to spare Marjorie's pride, but she also knew that even though she was helping some, her presence likely slowed Marjorie down; not that Marjorie would ever be so unkind as to say anything. Without word or invitation, Carolina started plucking the purple leaves on the plant in front of her and putting them in the broken basket at Marjorie's feet.

"Thank you," Marjorie whispered as she continued. "Daddy expanded the crop by four rows this year and without any help—" She shrugged.

"I'd be glad to help," Carolina offered.

Marjorie dropped her leaves into the basket and tucked a stray tendril of hair back under the fraying edge of her blue bonnet. "I cannot allow you to do that."

"Why not? I have nothing else to do." She moved over to the next plant and started removing its leaves.

Marjorie twisted her lips and lowered her lashes as she went about plucking more leaves.

Carolina dropped everything in her hand and turned to face her friend. "All right then, if you don't wish for my help, I shan't offer it again. However, since you already know I am the most shameless, ill-mannered lady of your acquaintance, I shall be blunt and tell you I came today to seek your help."

"You want my help?" Marjorie asked in a voice full of surprise.

Carolina bit her lip and nodded. "No, I don't want your help. I need it."

Marjorie laughed for what Carolina assumed might be one of the only occasions she'd done so since her home had been destroyed in the final year of the war. "What could I possibly help you with, Carolina?"

Carolina smiled at her. Marjorie was the only person who'd ever respected her wish to call her by her full name. Except John. Even after everyone else started calling her Lina in his presence, he'd continued to call her Carolina like she'd asked. Except when Gabriel first introduced them, but she assumed he did that just to irritate her—

Marjorie's cough reminded Carolina of her purpose. "I don't know how to say this..."

Marjorie laughed again. "Oh, Carolina, I don't believe that.

You've never lost your tongue before."

Carolina twisted her lips, but charged forward. "This is different." She casually turned to face the *Indigofera tinctoria* plant in front of her and began plucking off the purple leaves. "This is about a gentleman."

"Ah," Marjorie said, continuing where she'd left off with her work.

"I was hoping you could give me some advice," Carolina said as she plucked a little cluster of three leaves from the plant.

Marjorie's lips thinned. "I'm not sure I can give you any advice."

"Yes, you can," Carolina protested. She dropped more leaves into the basket and started pulling them from the next plant. "You were engaged to be married, were you not?"

"Engaged, not married," Marjorie pointed out before walking around to the other side of Carolina.

Carolina looked at her friend from under her lashes. Had she caught on to what she was doing? "But you would have married them."

Marjorie's hands stilled. "And it's for the best I didn't."

"Well, to be fair, the first one died."

Marjorie muttered something that sounded oddly like "might as well have" but before Carolina could ask her anything else, her friend spoke again. "What is it you wanted to know?"

"How to get him to admit his feelings."

"It's not a trick, Carolina. He just did."

Carolina frowned. That wasn't very helpful. "You mean you didn't do anything to Daniel to make him take notice of you?"

"Not unless you consider sewing him into the bedsheets doing something," Marjorie murmured.

Carolina sputtered with laughter. "W-what?"

"I sewed him into the bedsheets," Marjorie said with a shrug.

"Why?" she asked, drawing out the word.

"To keep him where he ought to be," Marjorie said with a

quick grin. "It's called a bundling bag. Mama said it was a Scottish tradition."

"And you sewed him into the bedsheets," she repeated, dumbfounded.

"Well, not him exactly. You just sew the sheets around him as if you're to make a sack and he's the goods."

All sorts of mischief cycled in Carolina's mind. "I'll have to wait a few more days to try that," Carolina murmured. "I sew him in the bedsheets and Bethel will never forgive me."

"Never is a mighty long time, Carolina."

"Yes, well, sewing a man into the bedsheets is a mighty hefty crime, so it just might fit," she said with a giggle as she pulled off another cluster of purple leaves and threw them down into the basket at Marjorie's feet.

"Perhaps so. But—" she plucked a few more leaves, moving much slower than she had been earlier, almost as if she was purposely going slow— "I think I might have some news that might make Bethel never grow cross with you or anyone again."

"Oh?" She clamped her lips together so she didn't look too eager for whatever it was Marjorie might want to share.

"Remember that secret?"

Of course, how could she not? "I think so..."

Marjorie snorted. "Carolina, you cannot fool me. I have a feeling that if it weren't for the young man you were speaking about a few minutes ago, whatever it was you thought I was hiding would have been the only thing on your mind."

Carolina cast her a mock scowl and plucked the leaves in her grasp with enough force the plant shook. "Think what you shall, but now I insist you tell me your secret."

"Well, if you insist, then I guess I'd better not tarry," Marjorie teased. "Remember I told you Daddy planted four new rows this year? Well, he said the crop could be good enough that he thinks he'll be able to afford to plant eight more next year, but he'll need some help."

Carolina knit her brow. Was this good news or bad news? More crops was a good thing, but as it was Mr. and Mrs. Reynolds and Marjorie spent all day every day tending to the rows they already had. How would they manage another eight? "That's good..."

"Actually it is." A slow smile spread her lips. "It means Silas will be able to return after Daddy sells this harvest in a few weeks. He'll be a free man, of course, earning a wage."

Carolina grinned. "I'm so happy to hear that," she said, hugging her friend.

"I'm sure Bethel will be, too," Marjorie said, winking.

"I hope you're right," Carolina said, sighing. "She might night not like it as much as we think she should."

"Why is that?"

Carolina exhaled and looked at a tree in the distance for a minute. "I fear her feelings for him aren't as strong as they once were."

"You mean because he's been away in Charleston the last five years?"

Carolina mindlessly picked the leaves in front of her. "Possibly. She hardly sees him. But what if it's more than just the time they've spent apart? Before the war, Bethel said they used to dream of getting married. Obviously marriage wasn't possible with them each on separate plantations, but they did get to see each other regularly and were as married as they could be, considering the circumstances. But what if it's different this time? He's free to come and go as he pleases, she's not. I just can't help but think it will create a chasm between them."

"I don't think so," Marjorie said softly. "I don't think he cares about the difference in their status, and since he'll be working here as an employee, he'll be able to go see her as often as he likes. Besides, Daddy said Silas was so excited at the prospect of coming here to work and being close to Bethel, I'm not so sure he wouldn't willingly work in your father's indigo fields if that's what it took to close that chasm you think might have been created by Silas' emancipation."

"He just might have to," Carolina said only half-jesting. "Mother would sooner allow me to marry John than allow Bethel her freedom."

"John? Is that your beau's name?"

"He's not officially my beau, but yes, his name is John."

"Is he the fellow your brother brought back with him?"

"Ye— How did you know Gabriel was back?"

"I must have seen him out working on the border between our plantations," she said evasively.

"Oh." Marjorie's unusual silence suggested there might be more than she was leading onto, but she knew better than to force her when it came to certain topics, and the look on her face made it quite clear this was one of them. Just like with the identity of the first man Marjorie had been engaged to. Marjorie told her nothing about him except that he'd gone off to war. A year after the war ended, she'd become engaged again. This time, however, the gentleman didn't end their engagement by dying an honorable death fighting for independence, but had been pursuing two young ladies at the same time and chose to marry the one with greater wealth.

"Carolina?"

"Yes?"

"What makes you think that you have to do anything to get his attention?"

"Because not doing anything isn't working."

"And what exactly have you tried?"

Carolina quickly told her about bringing him water and the picnic, conveniently leaving off a few irrelevant details of the picnic.

"That's all?"

Carolina frowned. "Well, I took him water yesterday while he was in bed with a sunburn," she said as if it were an afterthought.

Marjorie grimaced. "Lemon water is good to apply on sunburns. It should help it heal faster."

"Thank you. Mother bought some lemons last time we were in Charleston. I'll have to try that. I've tried my usual salve, but I'm willing to try anything else that might help. I've never seen such a bad sunburn." She moved to the next plant. "Do you have any other suggestions? For getting his attention not treating his sunburn, that is."

Marjorie looked like she wanted to say something, but just shrugged and shook her head instead. "Thank you for helping me today."

"You're welcome," Carolina said. She'd hoped her friend had been so distracted with their talking that she hadn't notice Carolina helping. Apparently not. "Consider it payment for the invaluable advice."

Marjorie lifted her eyebrows. "What invaluable advice?" Her eyes narrowed "You're not planning to sew him into the sheets the next time you see him, are you?"

"No. Not the next time; but I can't guarantee I won't the time after that."

~ *Chapter Sixteen* ~

John pulled his shirt over his head and sighed with relief when the coarse fabric rubbed his shoulders, but didn't hurt. Who knew the daughter of a wealthy plantation owner would actually know how to make—and be willing to apply—an ointment that actually worked. He snorted. That wasn't a mystery. Well, at least not the part about why she'd been willing to apply first the salve, then the lemon water; he was still astounded she'd known how to mix such an effective concoction in the first place. Her reasons for being kind enough to apply it to his blistered skin were obvious: she truly did fancy him.

He sighed. Were he just a common gentleman expected to work his life away in trade, she'd be the perfect wife: attractive and good-humored. And though he'd be reluctant to admit such out loud, he found her inability to be rattled, her unshakeable confidence, and her persistence to be admirable—and charming in a somewhat unusual way; which was downright odd, since he'd hated to associate with this type of creature while living in England. But there was something about Carolina that had set him at war with himself; from the day they'd met, he'd been battling between what he needed and what he wanted.

Abruptly, he shoved to his feet and walked from the room; it mattered naught that his body fired with need when he saw her, or that just the scent of her could make his heart pound. He couldn't marry her. Vicars didn't marry ladies who were so brazen and bold. They married quiet misses who could be a comfort to the ladies of the church and always set a good example with their proper manners and meek demeanor, something Carolina Ellis wasn't capable of; of that, he was certain.

"Are you sure you're well enough to work?" Gabriel asked.

John jumped. He hadn't heard Gabriel approach. "Yes, I believe I'm well enough." He'd been abed for two days, which was plenty of time to heal. Even if he wasn't completely well, he'd be out here working in order to be as far away from Carolina and her delicate touches and sweet smiles as possible. Another day of that and his resistance might crumble. Not to mention, Mrs. Ellis was planning a supper for some of the neighbors tonight and had told him in not so many words that he needed to be well and out of her house before the guests arrived. "What do you need me to do today?"

Gabriel scratched his head. "I don't. I thought you'd still be in bed today, so I already asked Lina to go."

"Go where?"

"To the Fields'."

John blinked at his friend. "While I admit your sister seems the sort to be a little unruly at times, I cannot believe you actually sent her to work in the indigo fields."

"Not those fields; I sent her to the Fields' Plantation. They're our northern neighbors." He chuckled. "I'd bet my entire inheritance had Lina known you'd be well enough to go in her stead, she might have done whatever you asked of her—including leaving you alone—to take her place."

What makes you think I want her to leave me alone? John started at the thought. "Er...is there a reason she doesn't like visiting the Fields?" he asked with a slight cough, while he beat his palm against his chest.

"I'd say so," Gabriel said with a grimace. "Apparently, Charlie's still sweet on her."

"And she doesn't like him," he ventured, chastising himself for caring so much about Gabriel's answer.

"No. He's proposed to her each time he's seen her since she was six."

"Six?" John repeated in disbelief.

Gabriel nodded slowly. "As you already know, Lina does nothing in half-measures, and following her clapping and cheering for him after he played the piano at our house when he was ten and she was six, he's fancied himself in love with her."

"Does he know she doesn't return the feeling?"

"I don't believe so, no." He shrugged. "Does it really matter?"

"No," John blurted; then flushed. "What I mean is, no, it doesn't matter to me whether or not she's informed him of her feelings."

Gabriel raised one dark brown eyebrow. "But only if they're not romantic feelings?"

John scowled. "I have no idea what you're talking about, and *you'd* better be careful what you're insinuating."

Gabriel chuckled. "Not to worry. She sees no reason to marry him while you're around. Mother, on the contrary—" He shrugged again as if that was a perfectly acceptable way to end a sentence. "You can ride over there if you'd like to give her an excuse to leave Charlie and Mrs. Fields' clutches before nightfall. And, to ensure she doesn't accept his proposal, of course," he added with a wink.

"I'm sure I'll find something around here that's in need of repair."

"Do as you'd like."

He surely would do as he'd like. He had no desire to chase after Carolina, and he certainly had no desire to "save" her from yet another unwanted marriage proposal. If he did that—even just to be kind, of course—she'd certainly think he had an interest in her. No, he'd go find something with which to occupy himself.

But doing what?

He walked to the barn to see if the roof was still in need of patching and frowned. Someone had finished his job. No matter. Perhaps there were more fence posts to drive. He walked the entire eastern perimeter and stared along the northern side. He came to an abrupt halt. If Carolina saw him here on her way back, she might think he was coming after her—which he wasn't.

John shut his eyes and sighed. He was being ridiculous. If she caught him over in that direction, he'd just tell her the truth: he was looking for something to do in order to earn his keep. *Is that so?* Shoving that traitorous thought from his mind, he pushed off from the fence and started toward the stables. If Gabriel didn't have any work for him, he might as well find something to do with his day, and the further away from Carolina, the better.

The day they'd arrived, Gabriel had allowed him to use the last stall in the stable for the black and white stallion he'd brought with him from Boston. Since then, he'd only taken him out long enough to brush him and take him for a few laps around the stable yard for exercise. Perhaps today he could take him down to the pasture and let him stretch his legs.

John saddled his horse and led him outside to the lush pasture before mounting. He filled his lungs with fresh air and tapped Hammond with his heels. Hammond took off running. The wind whipped through John's hair, blowing it every which direction. "Come on, boy," he urged.

Hammond ran faster and the grin he knew had to be splitting his face widened. It had been so long since he'd ridden his horse as if he hadn't a care in the world. Gabriel had offered to buy Hammond on more than one occasion, but John refused to sell such a fine piece of horseflesh and planned to take him back to England when he went.

Along the southern side of the pasture was a three-tiered fence. Gripping the reins a fraction tighter and lowering his upper body closer to Hammond's mane, John squeezed his legs together and sailed over the fence. When he pulled the reins, the horse slowed to a trot and then to a canter.

John led Hammond into a nearby grove of trees along a narrow, worn trail. With nothing but time, he went slowly, taking in the beauty surrounding him and the tranquil sounds of nature filling the air: three birds tweeting to each other, twigs snapping under Hammond's hooves, a rabbit or some other small critter running through a little cluster of dry, fallen leaves, the gentle splash of water. He froze. The gentle splash of water? He thought the pond was on the other side of the pasture. Had he gone in a circle?

He shrugged off the thought and continued forward. A break in the trees was ahead and he pulled Hammond to a stop, ready to turn around.

Just then, a movement caught his eye; then another. Interested in any distraction that would keep him away from the plantation longer and divert his mind from Carolina, he dismounted his horse and made his way up the small grassy hill in front of him.

He reached the top and his jaw dropped.

There in front of him in a small, open pond was Carolina. Naked.

Unlike him when he'd gone swimming in the pond sans clothing, she didn't stay in the deeper water where her body was fully concealed, so he was treated to a generous glimpse of her pert breasts as they came above the water every few seconds while she frolicked and swam. His body hardened instantly, and he swore under his breath. Did she have no shame? Apparently not, since she moved to float on her back, which exposed even more of her to his hungry gaze.

It took every ounce of control he possessed to turn away and walk back down the hill to his horse. But with every step he took, the memory of her deliciously bare body flashed in his mind.

Still in an uncomfortable state from his too-detailed memories when he reached the stable, he scowled at the boy who offered to put his horse away and then stalked off to hide himself in the little room where he bunked. One thing was for sure: although perhaps not done intentionally, Carolina would have an even easier time tempting him the next time she approached him. With a body as luscious and inviting as hers, only a blind man could continue to resist her.

~ *Chapter Seventeen* ~

Carolina wasn't getting out of the water until her skin had grown more wrinkled than her mother's face and had burned more than John's had. She hated what her mother was doing by getting Charlie's mother's hopes up about a marriage between Carolina and Charlie.

She flipped over onto her back and floated. So many times, she'd come to this little pond to escape her troubles. But none of her troubles had ever been as overwhelming as this one.

It had been a while since she'd seen Charlie, but today only confirmed her previous assessment that he would not make her—or anyone—a good husband; and it wasn't fair to anyone, especially Charlie, for Carolina's mother to play with the family's feelings when nothing would come of it.

Unfortunately, her mother thought otherwise and would likely do whatever she thought necessary to ensure Carolina married him instead of John.

The bottom of the sun fell behind the top of the distant line of trees that made up the western border of their land, an unspoken warning that dinnertime was growing near. Carolina jerked to a start. Dinner. She'd lost track of time, and if her latest—and hopefully last—plan to convince John to lay aside his pride and ask for her hand had any chance of working, she needed to find Gabriel.

She exited the water and dressed as quickly as her wet flesh would allow. She glanced at the sun and bit her lip. She had only two hours, at most, to bring her plan to fruition tonight—and there was little doubt in her mind that she'd *have* to do something tonight before Mother could further encourage a possible marriage between Charlie and Carolina.

Heedless of her unkempt appearance, Carolina ran toward the indigo fields. Father had told her Gabriel had gone there for the day when she'd gone to check on John and found he was no longer in bed.

A smile bent her lips when she spotted Gabriel by himself, shoveling some dirt at the end of a row.

"Can you do me a favor, Gabriel?"

"Does it have to do with John?"

"Yes."

"Then, no."

Carolina's smile faltered. "Please?"

Gabriel picked up his shovel and dug the tip into the ground. He bit his lip and, holding onto the end of the shovel with both hands for balance, used his foot to thrust the shovel into the ground, loosening a large clump of black South Carolina dirt. "What do you want me to do?"

"Tell him that Mother has requested his presence at her supper."

Gabriel dropped his newly scooped dirt, and it had nothing to do with his unsteady stance, but rather because he was howling with laughter. "My injury was in my leg, not my head, Lina. You'll have to do better than that."

Carolina pursed her lips. She should have known he wouldn't believe her. She'd considered telling him Mother wanted to discuss John's state of employment, but feared that John would just decide to go find work elsewhere rather than face Mother.

Her brother dropped the rusty shovel to the ground and sighed. "Lina, you must leave the man alone."

"But only a few days ago, you said to pursue him."

"I know," he agreed, "but have you forgotten what I said about letting him come to you?"

She frowned at him. "No. And I plan to, but I need your help."

"My help?"

Carolina fidgeted with the ruffle on her left sleeve. "I just need you to give him a gentle shove in my direction."

Gabriel arched a single brow, "A gentle shove?"

"Perhaps a nudge?"

"Shove or nudge, call it what you want; but what is it you want me to do?"

"I want you to invite him to supper tonight."

"No."

"Please?"

"I like the man far too much to expose him to that amount of suffering," he said, reaching for his shovel.

"Oh, it won't be so bad," Carolina countered with false bravado.

Gabriel shot her a dubious look then slowly dug out another shovelful of earth. This time, she kept quiet so not to say something to make him drop his dirt again. He lifted his shovelful of dirt and took an unsteady step to the right before dumping it out.

Carolina released the tight fists she wasn't even aware she'd made. Gabriel had always been her strong older brother. The one person in her family she'd always looked up to. Watching him struggle to do things most men could do without any effort was heart wrenching. But watching him find a way without help or giving up was even more heart wrenching.

"What makes you think it won't be so bad?" Gabriel asked, startling her.

She bit her lip. "John's biggest argument is that Mother doesn't like him. I just thought perhaps if she got to know him for the gentleman I know him to be, she'd alter her opinion of him and he'd stop pretending not to be attracted to me."

Gabriel's lips formed a thin line, and he stared at her with a blank expression on his face. "And if I told you Mother had already asked me to invite him?"

Carolina's heart skipped a beat. "She did?"

"Yes," he said flatly.

"What did he say?"

"I haven't asked him yet."

Carolina rolled her eyes and groaned. "What are you waiting for?"

Gabriel grumbled something, but she didn't bother to care what it was. Her mother had invited John to dine with them. She didn't know why, nor would she question it. As Father would say, one should never look a gift horse in the mouth, and this was one gift horse she had no intention of looking at anywhere near its mouth.

Unfortunately, an hour later, she wished she'd examined the teeth of that gift horse, or quite simply demanded to know why John had been invited and then talked Gabriel out of inviting him.

For just as she'd finished changing into a clean gown for dinner and pinning her hair in a coif she'd overheard a lady in Charleston describe as the height of fashion for ladies in Paris, doom set in with the sound of a team of neighing horses.

Carolina poked her head out her window and gasped. The Fields were here.

Pulling on her gloves, she ran down the stairs, taking them two at a time and silently praying Gabriel wouldn't be able to convince John to come tonight.

No such luck.

Standing in the hall by the front door wearing a set of Gabriel's finest clothes was John. Her breath caught. Even though the sleeves of his borrowed coat didn't quite reach his wrists and his shoulders appeared to be stretching the seams of the fabric, he looked dashing with his hair slicked back, exposing his clear blue eyes and his stoic face.

The moment ended too soon for Carolina's liking when a *thwack, thwack, thwack* reverberated from the door.

"I's a'coming," Lamar shouted, running down the hall.

Carolina stepped back onto the lowest stair to get out of the butler's way but didn't take her eyes off John who seemed to have an intensity in his eyes she hadn't noticed before.

Suddenly, the commotion of their guests being let in the front door ended the moment she and John shared, forcing them to redirect their attention to the intruders.

"It's nice to see you again, Mrs. Fields," Carolina said, accepting the older woman's embrace. She turned to the side and greeted Lucinda, Charlie's sister, and then their cousin Hannah. Mr. Fields stood with Charlie just inside the door. "Mr. Fields, Charlie," she murmured with a slight curtsey.

"Lina," Mr. Fields greeted before nudging his son.

Charlie looked at his father and then turned back to Carolina with the same empty expression he always wore. "Lina," he slurred.

"Come in, come in," Mother encouraged. Even when trying to sound sweet and inviting, she didn't. Perhaps it was because she'd dripped so much vinegar through the years, she was incapable of producing the minor amount of sugar it would have taken to sound sweet. Who really knew? What Carolina did know was the reason Mother had invited John. The smug smile on her face when Hannah Fields came in told Carolina all she needed to know: Mother intended to push him off on Hannah, a poor relation of the Fields, to get him away from Carolina and force Carolina to accept Charlie.

Carolina bit her lip to contain her laughter. The likelihood of that happening was the same as Mother learning to shoe a horse.

Now, the likelihood of torturing Carolina and making her jealous all evening was decidedly in Mother's favor.

"Hannah, why don't you sit there? Then we'll put John next to you. And, Lucinda, why don't you sit on the other side of John?" She grinned at Carolina then rushed from the room to greet another set of arriving guests.

Carolina ground her teeth. Apparently, while Carolina had been forming her plan this morning, Mother had, too.

"Sit, Lina" Charlie commanded loudly, but not unkindly.

Carolina offered him her best smile and sat in the chair he was pointing to. It wasn't his fault he was so blunt and impersonal. Truly, she had no idea why he was that way. He just was and had been his whole life as far as she knew. "Thank you."

He nodded stiffly and took his seat. As she expected, he took an instant interest in his dinner plate. He picked it up and then turned it over and over in his hands. He set it down and picked up the dull butter knife to the right of his plate. Turning it this way and that, he watched in amazement as the light from the chandelier that was reflected on the silver moved up and down the side as he moved it in his hand. "Watch, watch," he said, slapping her arm with the back of his hand to gain her attention.

She bit her lip so not to grimace in pain. As he continued to slap her, Carolina gently placed her hand over his to still his movements. "What is it, Charlie?"

"Watch," he commanded again, his eyes fixated on the knife in his other hand.

"That's very nice," she complimented. "Would you care to see another trick?"

He turned his wide-set green eyes toward her. "It better?"

"Better than yours?" she asked for clarification.

He nodded slowly.

"Of course not," she said, taking the knife from him. "Yours is by far the best trick I've seen. But this is just a bit different." She dropped her voice to a stage whisper. "It never hurts to know more than one trick when entertaining."

Nothing about his expression changed. But that was no surprise. She'd never seen him smile or frown, laugh or cry, appear confused or certain. No matter what the situation, his expression stayed the same: disinterested. Even if he was interested or did feel one of those emotions, you'd never know it by looking at him, only by listening to his words; which unfortunately for Charlie, was something very few people ever did.

"Show me!" Charlie demanded.

"Watch over there." She pointed to a little spot on the far wall, waited for him to fix his eyes where she'd pointed, and then turned the knife at an angle that would catch the light from the chandelier and reflect it on the back wall.

Unintelligible, high-pitched squeaks filled the air and Carolina grinned. He liked her trick, and if the noises he made weren't enough confirmation, the way he wildly bounced up and down in his seat certainly was.

"Would you like to try?"

Charlie's noises grew louder and he reached for the knife.

Carolina brought the knife against her chest. "You need to sit still first."

He didn't stop right away and reached for the knife, nearly mauling her chest as he did so.

Had he been anyone else, she'd have been horrified that he was practically touching her breasts. But he didn't know any better, and despite the muffled giggles and gasps coming from his sister and cousin, she didn't feel it was appropriate to shame him for what he didn't understand. Instead, she fought to keep the blush from her cheeks and used her free hand to push at his wrists. "You need to sit still and put your hands in your lap, Charlie. I'm not going to give it to you until you do."

He struggled against her another ten or fifteen seconds, but she continued to hold the dull knife against her chest. He let out a scream she knew to be of frustration, though he didn't look frustrated, then turned and put his hands in his lap. He clenched them together tightly and persisted to let out a series of short shrieks.

"You have to stop doing that, or I won't give it to you," Carolina warned. He reached out to grab the edges of his plate, but Carolina's hand shot out faster than his, and she covered the top of his plate with her open palm, holding it in place. "No."

He let out one more shriek and then dropped his hands to his lap, resigned.

Carolina waited a few seconds to make sure he'd calmed down. She hated treating him this way, but it would seem nobody else—including his own parents—had any interest in his behavior and would rather ignore him than even attempt to help him. She pushed aside her bitter feelings about the situation and pulled the knife away from her chest to hand it to Charlie, only to be stopped a second later by a shriek that sounded more appropriate for a murder scene than a dining room.

"You know better than to play with your knife, Lina," Mother snapped, from where she stood just inside the door with the last of her guests. "You're so careless you're likely to cut your finger off. Give that to me."

Heat crawled up Carolina's face at her mother's words, and she gripped her knife tighter. "It's not even sharp, Mother," she pointed out.

"Give me the knife," Mother demanded again, opening and closing her hand.

Just then, Charlie decided to grab the knife; whether to give it to Mother or to try to make the candlelight reflect on the back wall, she didn't know. "Let go, Lina," Charlie said, yanking on the knife.

Carolina didn't know whether she loosened her grasp or the moisture on her palm made it harder to hold, but somehow Charlie tugged it loose and sent it flying across the table to create an ear-piercing screech as it nicked John's wineglass then clattered against his plate.

Always the helpful young lady, Lucinda picked up the utensil and handed it to Mother. "Here, Mrs. Ellis." She turned her laughing blue eyes to Carolina. "Don't worry, Lina. I'll be sure to dispose of all of the knives in the silver set Mother plans to buy for you and Charlie as a wedding gift. It would be tragic if either of you were to hurt yourselves."

As if that was the most humorous thing ever spoken, Lucinda, Hannah and perhaps a few other guests broke into peals of laughter. She doubted John was laughing, too, but refused to look up for confirmation, especially since tears were stinging the back of her eyes and would likely fall if someone mentioned her obvious discomfort. John didn't seem the sort to laugh at another's expense, and there was no denying that this jest was certainly at someone else's expense. Ironically, Carolina didn't honestly know who was more the object of the jest: her or Charlie, or if perhaps they shared that honor equally.

Suddenly, two heavy arms wrapped around her and squeezed her too tight for comfort. Though terrible at expressing his own feelings, Charlie had an eerie perceptiveness when it came to someone else. He must have sensed her hurting and thought to offer her comfort. Heedless of what was proper or what anyone else would say or do, she reached one of her arms up to wrap it around his neck and leaned in close to him in the best attempt at hugging him back she could manage.

He might not understand that he, too, should be hurting because he'd just been cruelly insulted by his own sister; but Carolina knew; and even if nobody else thought enough of him to show him any compassion, she did.

~Chapter Eighteen~

John's heart slammed in his chest as full understanding finally took root in his brain. Though Carolina hedged on the side of overzealous with her constant prattle and scandalizing boldness, she was only that way because it was who she was. She wasn't *trying* to be annoying or insincere. It was just that her heart was the size of the ocean and knew no boundaries. A trait he'd overlooked before, but never would again. Not that he thought for one minute he'd ever be able to overlook anything about her ever again, as it was.

Below the table, he clenched his hands into fists to keep from strangling someone. And there were many people who needed a thorough strangling: Gabriel, for not telling him the truth about Charlie, but letting him believe Charlie was a genuine suitor; Mrs. Ellis, for being so cruel to Carolina; or the two impertinent chits he was seated between, who thought it amusing to poke fun at someone who clearly didn't understand their cruel intent as well as someone else, only because she was the object of the other's affections.

He swung his gaze to the young man's parents. Neither seemed to find anything unusual in what had transpired. Mr. Ellis looked impassive and Mrs. Ellis had a rather pleased look on her face. John shook his head and thought of what to say, but nothing he thought of could possibly make the situation better.

"Thank you, Charlie. I feel much better now," Carolina murmured, patting one of his large arms.

Charlie let go of her and straightened in his chair, then picked up his spoon.

John didn't bother to find out what he planned to do with that;

he only had eyes for Carolina, who for the first time since he'd met her, didn't seem interested in him.

To his misfortune, the annoying chits on either side of him did and prattled on about one inane topic after another.

Between bites, he'd nod or murmur something that could pass as an answer; meanwhile, he tried not to act too obvious about staring at Carolina. He noted the red hand marks Charlie had left on the bare skin of her arm from his tight grasp. He also noticed, much to his utter amazement, that Carolina never seemed upset or bothered by Charlie's less-than-gentlemanly eating habits. She just wiped away whatever he happened to get on himself (or her) and helped him hold his spoon better. Of course, that would only improve the situation for a minute or two, then he was making a mess again.

By the time dinner was finished, his brain was numb from the awful conversation and his blood was pumping at the fury he felt on Carolina's behalf.

"Gabriel," John barked, as the group was making their way down the hall to the parlor for their after dinner entertainment.

Gabriel turned around and forced a thin smile.

John jerked his thumb in the direction of an empty room.

Gabriel frowned but followed him into the room.

"What is going on?" John demanded without ceremony as soon as he shut the door.

"You're earning your wages."

John nodded once. Gabriel had tried many ploys to get John to come tonight, but it was his offer to pay him handsomely that got John to don a dinner costume more than twenty years past fashion in London and suffer.

"Why didn't you tell me the truth about Charlie?" he demanded.

A smug smile bent Gabriel's lips. "Why does it matter? I thought you weren't interested in her."

"I'm not," he burst out, running his fingers through his hair. "I just don't understand why everyone thinks they should make a match."

"It's not everyone. It's just their mothers." He twisted his lips. "Mine feels Lina has lost her chance to be a Charleston man's wife due to her public display of interest in you, and Charlie's feels Lina is a good match because she treats him well."

"Yes, I noticed," John said flatly. "I find it interesting she has a care one way or the other how he's treated, when she and his father don't seem too interested in him."

Gabriel frowned and nodded. "They like to pretend nothing's wrong. They've always been that way." He shook his head and glanced out the window at the sunset. "When we were younger, Lina would ask me the whole way home what was wrong with Charlie and why nobody else seemed to notice. Of course, I'd noticed, but tried to pretend not to while he hurled his toy soldiers at my head. I thought perhaps if I didn't draw attention to it, he'd stop. His parents, however, have either gotten so good at pretending not to notice that they don't see it anymore, or they're so eager to pretend nothing is wrong that they think if they ignore him or don't get involved in one of his tantrums, it isn't real.

"Truly, I don't know which it is. Lina is the only one who has ever come close to understanding him or getting him to calm down, which is why they think she'd be perfect for him."

"You don't really mean to force her to marry him, do you?"

Gabriel leaned his shoulder against the wall. "Why do you care?"

John sighed and dropped his gaze to the floor. "I might not wish to marry her, but I don't think it's fair to condemn her to a life as a nursemaid."

"She might enjoy being his nursemaid. You might not believe this, but in the world we live in, our families don't inherit large fortunes and use them to provide for everyone in the family. There are many local young ladies who'd be tripping over themselves to marry him, if it meant she'd get her own home and all the luxuries that go along with marrying a wealthy indigo farmer; should his father continue to see prosperous years until he passes, that is."

A knot formed in John's gut. When John and Gabriel met, they were just two young men struggling to survive by working in the same Boston warehouse. John had been an outcast of sorts due to his strong connection with England and was only tolerated by the other workers only because he was an honest worker. Gabriel had befriended him because, well, like Carolina, he wasn't one to see the same boundaries or form the same opinions as the majority. He cared only for the man himself, not what society thought of him. Little did John know at the time it was really Gabriel who was in need of a close friend. Though Gabriel would never admit to such, he'd been as much, if not more so, an outsider as John was, but not because of his position or wealth, but the choice he'd made not to return to his family and to work for just enough of a wage to get by in a miserable Boston warehouse.

But both being without the favor of Boston's elite hadn't mattered. Neither cared about social standing while in Boston. To them, they were just two young men getting by in this world. Then, when John told him he was planning to return to England and explained that his brother held a title and what it meant for John in English Society, Gabriel seemed to have changed. It was almost as if there'd been a barrier erected between them. One which John had no idea how to break down. So when Gabriel challenged him to see the hardships those who owned large estates in America suffered in order to make their way, he saw no reason to refuse.

His challenge wasn't issued out of hatred or jealousy, mind you, but perhaps understanding. It had been John who'd helped Gabriel through a difficult time in Boston, and now Gabriel saw the chance to help John understand those who were not born to the same wealth and position as himself. The very same kind he'd one day be preaching to. And while he had a greater respect and understanding of the hard work that the majority of the world faced, he couldn't help but wonder if there would always be a slight chasm between the two.

"I didn't mean to insult your family or belittle the life you'll one day inherit," John said quietly. "My point is that I don't think anybody should be forced to take on such a task."

"She's not being forced," Gabriel corrected, opening the door. "She has a choice, and the last time I spoke to her about it, her choice wasn't Charlie."

John stood in silence as Gabriel made his exit. It wasn't his place to question things he had no intention of changing.

He walked into the parlor just in time to hear Mrs. Fields brag about what a wonderful pianist Charlie was and urge him over to the pianoforte.

John cringed, as did the rest of the room, he imagined, as Charlie began banging on the keys and half-sang, half-screamed words nobody seemed to understand.

Charlie's sister and cousin giggled again, as if they believed this to be a scene from a never-ending comedy. The rest of the room stared in shock, grimaced in pain at the torture that was assaulting their ears, or stared at Charlie dumbfounded.

When it was clear Charlie had no intention of stopping and the crowd was growing less restrained in their reactions, Carolina was at his side. "Shall we play Greensleeves?"

"I am," Charlie shouted, not stopping his clanking.

Carolina smiled at him and then went on to play Greensleeves flawlessly despite Charlie's help.

When she was finished, she placed her hand on top of his to still it, then did the most unexpected thing: she slid her hand into his and gave him a slight tug. Seeming to understand what she wanted, he stood up with her and took a bow when their audience began applauding.

"What of another?" Charlie's cousin suggested.

The crowd grumbled, and understandably so.

"No, I think that was quite enough," Mrs. Ellis said, forcing what might pass as an apologetic smile. "While Charlie's playing was exceptional, we wouldn't want Lina to deafen anyone."

"Then what of a play?" Mrs. Fields suggested.

"I'm afraid I won't be able to participate in a play, Mrs. Fields," Carolina said. "I think I played too loud and now my head hurts. I think I should retire for the evening." She cast a glance at Charlie that John couldn't see, then struggled to free her hand from his grasp and fled the room, brushing past John as she went.

Had the circumstances been different, a tendril of hot desire would have coiled in his abdomen at the feel of her soft body pressing against his; but instead, it was fury that coiled in his gut at the sad expression on her face and the unshed tears in her eyes.

~ *Chapter Nineteen* ~

Carolina was almost to her room when Bethel's heavy footfalls sounded down the hall.

"'Mere, chile," she said, wrapping Carolina in a tight hug.

Carolina didn't care how much her mother hated it when she showed any affection toward Bethel; she hugged her back, taking comfort in her embrace.

"It be a'right," Bethel soothed, rubbing her back. "Let's gets yous in bed."

Carolina let Bethel lead her into the room and help her change out of her gown. She pulled on her nightgown and slipped into bed. Bethel sat down beside her and smoothed over the blankets, then idly scratched Carolina's scalp and ran her fingers through her hair the way she had so many times to help her fall asleep after a bad day.

Tears streamed from her eyes in two steady currents, wetting her cheeks then running down to her hair-covered pillow. "I j-just don't understand," she sobbed through the emotion that was clogging her throat.

"Nob'dy do, chile," Bethel said.

That was the last thing she remembered before closing her eyes tightly and wishing that things would be different.

A bright light entered the room and she blinked her eyes open only to realize it was morning. She closed them again and fell back against her pillow. She hadn't actually had a headache when she'd gone to bed, but she certainly had one now from all the crying she'd done last night. She pushed the tips of her fingers against her eyes and rubbed, noting the stiffness of her eyelashes. With a sigh, she sat up and climbed out of bed, no less upset than she'd been the night before.

Why, after all these years, had nobody bothered to inform Mr. and Mrs. Fields that instead of helping Charlie find his way in the world, they were allowing him to be made into a laughingstock? And why did her mother think it was perfectly acceptable to invite him to the supper, when she knew he'd make a fool of himself? Did her mother have no consideration for anyone except herself and her own motives?

Anger bubbled inside of her, ruining any appetite she might have. She glided down the main stairs toward the porch, where she'd swing until it was time to take John his glass of water. He might not have acted overly gracious the first few times she'd brought him water, but it was no secret that she still enjoyed bringing him water, since it afforded them a few minutes of conversation—even if they did argue half the time.

"Dalton will be 'round with the buggy in a few minutes," Mother said coldly, catching her right before she stepped onto the porch.

"All right."

Mother placed her cold hand on Carolina's arm. "You will be riding over to the Fields' to apologize and accept Charlie's marriage proposal."

Carolina stiffened. "No. I will not. That is not my apology to make; it's yours."

"It most certainly is not. He was your guest, and you abandoned him to pretend you were unwell with a headache."

Carolina stared at her mother. "He was not my guest; he was yours. You invited him to prove a point, and it didn't work. But my 'abandoning' him, as you put it, wouldn't have happened had you any semblance of a heart and had not invited them last night."

"That boy wants to marry you, Lina. I couldn't very well not invite him."

"No, you're wrong."

Mother arched a brow. "Oh, and what do you suppose I would

have said to Mrs. Fields when she asked why I didn't invite their family?"

Carolina narrowed her eyes. "That's not what I meant and you know it. Charlie doesn't want to marry me. Frankly, he doesn't know what he wants, and the only reason he thinks he wants to marry me is because you and Mrs. Fields have convinced him he does."

"That's not true," Mother argued. "The first time he asked, it was because he wanted to."

"Yes, and since he was ten, I'm sure he knew exactly what he was asking."

Mother shrugged. "Sometimes when you know, you just know."

"No. He just knows his parents are married. My parents are married. Every adult he knows is married. So to him, he thinks it's normal to get married."

"Isn't it?"

Carolina wanted to groan in frustration. "Yes. But what you and Mr. and Mrs. Fields fail to accept is that Charlie does not understand what marriage is. He can't." Tears burned the back of her eyes. "He has no conception of what marriage means. He just knows to say the words, 'Lina, marry me'. He doesn't mean them any more than he knows what being a husband means."

"And you think that transient, John Banks, better understands what being a husband means? I doubt it. He seems the sort to be faithful to one woman for as long as Charlie can carry a note," she said, shaking her head in disgust.

"Why do you even care?" Carolina burst out. "If you have no problem marrying me off to a man who is likely only to remain faithful because he doesn't understand the difference between the words faithful and unfaithful, then why do you care if I marry one who isn't?"

"Because I have a reputation to maintain," she said, lifting her chin a notch. "I don't want to be shunned from the homes of my friends because it's well known that my daughter's husband visits brothels."

Carolina stared at her mother in awe. "And you know for a fact he makes frequent visits to brothels now?"

"No. If he did, he'd lose his job."

Carolina was so close to giving in to her urge to groan it was almost overwhelming. "You make no sense."

"I make perfect sense," Mother snapped. "It's you who is too naïve and free with your affections to see reason. That boy is the worst kind there is. He has no regard for anyone but himself, and if you don't watch out, he'll hurt you."

"That's impossible. He wouldn't hurt anyone."

Mother looked doubtful. "It doesn't matter anyway, because I have no intention of giving him my permission to marry you. Now, go apologize to Charlie and accept his offer."

"No. I don't wish to marry him."

Mother's lips thinned. "Then you shall remain unwed. Is that what you want?"

Carolina clutched the fabric of her skirt and met her mother's cold eyes. "If the choice is to marry Charlie or no one at all, I'll remain unwed. But that isn't the only choice at hand."

"It's the only choice you have," Mother said sharply. "He might have a few unusual tendencies, but given his family's wealth, he is a far more respectable choice; and since you refused every man in Charleston, he's the only choice you have left."

"I still don't see why you dislike John so much," she said without thinking. Truly there was no reason to continue to argue her point right now, other than she just couldn't stop herself. Charlie might be kind and sweet, for the most part; but it was in an unabashed innocent way, not in the way that a husband would act.

"John Banks is a worthless beggar who'll never amount to anything."

"You're wrong," Carolina fired back; her blood boiling with outrage. "It's the hardworking men like him who built our city and our country. Not everyone can come from wealth and own a plantation. Someone has to build that plantation."

"Yes, and we call those people 'hands', Lina."

Carolina sucked in a hard breath. "He's none of those vile things you say about him."

"He is, and I don't like him here. I've only allowed him to stay because—"

"You didn't allow him to stay, Gabriel did," Carolina snapped. "If it were up to you, he'd have died of thirst while walking back to town after helping Gabriel return home."

Mother frowned. "Don't be so nonsensical. I won't deny that I don't like his presence, but I would never be so cold as to throw him out."

"Yes, you would," Carolina mumbled under her breath, because heavy steps could be heard down the hall and Carolina didn't want anyone to overhear their argument.

"No, I wouldn't; but as soon as he's earned his fare, he'll be gone. And don't you dare try to do anything to encourage him to stay longer," Mother warned, wagging her finger.

"I—"

"Miss Lina," Bethel called.

Carolina's eyes widened in terror. "I'm coming, Bethel," she called back, hoping Bethel would stay put and her mother wouldn't follow her.

"Where do you think you're going?" Mother grabbed her arm to stay her. "I'm not satisfied you understand my warning."

"I understand," Carolina blurted, throwing a glance over her shoulder to see if she could catch a glimpse of Bethel, who likely hadn't heard her command.

Mother placed her hands on her hips and unease washed over Carolina. "What's the meaning of this," Mother demanded of Bethel as soon as she came into view holding a large tray with two glasses of water.

"I asked Bethel to prepare some water for Gabriel," Carolina answered, as her blood began to race.

"Do you think I'm a fool, Lina?"

"N-no."

"Then don't treat me as such."

Carolina swallowed convulsively. "I didn't."

"You insult my intelligence with your lies. And you—" she turned toward Bethel with a lethal stare— "have you forgotten who you belong to or do I need to remind you again?"

Carolina's blood turned to ice. "No!" she said, jumping in front of Bethel. "She knows."

"I don't think she does, or she wouldn't be taking orders from you."

Behind her, the glasses of water rattled on the tray as Bethel's hands trembled. Carolina's heart crumbled. They both knew what was to come. There was little more that Mother loved than demonstrating her authority.

"Go get me the strap, Lina," Mother commanded.

"No."

Mother's lips formed a tight line. "Don't defy me, Lina. This is your fault anyhow. Now get me the strap."

She took a step backward to better shield Bethel, which only served to infuriate her mother more. Tears stung her eyes. "Strap me," she said on a sob. "Let her go. This is my fault and I should be the one punished."

"No. She did wrong and she'll never learn if she's not punished."

"Move 'side, chile," Bethel said softly. "'T'll be a'right."

"Very good," Mother clipped, before turning to walk toward the kitchen where she'd ordered the strap hung as a subtle reminder of just whose house this was.

Carolina's vision blurred and she blinked rapidly to clear her eyes. She wanted so badly to protect Bethel, but they both knew her efforts would only be temporary. On more occasions than she cared to remember, she'd found herself in this very position, only to have made things worse for Bethel by further inciting her mother's wrath. But that was when nobody else was here to stop Mother. Father was physically unable and none of the other house servants would dare cross Mother.

But what of Gabriel?

She'd never know if she didn't at least try.

"I'm so very sorry," she choked out; then not waiting to hear Bethel's response, she ran down the hall and out the back door, sobbing her brother's name as she went.

~ Chapter Twenty ~

Just as John and Gabriel approached the little series of three steps that led to the back entrance of the big house, Carolina came tearing out the door and ran down the stairs, shrieking Gabriel's name and the word help as two torrents of tears streamed down her bright red face.

She must not have seen them standing next to the stairs, because she didn't stop, she only swiped at the tears on her cheeks and ran toward the indigo fields where he and Gabriel had been working earlier.

"I wonder what's happened to her," John said.

Gabriel shrugged his response, but didn't look too concerned by Carolina's theatrics.

Just then, the unmistakable sound of leather slapping skin rang through the air.

"I'll go after Carolina," John said automatically, as his friend stumbled up the stairs. "Wait, Carolina," he called as he chased after her.

She didn't slow.

He sped up his pace. She didn't have that much of a lead on him, besides she was wearing slippers and a skirt!

He continued to run after her and grimaced every time she stumbled or tripped. But she kept running and he stayed right behind her. "Carolina, stop."

She didn't.

She was within arm's reach now, and he reached for her, grabbing a fistful of fabric and bringing her to the ground with a strangled whimper. "Let me go. I must find Gabriel," she cried, trying to break free of his hold.

"He already knows."

"Are you sure?" she choked between sobs as she took to her feet and wiped her eyes.

John nodded. His mother had been prone to vapors—leaving him with just enough knowledge to comprehend that when these moods hit, it was best to stand there quietly and not say anything, lest you upset them further.

"Stop staring at me!"

Or perhaps he was wrong. "I'm not staring," he said slowly.

She sniffled and used the heel of her hand to dry under her red-rimmed eyes. "Yes, you are. Now go away."

"I came—"

"To tell me Gabriel knows..."

"No," he said gently, stepping closer to her. "I came because I thought you might like some company."

"For once, John, I don't want your company."

He was taken aback. The past few weeks, he'd tried everything he could to avoid her company, and now she was telling him she didn't want his? "Then what do you want?"

"To go far, far away," she said with a sob.

He started. Her broken tone would suggest she wasn't jesting. "Carolina, what's happened?"

Sobs wracked her body again, and she crumpled to the ground before him.

He sank down next to her. "Shh," he crooned in her ear, taking a seat on the grass as close to her as he could. "It'll all work out."

"No, it won't," she said between sobs.

On impulse, John wrapped his arms around her and pulled her onto his lap, then bent his head and pressed his cheek atop the crown of her head. Her soft, curly brown hair felt good against his skin. He closed his eyes. He was here because she could use a friend, nothing more, he reminded himself as he began to rock her from side to side.

Carolina leaned closer to him, pressing her face against his chest. "I hate her," she whispered.

"Who?"

"My mother."

Well, that wasn't an unexpected discovery. There were very few people he'd ever met that he wasn't particularly fond of, and Mrs. Ellis was certainly one of them. "Surely, you don't hate her," he said softly. "You might not like her, but you don't hate her."

"Yes, I do," Carolina insisted. "She's so cruel."

"Is this because she's forcing you to accept Charlie?" He didn't know why those were the first words out of his mouth, and he hoped she wouldn't question him further. Her possible impending marriage to a simpleton or the tender moment they shared now changed nothing between them, and he'd do well not to lead her to believe his feelings for her were anything other than that of a friend.

"No. It has nothing to do with that. It's something else."

He rubbed long strokes up and down her back with his open palm. "What did she do to you?"

"Nothing," she said on a sob. "It's Bethel."

John nodded. He'd noticed the closeness between the two but had never thought too much about it. He, too, hadn't been very close to his own parents; but instead of being close to a servant, he'd sought his brother's favor. "What's wrong with Bethel?"

"She's getting the strap, and it's my fault," she said in a voice that was nearly inaudible.

A knot formed in his stomach. That explained the noise he'd heard earlier. "I'm sorry," he whispered around the lump of emotion that had taken root in his throat.

"It's not your fault; it's mine," she said.

John stilled and tightened his hold, hoping she'd find the comfort she needed. Then before he could stop himself, he leaned forward and dropped a kiss on the crown of her head. "It'll be all right, Carolina. Gabriel went in there after you left. He'll stop her," he whispered against her hair.

Carolina sniffled. "No, it won't stop. He might stop her now, but she'll just do it again when he's not close to the house."

John shut his eyes and rocked her sobbing form. "Is there anything that can be done?"

"No," she said so softly he might not have heard her, had his head not been so close to hers. "Mother and Father refuse to grant her freedom because she does so much around the house. She's nothing but a machine that breathes to them."

John's heart clenched, for as willful and spirited as Carolina seemed, she had a good heart. First, it had showed with how she'd treated Charlie, and now with Bethel.

"Was it always like this?" he asked before he could think better of it. In just his short amount of time here, he'd learned many things had changed following Mr. Ellis' return from war—but nobody dared speak of it.

"With Bethel, yes." She swallowed convulsively. "Mother resents her."

"Because you're closer to her?"

Carolina nodded against his chest. "Her skin might be a few shades darker than mine, but in my heart, she's my mother. That's why she's doing this today," Carolina whispered. "She knows it hurts me more than it does Bethel."

"I'm sorry," he said for lack of anything else to say. "I don't know what I can do to help make it right, but I will always be here for you." He clamped his mouth shut. That was a promise he had no business making to her. He couldn't always be there for her. Their lives were far too different.

"Thank you," she said; her face pressing against his dingy shirt muffled her words a bit.

John continued to hold and rock her. He couldn't do anymore than that. He'd never experienced anything like she was experiencing right now. All of the servants he'd ever known were given wages for their work and were free to leave if they so desired. Bethel wasn't. She had to stay, no matter what she was asked to do or the punishment she'd incur for not. However, as much as he wanted to help, he just couldn't.

Time dissolved in that hot South Carolina field, and finally Carolina's sobs and sniffles subsided. He turned his head to the side to peek down at her and felt a bittersweet smile tug his lips when he realized she'd fallen asleep.

Nobody who might be around to see them was the kind who'd say anything, so he saw no reason to wake her up. Instead, he continued to hold her, loving the way she felt in his arms. He'd never fully understood slavery until he'd come to the plantation. Of course, while in Charleston, he'd actually met a few freedmen, such as Silas, who were working for their employers and collecting a wage, but that was rare. He'd also encountered a few field hands at neighboring plantations who seemed to like working for their "massas".

The same could not be said for those who worked these indigo fields. Gabriel's insistence to work alongside them—which he learned was actually more common on plantations that had too few hands than he originally thought—had raised the morale and smoothed things over a little. But there was still a lot of resentment among the field hands toward Mrs. Ellis. Gabriel had mentioned that prior to his father's accident, they'd all been treated very well, and he was surprised there hadn't been a slave rebellion when Mrs. Ellis took over. Perhaps that was because they all seemed to love Carolina, and she them.

"John?"

John jerked at Gabriel's voice. "Carolina," he whispered, gently brushing her cheek with his lips. "It's time to wake up." When she didn't immediately wake, he gave her a little shake.

Her eyes fluttered open and she looked from Gabriel to John, her tearstained cheeks turning red.

"I think Bethel would like to see you." Gabriel's voice sounded as though it was full of gravel.

John helped Carolina off his lap and then gained his feet.

"Don't," he warned Gabriel, when Carolina had run far enough to be out of hearing distance.

Gabriel threw his hands into the air in a show of mock innocence. "I didn't say anything."

"No," John allowed, dusting off his backside. "But you were about to."

"About to what?"

"Demand I marry her."

Gabriel lifted his brow. "Why would I do that?"

Scowling, John folded his arms. "We were doing nothing wrong. I was just trying to console her."

"Why do you fight it so?"

"Fight what?" John burst out.

"Your obvious attraction to my sister."

John blew out a breath. He couldn't deny it. He was becoming more attracted to her with each passing day. But he still couldn't marry her. "I can't marry her."

Gabriel rolled his eyes up toward the sky and twisted his lips. "I know she's annoying with her incessant chatter and never-ending theatrics; and I'll even grant you she has the ability to drive a man mad with her tendency to appear at the most inconvenient time possible. But she doesn't do it with the intention of being an annoyance, it's just who she is."

"I know that." And dash it all, it was *those* very things about her that entranced him more than anything else. He might have found it awkward, at first, that she kept bringing him water, but he'd loved standing there talking with her as he drank it, just like all the other times they'd talked. He enjoyed her being her, but her being her did not bode well for the wife of a vicar.

"Then what keeps you from marrying her?"

John shoved his right hand into his pocket and idly turned his pocket watch over in his hand. "I just can't."

"Can't or won't?"

"Can't."

"I don't believe you."

John scowled. "You can believe whatever you want, but that's the truth. I'm financially not in a position to take her as my wife."

Grimacing, Gabriel readjusted his stance. "John, listen to yourself. You told me only days ago that the reason you couldn't marry her was because she wasn't meek and mild like all the proper ladies of England, and now it's because you don't have the funds." He lifted a single hand into the air to stop John's rebuttal. "Frankly, I don't care which it is. Both of them are excuses, and they're both weak. If Lina only cared about money and living the carefree life of a wealthy landowner's wife who only had to worry about hosting parties and commanding her household about, she'd have accepted Charlie by now. He might not be the most appealing gentleman, but he has enough wealth to command the respect due him.

"Having grown up with her, I know better than anyone how uncomfortable it is to claim a relation to the girl who goes around as if the world is her stage and she is the lead actress in a melodrama. But you've already acknowledged that you understand that's just who she is. What *I* don't understand is why you'd care so much what others think of her to throw away your own happiness."

"It's not for me I fear public ridicule. It's for her," he said defensively. "I love her enough not to care what others say about her, but how will she feel when she's mocked for her vibrant personality or is whispered and laughed about behind fans?"

Gabriel looked him right in the eyes and asked, "Do you think she's the kind who'd care?"

~Chapter Twenty-One~

Carolina pulled the crisp sheet and soft blanket up to her chin and closed her tired eyes. So much had happened today, and all she wanted now was to close her eyes and fall asleep.

John's handsome face with his high cheekbones, chiseled jaw, clear blue eyes and crooked smile formed in her mind. A poor transient, or not, he was still attractive, which was only compounded by his kind personality. He might seem a little brash at times, but that wasn't who he truly was. Today, she saw him as she knew he'd be: a sweet and compassionate man she'd only been able to catch quick glimpses of when he'd been trying to put her off, a task at which he still seemed most persistent.

Not that it mattered overmuch tonight. There was always tomorrow.

She jolted. It *did* matter. Her mother had been so furious with her for what had happened today, she had said they'd both be going to the Fields' tomorrow in order for Carolina to accept Charlie's suit. That meant if she didn't get John to lay aside his pride tomorrow morning, she'd officially be engaged to Charlie before the sun set; and while she'd only be engaged and not actually married, it would take nothing short of a Divine Intervention to free her from an unwanted marriage at that point.

The thought gave her a colossal surge of energy; she leapt from her bed and began walking the length of the large plush rug in the middle of her room. Drawing her lower lip between her teeth, her mind raced. What could she do now? She would literally only have hours before Mother would insist it was time to pay a call on the Fields to make their engagement official.

A sound outside caught her attention, but she ignored it and continued to pace. She'd taken John water, brought him a picnic—which he didn't even eat, spoke candidly to him, and nothing seemed to have caught his notice. What a lot of good Bethel, Gabriel and Marjorie had been. Not one of them had offered her a solution that seemed to make him take anymore notice of her than he had before.

Whatever she did tomorrow would have to be revolutionary, something so big and important that he wouldn't have a choice but to acknowledge his interest in her; but what? She had no more ideas on how to tempt and sway him than she had when she first started. Something hit her window, startling her. She scowled. There must be a storm nearing to cause so many acorns to be hitting her window.

She sat down on the edge of her bed and resumed thinking, her fingers idly twirling the purple silk of her nightgown. What hadn't she tried yet? She sighed. Nothing. She'd tried everything. Well, maybe not everything, she amended with a blush. But there were some things even she wouldn't do.

Carolina fell back against her mattress, tears stinging her eyes. Was that it, then? She could either seduce him, offering him her virtue in hopes that he'd be the gentleman he'd claimed to be, or be pressured to accept a marriage to Charlie?

She released a weak, wavering breath. Why was it in Charleston, the gentlemen flocked around her like mosquitos to rice fields, but John seemed completely unaffected by her? What was the differ—

A loud, sharp crack came from the side of her room, scaring the wits out of her and extinguishing her thoughts. Slowly, she turned toward the window to see what had made the sound and frowned. The tree closest to her didn't appear to be swaying with the wind. How odd.

Just then, something else hit her window; then again; and again; almost like it was raining small stones. Somebody clearly wanted her attention; but who, and why? Had one of the hands been injured today and in need of her salve? Her blood turned to ice at the thought, and she shoved the window up as fast as she could. "Who's there?"

"Shh," was the only response.

Carolina scanned the moonlit ground outside her window. "Who's there?" she asked again, whispering this time.

"Me."

Carolina's breath caught. "John?"

"The very one," John said, stepping out into the moonlight from a little grove of bushes.

"What are you doing?"

"I came to talk to you."

"Talk?"

A series of soft thuds sounded, presumably created by the rocks he'd been holding hitting the ground. "And possibly something else."

Carolina's chest tightened painfully. "Does this something involve a bed?"

"Gads, Carolina," he burst out in a harsh whisper. "Must you always be so forward?"

Stung by his harsh words which only compounded the hurt she'd already felt from his not-so-subtle insinuation, Carolina gripped the edge of the window pane and brought it down decisively.

Immediately, rocks or acorns, or whatever it was he was throwing, started pelting her window again. Thank goodness her room was the only one on this side of the house and her mother was a sound sleeper, or they might have a visitor.

A slow smile spread across her lips. He was mighty determined to talk to her. Slowly, she eased the window back open.

"Did that make you feel better?" John asked from below.

"Perhaps a little."

John shook his head and took a step closer to the window. "All right, just jump whenever you're ready."

"Jump?"

"Yes, jump," he confirmed. "I originally thought I'd scale the wall and convince you to leave with me in a dignified manner, but then I realized you'd probably find jumping all the more romantic."

"And why would I be jumping?" She cringed at her tone. It was that same sarcastic, condescending tone Mother used when speaking to anyone she felt inferior.

"So you can ride off with your prince—or should I say, me—into the moonlight."

"Wh-what?"

John ran his hand through his hair. "You were right, Carolina. Must I say more?"

"Yes. I think you must."

"Of course you'd think so," he muttered. He blew out a deep breath. "Carolina, I want to marry you."

"You do?"

"Didn't my eyes tell you that already?" he teased.

"Well, yes, but your mouth has refused to acknowledge it. Usually, it settles for an unflattering statement—"

"Do you plan to recount all of my faults, or do you want to get down here so we can leave for town before anyone catches us?"

His words ran through her head. *Leave for town before anyone catches us.* "You mean to elope?" she asked with a slight squeal.

"That was my plan for the night." He did a slow sweep of the windows of the lower level of the house. "What was yours?"

"I don't know. I didn't have one."

He shook his head. "I find that hard to believe. You always have a plan."

"I know," she said pertly. "But I didn't realize yours was to run away with me tonight, when you threw rocks at my window."

"And what did you think my plan was?"

"To seduce me."

Cicadas and crickets chirping in the grass was the only sound.

"I didn't realize you thought so poorly of me," John said at last; his tone low and serious, a stark contrast to how he usually spoke.

"It's not that I think poorly of you, John. It's just that when a young lady is drawn to her window by a pebble-throwing suitor and told his plans include to talk and 'possibly something more', she assumes he..." Her face burned and she shrugged, unable to voice the words of explanation.

"Plans to ravish her," he finished for her. "Don't worry. I do plan to do that, but first I plan to take you to town and give you my last name; however, if you continue to waste precious time, the only place we'll be going tonight is to the woodshed with your mother."

A small burble of laughter passed her lips. "You know her very well."

"Too well," he retorted. "Now, would you like me to climb up there and help you down, or do you wish to chance the stairs?"

"I'll just jump down."

"I was only jesting when I suggested you jump," John rushed to say.

"Don't worry. I've jumped plenty of times. It's not that high."

"It's two stories," he pointed out.

Carolina ignored him and reached under her bed for one of the pairs of leather shoes she'd hidden and claimed she'd lost, so she could give them to one of the field hands' children who often outgrew their shoes long before May, when they all received a new change of clothes. She slid her feet into them, then went to the window on the adjacent wall and opened it, and reached for the thick tree branch that grew so close to her window. Using the skills she'd perfected from many nights of sneaking out to sleep under the stars, Carolina climbed down the thick branch as agilely as a cat. When she reached the tree trunk, she jumped the remaining four feet to the ground and then walked around to the side of the house where John waited.

"Are you ready?"

He jumped and then his gaze shot to her. "How did you get down here so fast?"

"I told you. I climbed down."

Nodding, he said, "And did you happen to drop a bag of clothes down, too?"

"No. You said to hurry. I didn't think I had time to pack."

"That's all right," he said slowly, his eyes traveling up and down her barely covered form. "What you're wearing is more than appropriate for tonight."

A measure of pride shot through Carolina. He desired her. And even better, he wasn't denying it. "What of tomorrow?"

"Don't worry about tomorrow, either. You're perfectly dressed for the rest of our lives, as far as I'm concerned," he said thickly. He jerked his eyes away and swallowed. "But first we need to go find a Mr. Murphy. Come." He led her toward the pasture where he'd tied up his horse.

John picked up the dark green bag he'd set next to the tree and dug through it until he found what he was looking for.

"What's that?"

"A coat," John said, airing it out. "You'll have to wear something while we travel and see the judge."

She flushed. "Of course." She took the garment from John and slipped it on. Naturally, it was too large for her, and with only the moon for light, it was obvious the coat was dirty and ragged, but that didn't matter; she was proud to wear it.

John helped her mount the horse, then untied him and climbed behind her, nestling his body against hers. His large hands came around her and took the reins. When he flicked the reins, the horse began to walk and then run.

Carolina leaned against John's large body, pressing herself against his chest. The scent of his coat filled her nostrils. She loved the way it smelled of sandalwood and fresh grass, just the way John always smelled. She pulled the garment tightly around her, barely believing what was happening, but not daring to question it, too afraid she'd wake up to find that it had all been a dream and she was still lying in her bed.

But it wasn't a dream, and her confirmation came only a short time later when she was awakened by a softly whispered, "We're here," followed by a warm kiss just behind her ear that made her skin prickle with excitement.

John dismounted and then helped her down.

With as much grace as a lady could possibly possess at an hour when the moon was ruling the sky, Carolina dismounted the beast.

John's arms wrapped around her to steady her. "You're all right. I've got you."

She nodded and regained her balance. "Thank you."

He pressed a quick kiss to her brow. "You're welcome. Now, let's go get married, shall we?"

~Chapter Twenty-Two~

John flexed his fingers to get the blood flowing to them again. He'd been so nervous during his impromptu wedding ceremony that he'd clasped his hands too tightly to conceal his nerves and had cut off the circulation.

Carolina peeked up at him from beneath her lowered lashes, her full, pink lips beckoning his to take them in a passionate kiss to mark the start of their marriage.

He couldn't deny her that, could he?

He reached forward and cupped her face with his still numb fingers then pressed his lips to hers. Reluctantly, he pulled away, reminding himself it would only be a little while longer before he could explore every inch of her and make her his.

The blush that stained Carolina's cheeks was his reward for being patient, he supposed.

"There's a little place called Tuffy's just up the road a block or two," said Mr. Murphy, the man who Gabriel suggested he seek out to marry them. He put his pipe back into his mouth and then added, "It's not much, but it'll do for a pair of young, penniless newlyweds, I should think."

Had John thought Carolina actually cared about this man's opinion of her, he'd clarify that there was no reason for a hasty marriage other than genuine feelings between them. Instead, he briefly exchanged nods with the dark-eyed stranger who appeared anxious to get back to his game of cards, then took Carolina's clammy hand and led her outside where Hammond was waiting.

"Your steed, Mrs. Banks," John said, helping her onto the horse.

She giggled and a broad smile took his face. "Thank you, Mr.

Banks."

John mounted Hammond and they headed down the street to the inn Mr. Murphy had indicated. A cry that sounded decidedly like that of woman of ill-repute entertaining a customer filled the air.

"What's that?"

"Nothing," John said. He cleared his throat. "Perhaps there's a stray cat in heat around here." It was an attempt to satisfy her curiosity and not scare her at the same time.

"Not that. Lord knows I've heard Silas and Bethel getting 'better acquainted with one another' more than enough to know what *that* was. I was curious about *that*."

Praying he wouldn't regret what he was about to see, John followed the imaginary line from her outstretched finger to the boardwalk beside them where a small, brown triangular object lay.

"It looks like hair," she said before he could form a response. "Like the hair that's—"

"It's a toupee," John blurted, choking—whether due to his indirect lie or from shock at seeing a merkin just lying on the ground, he'd never know. He slapped his chest twice with his open palm, but it did nothing to relieve the pressure that was clogging his throat and crushing his chest.

"What's a toupee?"

"Pardon?" he croaked. "Oh, right, it's a wig." That was true enough. Unfortunately, this particular wig was not worn by a man, but was definitely *for* a man. That made it qualify as a toupee, didn't it?

"I've never seen a wig like that before. Where does one wear it?" The innocence in her voice brought him from his fog.

He gave her an affectionate squeeze. "That's enough, Carolina. Sometimes there are things you don't want to know the answer to, and I can assure you, that question is one of them." He was pleased beyond measure that she didn't question him any further, because he doubted he'd be able to make up anymore lies to avoid explaining exactly what kind of wig that was and why it was used. "Let's be off. I know of a superior inn we can stay at."

"We don't have to stay in something so fancy," Carolina said as they approached an inn across town.

John chuckled at her weak protest. "Of course we do. It's only fitting for a groom to take his bride to the best lodgings available on their wedding night."

"Does that mean we'll have to spend tomorrow night in that other place?"

He shuddered. "God willing, neither of us will ever have to clap eyes on a place like that ever again."

Carolina looked at him in interest, but didn't ask anything.

But he'd have told her if she had. She was his wife and he owed her that.

Brushing away a fleeting thought of uncertainty, he flashed her his best smile and escorted her inside the inn.

"We'd like a room," John said, approaching the counter.

The grey-headed man behind the counter looked at him through his spectacles, pursing his lips.

John pulled a handful of change from his pocket and slid two coins in the innkeeper's direction. "I can pay upfront, if you'd like."

"No, no, that won't be necessary," the innkeeper said. He flipped open his log book and ran his finger down the page. "You're in luck. We have a vacant room on the third floor."

"Very good; we'll take it." John slipped his coins back into his pocket. "And a bath, please."

The innkeeper nodded and handed him a brass key from one of the pegs behind him. "Fifth door on the left from the top of the stairs."

John turned to Carolina and scooped her up.

"What are you doing?" she said laughingly.

"Carrying my bride to my bed," he whispered in her ear. Ignoring the stares they were receiving from the onlookers they passed, he brought her to their room and, with minimal help unlocking the door, carried her over the threshold and to the bed. "Are you crying?"

Carolina wiped away a tear. "Yes, John, I am. I know you, being a gentleman, don't understand feelings and emotions, but I find this all very romantic."

He shook his head. It was always one emotion or the other where Carolina was concerned. He placed one forearm on either side of her and brought his face closer to hers. "As long as that's the only reason for your tears tonight, I'll gladly offer you my handkerchief."

***

"You don't think I'll regret what happens between us tonight come tomorrow morning, do you?" Carolina asked, pushing a swath of his blond hair away from his eyes.

A shadow crossed his face. "I hope not." He pressed his lips into a thin line. "I know you've dreamt up some version of love at first sight from the moment I entered that ballroom, but you might regret your decisions when I cannot keep you living in the same style you are accustomed to."

His solemn, honest statement made her heart ache. "Never," she murmured before giving into the temptation she'd been fighting all night and brushing her lips across his.

John's blue eyes grew darker and more intense, holding her captive. Before she could even think to move away, John's lips were back on hers, kissing her in a way that was more demanding than he had before. He ran his tongue along the seam of her lips, and she gasped his name.

"Carolina," he whispered in return, framing her face with his large hands. His heavy body pressed against hers, crushing her swollen breasts against his hard chest and setting her blood to simmer in her veins at his closeness. He drew her bottom lip into his mouth and raked his teeth across it, exerting just enough pressure to make her gasp his name again.

He released her lip and sought to deepen their kiss. She froze at the sensation of his tongue exploring her mouth, but her uncertainty didn't last long and she boldly pushed her tongue past his lips to mirror his actions.

A gasp, followed by a groan sounded, but Carolina didn't know who'd made which noise, nor did she care. John's left hand was suddenly on her right breast. Instinctively, she arched her back, pressing her breast more firmly against his palm.

He pulled back, panting. "Too many clothes," he rasped. His Adam's apple bobbed as he swallowed audibly and reached for the buttons that went the length of the coat she wore. He leaned forward and pressed a slow, lingering kiss to her lips each time he slipped a button free. Then, when he'd undone the last, he straightened to his full height and pushed open the coat. He lowered his lashes and held his hand down toward her.

She accepted his help to stand and then stood stock-still as he bent to remove her boots and peel her coat from her. She remained motionless as nothing more than a thin piece of silk, which was soon to be removed, stood between his eyes and her body.

Nervous excitement set her pulse to race as he lowered his lashes and pushed the straps of her nightgown from her shoulders, baring her to his hungry gaze in one short second.

John's eyes swept her from her flushed face to her swollen breasts, then all the way down to her toes.

"Am I what you expected?" she forced herself to ask to fill the intense silence.

"Better," he growled, capturing her lips in another demanding kiss.

Carolina wound her arms around his neck and shamelessly pressed her bare breasts against his hard chest, the coarse fabric of his shirt lightly scratching her sensitive, erect nipples; but she didn't care, she wanted more. More of his kisses. More of his touch. More of him.

He pulled away again and yanked his shirt over his head in such haste the seams along the shoulder split. Seemingly oblivious to the recent destruction of his shirt, John pulled her to him again; this time the soft skin of her chest was pressing against the smattering of wiry hair that covered his.

His large, callused hands roamed up and down her back while she kneaded the hard muscles in his broad shoulders and back. He ran his fingertips up and down her spine, making her shiver. She leaned forward and pressed her forehead against the wide plane of his chest, succumbing to the delicious sensations his wandering fingers created in her.

Pressing a row of kisses along her hairline, John pulled a pin from her long, curly hair. Then another. And another. Never had she taken her hair down in front of anyone except Bethel, and then it was only to wash or comb it. John pulled another pin free and dropped it to the floor with a soft *clink*.

Carolina closed her eyes and let the comfort and excitement from his touch envelope her, sighing with both pleasure and relief when he'd pulled loose the final pin and combed his fingers through her locks, freeing them to fall completely.

He leaned his face closer, burying it in her hair and inhaling. "Mmm."

Carolina swallowed, her body reeling at the simple gesture.

John moved her backward until she felt the edge of the mattress against the back of her legs. He pulled back then, putting about a foot of space between them, and unfastened the flap of his trousers then lowered them to the floor.

He broke eye contact with her, his eyes sweeping her naked body once again. Abandoning all shame, she did the same, taking note of the rigid planes of his chest and the large, rounded muscles of his shoulders and arms. His stomach was flat with twin ripples of muscles that started just below his ribs and stopped at his waist. Between his two muscled thighs, rested a large patch of brown, curly hair that surrounded his long, thick erection. She swallowed past the lump of unease that formed in her throat. She'd grown up on a plantation seeing plenty of farm animals procreate, so she knew what it was for. She just didn't believe for one second that it would fit where he was intending to put it.

The thought was pushed from her mind a moment later when his warm hands found that sensitive dip just above her hips and applied the slightest amount of pressure before slowly moving up her sides to skate over her ribs. He stilled his hands and brushed both of her hardened nipples with the callused pads of his thumbs. She gasped at the sweet torment. A wolfish smile took his lips; then he did it again, harder and with a longer stroke this time. She was prepared for it this time and bit her lip to keep from calling out, but it mattered naught for her body jerked on its own accord, revealing to him just how much she enjoyed his touch.

Would he enjoy hers just as much? Moistening her lips, she reached her hand forward and trailed her fingertips down the front of his body, loving the way his body tensed and his muscles leapt under her touch. She made ten slow paths all the way down to his waist, taking her time to feel every edge, plane, and dip of his chest and abdomen along the way. She had no idea who this excited more: him or her. The fact that she could hear his ragged, uneven breathing over the sound of her blood pounding a loud, steady tattoo in her ears might suggest it was him; but only marginally.

He lowered his head, his eyes fastened on where her fingers had stopped just above his waist, and he moved his hands to gently grip her hips, keeping her from moving away from him.

With a deliberate slowness that went against every ounce of curiosity she possessed, she moved her right hand down and wrapped it snugly around his erection.

His loud groan and tightened grip on her hips emboldened her more. Keeping her firm hold on him, she glided her hand up and down his length. Another groan passed his lips, and his shaft grew thicker—if such a thing were possible.

She slowed her movements, taking her time to go all the way down to the base, then up to the tip where a little pearl of moisture formed at the slit when her fingers reached the tip. She brushed her thumb over the drop of fluid and watched it dissolve on the velvet-soft skin at the tip of his erection, barely registering the hitch in his breath as her thumb moved across his swollen flesh. She moved to do it again; even slower this time.

His hand suddenly encircled her wrist. "Stop."

Carolina's body soared at the sound of the ragged command torn from his chest.

"Why don't you lie down," he encouraged in a voice she hardly recognized—one raw and filled with naked emotion. Without waiting for her to move, he helped her up, then joined her.

Carolina looped her arms around his neck, drawing him as close to her as she could. His large right hand caressed up and down her thigh, easing her legs apart. He positioned himself between her parted thighs and, without so much as a muttered word of warning, pushed his length fully inside her.

~Chapter Twenty-Three~

Carolina's high-pitched shriek was the equivalent of an ice bath, jerking John straight from a lusty haze and extinguishing his ardor.

"Did I hurt you?" he asked, his face heating in embarrassment at such a stupid question. Of course, he'd hurt her. The tears coursing down her cheeks weren't put there by feelings of joy, of that, he was quite certain; but why? Though not something he'd like to admit to anyone, he'd once witnessed a couple engaged in coitus, and she hadn't reacted this way when her partner had entered her in such a manner. In fact, she'd acted just the opposite, shrieking in what John assumed to be pleasure, not pain.

"I'm sorry," she said on a sob.

John wiped away the tears from her cheek. "You have no need to be sorry. I do. I should have..." He had no idea what he should have done differently, and perhaps that was the bigger problem. He separated their bodies, and instantly his eyes widened and his arms trembled in time with Carolina's lower lip as he caught sight of the blood. It wasn't a lot, thank heavens, but there was clearly a little puddle of it on the sheets that hadn't been there before.

His heart ached with guilt for the pain he'd caused her. "That bath will be here shortly," he whispered, pulling her onto his lap.

"John, we can continue, if you'd like."

He let out a harsh bark of laughter. There was no way that would be possible now. "That's not necessary."

"Isn't it though?"

John brushed a kiss on her brow and pulled the sheet up over them. "No."

"But isn't that what has to happen for us to have children?"

A hard knot formed in his stomach. She was right, of course. They'd have to try again if they wanted children. "That's not important tonight, Carolina. We still have plenty of time to worry about having children."

She shifted in his hold, which would have sent him into a state of need in a second only a few minutes ago, but now only served to make him loosen his hold on her until she was more comfortable. "Of course, we have plenty of time; but how much time did you plan to wait?"

"Enough," he bit off. Before he'd left for America, Edward had initiated yet another conversation with him about what he should expect to encounter on his wedding night. And just like all the other times Edward had tried to have this discussion with him, he'd declared there was no need for Edward to explain anything to him —he knew all he needed to know already—and left before Edward could ruin John's good image of Regina. Now, he wished he'd listened rather than relied on the memory of what he'd witnessed that dreadful night long ago.

"The bath is here." Carolina's murmured words brought John from his thoughts.

John called for the servant to enter and simultaneously held the sheet over Carolina as tightly as he could so not an inch of skin beneath her chin could be seen.

As soon as the bath was filled and the servant was gone, John released the sheet and stood up. He carried her to the copper tub that had been placed in the middle of the room and set her down next to it.

He held her hand as she stepped into the steaming tub, then dropped to his knees beside the tub. He lifted her leg closest to him and propped it up so her ankle rested on the far rim of the tub. Not yet able to meet her eyes, he picked up the cake of soap that had been left with the tub, dunked it under the water, and spun it around in his hand until he'd worked up thick, creamy lather, then set the soap down and ran his sudsy hand up her exposed calf.

"I didn't mean to hurt you," he said as much for his benefit as for hers. "I'd never intentionally do anything to bring you pain."

She placed her hand on top of his, stilling his movements. "I know that. It truly wasn't that bad, John. We could have continued."

He brushed his lips across her row of knuckles. "You don't have to say that to make me feel better. I saw your tears, Carolina. I know it hurt. We can wait for another time."

Carolina pulled her hand from his and dropped it back into the tub. "I don't know what waiting will accomplish. Surely, now that I know what to expect, I can prepare myself for it and it won't feel so much like a battering ram."

John choked. Then coughed. "Carolina, while I am flattered you'd compare my rod to such a large and powerful piece of military equipment, you shouldn't have to prepare yourself so it won't hurt. It shouldn't have hurt the first time."

"And you'd know this based on your vast experience?" she asked, lifting her brows.

He turned his attention back to her leg. "I'm physically no more experienced than you," he said unevenly. He forced himself to meet her eyes again. "But like other boys, I did have my curiosities, which I fulfilled. Or at least I thought I did," he added, mumbling.

"I'm getting the impression this is another one of those topics about which I don't want the details," she said, her face turning a pale pink.

"I'd say it fits firmly in that category," he agreed, relief flooding him at her easy dismissal of the topic. He *would* tell her, just not tonight. For as bold and carefree as she seemed to be, this was not something any new bride wanted to hear on her wedding night.

Carolina shifted in the tub, splashing a bit of water over the edge and onto him. Her far leg relaxed and fell open, revealing herself completely to him. He tried not to stare, but that was like asking a man dying of thirst to wait an hour longer for a glass of water.

Moving slow so not to startle or hurt her more than he already had, he ran his hand behind her knee and then along the inside of her thigh.

She sighed and lowered her lashes, her head falling back against the back of the tub. He moved his fingers closer to her body's core. With his free hand, he reached up and combed his fingers through the side of her long, silky hair that hung over the back of the tub while he brushed the fingertips of the hand still in the tub against the outer edge of her most intimate area. Her breath hitched, and consequently so did his.

He did it again, applying more pressure this time. Her eyes remained closed, but her breath hitched again, accompanied by a quiet, suppressed groan.

Blood fired in John's veins, and he became bolder in his touches, rubbing here and massaging there, with no set pattern or pace. He feasted on the sight of Carolina's budded, pink nipples rising in and out of the water each time her body bucked and arched in response to his touch. With a silent prayer he wouldn't ruin everything, he slid a finger inside of her. She stilled. He thought she might request he stop touching her and started to remove his hand on his own accord, but stopped only when she rasped, "Don't go."

"Never," he whispered, not trusting his voice to speak louder. He pushed back in as far as he could, then slid out, imitating the movements he'd made earlier using another part of his anatomy. Her skin flushed and she bit her lip as he pushed forward again. "Do you like this?"

"Yes." Her response broken, ragged.

He increased his rhythm and was rewarded with a sweet sigh in the midst of her labored breathing. Her left hand gripped the edge of the tub and her right found his shoulder to hold onto, as if without it, she'd fall into the tub a boneless heap and drown. Her nails bit into his skin, bringing him the most enjoyable pain he'd ever experienced. "That's it, Carolina," he encouraged as her hips bucked wildly, matching his thrusts. He slipped his arm behind her neck to keep her from hitting her head on the edge of the tub as a result of her fevered movements. "Fall; I have you."

Just then, she did. Her nails dug even deeper into his skin, and her body tensed, then spasmed. He slowed his movements, but held his position until she opened her dazed eyes.

"I—I— D-did you— Have you—"

John kissed her parted lips to put an end to her incoherent stammering. When he pulled back, that faraway look was still in her velvet brown eyes and her face was still flushed with pleasure. Wordlessly, he lifted her from the tub and dried her off, then carried her to the bed.

Carolina's breath caught as her husband covered her body with his own. He whispered soft words of love in her ear before his lips found hers again. He kissed the center of her lips, then the corner, and then made a path of kisses all the way down to her jaw; his hands skimmed up and down her sides, his fingers brushing every inch of her they could touch, from the bottom curve of her breasts to the dips just above her hips, searing her with each pass. His kisses became more urgent, as did his caresses. He reached his right hand up to cover as much of her breast as would fit in his palm, then squeezed. Sparks of desire fired through her, and she pressed her breast more firmly against him, silently praying he'd do it again and again.

He shifted, releasing her breast as he repositioned himself. The arrogant man dared to smile when she whimpered at his absence.

She placed her hands on his shoulders, bracing herself for his intrusion.

This time, he pushed inside slowly taking great care to be gentle. Her muscles grew tense the further in he went and the more her body had to stretch to accommodate him. When at last she didn't think she could take anymore, he stopped moving and held still, holding her gaze.

She refused to ruin everything again with another outburst, but she'd be lying if she didn't admit it was uncomfortable—but not nearly as painful as last time, to be sure.

"I'm going to move now."

His strangled voice sent a surge of feminine pride like she'd never experienced before through her. She loved it that she could have this affect on him. That she, Carolina, could make his eyes take on this intense gleam of want, turn his body rigid with need, and cause his breath to become ragged with desire. More than that, she loved knowing she'd be the one to fulfill his wants, needs and desires for the rest of their lives.

A moment later, her thoughts of love and his desire and fulfillment were gone, replaced instead with wonder at how his movements had gone from causing her discomfort to suddenly bringing her the same internal pressure she'd felt when he'd touched her in the tub. She squeezed his shoulders, a silent command for him to move faster, harder.

He did, and her hips bucked on their own accord to meet his movement. A shower of hot sparks shot through her, followed only a split-second later by another round when he thrust again. Carolina groaned his name and tightened her grip on him until she was certain he'd have two hand-shaped bruises on his shoulders before the night was through.

She matched his movements, thrust for thrust, passion for passion. The pressure in her midsection mounted more with each of his strokes until finally she couldn't contain it anymore, and with a muffled cry against his shoulder, the most delicious pleasure swept over her, taking her—and him—into that delirious state of completion.

Breathless, they both fell to the pillows in a sweaty, tangled heap.

"I do believe I shall enjoy this aspect of marriage more than I originally thought," Carolina said between deep breaths.

"Comparing my tool to a battering ram and complimenting my prowess in bed, you certainly know a thing or two about flattery, m'dear," he said, rolling off to the side and propping himself up on his elbow.

"No, not flattery, just practicing your near honesty," she said with a wink.

Something unnameable flashed in John's eyes. "'Near honesty', you say? Perhaps now would be a good time to perfect my deficiencies."

Carolina ran the back of her index finger along the edge of his stubble-covered jaw. "Promise?"

"That, and more," he said with a savage growl before proceeding to show her he was the sort of man who made good on his promises—no matter how deliciously wicked they were.

~ Chapter Twenty-Four ~

If Carolina didn't have a spawn in nine months, John would need no further proof to convince himself that she was barren.

"Will clothes be optional for breakfast again this morning?" she asked when he rounded the dressing screen after his bath wearing precisely the same thing he'd been wearing before his bath: nothing. Come to think of it, for the entire week they'd been married, neither of them had worn anything, except when he'd gone downstairs to request their meals be sent up and when a modiste had come to visit four days ago to take Carolina's measurements.

"Absolutely." His grin at the sight of her lounging naked on the bed faded a hint. "But we'll have to be fully dressed for lunch, I'm afraid."

Carolina climbed out of bed and padded over to him. She skimmed her hands down his chest and stomach, then toward his waist. "Must we?"

He lowered his lashes and swallowed but didn't move to stop her wandering fingertips. "I suppose you could dine naked for lunch, but I doubt you'll want to. Today we need to go see your father and collect your things."

Carolina dropped her hand and scowled. "Can't we stay here a few days longer?"

John shook his head. It was only because Gabriel had given him half the price they'd agreed Hammond was worth that he'd had enough funds to pay for the hotel. He needed to deliver Hammond to Gabriel to complete the sale and collect the other half of the money so they'd have enough funds for passage to England, where a place to stay and a job waited for him. "No, I'm afraid not. Is something wrong?"

The tip of her pink tongue darted out and licked her lips. "No. Not wrong. I just don't want to see them again, that's all."

"But you need your clothes, and I need to make good on a promise I made to Gabriel," John pointed out. He stepped closer to her until there were only mere inches between them and brought his hands to her face, caressing her cheeks with his thumbs. "Besides, we're married now. Your mother has no control over you any longer. You're mine now, and if I haven't proven that to you already, I'd be glad to give you another demonstration."

She smiled and shook her head. "I think you've demonstrated that fact quite adequately already. It's just—" She shrugged. "They'll all know we've been alone together for the last week."

"Indeed."

Carolina pressed her forehead against his chest.

"Surely you're not actually worried about that, are you?" He tipped her face up toward him, marveling at what a strange, complex creature she was. Before they'd married, he thought her incapable of being embarrassed or put off by anything. Apparently, she was a good actress. "Almost every new bride has to face her family, Carolina. Nobody will think poorly of you. We were married. That's all that matters."

A peal of her throaty laughter filled the room and sent a hot tendril of desire to coil in his gut. "I don't care about *that*. It's Bethel."

"Bethel?" What did she have to do with anything?

Carolina seemed to find something about the wooden floor plank under their feet vastly amusing. "I'm sure she paid dearly when I disappeared the first time. I'm afraid if I go back, Mother might take her anger out on her again."

John pulled her in a tight hug. "I won't let that happen, Carolina." He didn't know what he'd be able to do to prevent it, but he'd think of something. "Now, let's have breakfast then we'll get ready to go."

The solemn look on Carolina's face during breakfast tore at his heart. She was truly worried. Of course she was. Bethel was more of a mother to her than her own mother was.

After they finished their meal, John excused himself behind the screen and came back with a small parcel. "I hope it fits," he said, handing it to her.

Carolina's slender fingers freed the knot in the twine and pulled the paper away. "When did this arrive?" she gushed, grabbing the top of the folded gown that had been delivered.

"Not long ago," John said evasively, shrugging.

Carolina swatted at his shoulder. "You weren't hiding it, were you?"

"Of course not; what kind of husband do you think I am?"

"The kind who likes to see his wife spend her days dressed in the same costume she wore when she entered the world."

"You can't blame me, can you?" he asked, sweeping her naked body with his eyes. "What man would want his wife to cover her body when it's as beautiful as yours?"

Her skin grew pink. "That will be enough of that."

He laughed at the way her voice hitched on those words. "You know you wouldn't want me any other way."

She came up on her toes and pressed a soft kiss to his lips. "You're right. I wouldn't want you any other way. But that doesn't mean I want to go see my parents today."

"Don't worry, Carolina. It'll be fine."

***

He couldn't have been more wrong. Everything was *not* fine.

In fact, it was the furthest thing from fine as something could possibly be.

"What did you say?" John demanded of Gabriel, stealing the words straight from Carolina's sputtering lips.

Gabriel took a deep, unsteady breath and handed John a tattered copy of the *City Gazette,* one of Charleston's most prominent newspapers.

John snatched the paper from Gabriel and started reading while Carolina peeked over his shoulder, trying to make sense of what they'd just been told. Surely Gabriel had been mistaken, hadn't he?

"I don't believe this," John whispered as the paper slipped from his fingers and drifted to the floor. He swallowed hard and scrubbed his face with his fingers.

Another wave of nausea washed over Carolina. Gabriel's claim was true. They'd not actually met with the real Mr. Murphy who was rumored to help young lovers marry under the blanket of darkness, but with the man who was pretending to be him and tricking unsuspecting lovers into paying him for services he was not authorized to perform.

"I don't see why you wouldn't believe it," Mother said. "It would seem that you'd understand a member of your own kind better than any of us."

John tensed and speared her with his icy gaze. "Madam, has it occurred to you that had I known I did not legally marry your daughter I wouldn't have brought her by to see you?" His tone held a sharp edge Carolina had never heard before.

"Didn't you wonder why you weren't given a certificate?" a pale faced Gabriel asked quietly.

"I didn't even think about it," Carolina said defensively. "I've never been married before, how was I supposed to know what to expect?"

Mother twisted her lips as if she'd just bitten into a lemon. "Either way—"

"That's enough, Mrs. Ellis," Father said. "The fact is, they're not actually married. There's nothing we can do to change what's already happened, instead we need to discuss what will happen now."

"We'll go back to town and make it right," John said easily.

"You most certainly will not," Mother said. "If you didn't do things right the first time, what makes you think I'll trust you to do right by her now?"

John bristled. "I didn't know that man was a fraud. I went to the address Gabriel gave me. How was I to know I was meeting with an impostor?"

"I don't know. But this wouldn't have been a problem had you married her the right way the first time and not run away like the thief that you are," Mother retorted.

Color rose in John's cheeks, but he ignored her accusation. "And had I asked for her hand, would my request have been accepted?" The challenge in John's voice matched the one in his eyes.

"Well, no," Mother said airily. "You are a completely unsuitable choice for my daughter. She might not have had a chance to reel in the finest catch Charleston has to offer due to her unbecoming behavior and unimaginable interest in an English vagrant such as yourself, but she still had prospects; something that you've once again managed to rob her of."

"Rob me?" Carolina argued. "If the prospect you speak of is Charlie Fields, then I'd say he did Charlie a great favor."

"You'd be the one to think so," Mother said; her voice mixed with pity and condemnation. "But you're charitable—"

"Mrs. Ellis yous hab a vis'tor," Bethel said, coming to the open door of the parlor. Her solemn voice and swollen cheeks tore at Carolina's heart.

She swallowed the emotion in her throat and blinked back the tears in her eyes. Bethel had paid a heavy penalty for Carolina's behavior. And likely, it wasn't just once. John's knuckles brushed her arm, giving her an unexplainable amount of comfort.

"Have our guest wait..." Mother exhaled, casting a sharp glance at both Father and Gabriel who slept in the informal parlor due to their injuries. "Send them in, I suppose."

"Yessum."

"If you'll excuse us," John began, taking Carolina's hand in his, "we'll leave you to your company now."

"No," Gabriel said. "I know you mean to do right by her, John, and this is partly my own fault; but as her brother, I cannot let her be seen leaving here with you."

"You do realize she was just seen riding in—on the same horse —with me?"

Gabriel nodded. "That was unavoidable. But I will not—no *cannot*—let her be seen that way again. It might start some unsavory rumor."

An inappropriate burble of laughter escaped Carolina at Gabriel's implication. Or perhaps it was at the look of disbelief stamped on John's face.

"You cannot be serious," John said. "I intend to make things right, Gabriel. Nobody who will see us today will be of any import once we're in England."

"Is that so?" drawled a masculine voice from the door. "I happen to know a certain English Lord and Lady who some consider to be important. I believe you know them, too."

John spun around, his eyes wide with shock. "Edward? What are you doing here?"

Edward, who resembled John with his blond hair, blue eyes and tilted smile, came farther into the parlor, silently ushering a petite lady and a small child in with him. "I came to see my brother. I wasn't aware that had become a crime."

"It's not. Is everything all right?"

Edward waved him off. "We'll talk about my news later. I'm far more curious about the situation you've created where you're intending to make things right, Trouble."

Though his brother smiled as he said those words, John didn't. "You're not helping matters, Edward."

Edward's smile faded and he looked over to where Mother stood with a look on her face that might suggest she was suffering a condition that made her unable to use the chamberpot without the help of herbs. "John, are you in any real trouble?"

"I'd say so," Mother answered for him.

"And just what crime has my brother committed?" John's brother asked, his tone and expression cool as could be.

Mother cast him a look of icy disdain. "Abduction."

Edward didn't show a hint of emotion, just turned his eyes back to John.

"I'll explain when we're on the ship bound for England, but believe me when I tell you it's not nearly as bad as she's claiming."

Edward lifted his eyebrows, but didn't speak. "I hope you're right, because abduction is certainly a damnable offense."

A loud gasp rent the air. "You said damn," a little boy no more than three or four said in a stage whisper; his brown eyes wide with wonder. "Mama said damn's a bad word and that gentlemen shouldn't say damn in front of ladies."

Carolina smiled at the boy's mother whose face was now as red as her gown. "Alex," the other woman said gently.

He blinked up at his mother. "But you told me damn—"

"I know what I told you; but Papa didn't say that, he said damnable."

The boy's eyebrows drew together, and his mother threw a pleading glance at her husband who shrugged in response.

Ignoring everyone else in the room, John sank to his haunches in front of the little boy. "Damn is a naughty word because it implies you're condemning something because you're angry and annoyed, and you have no regard whatsoever for what your cursing. Damnable just means something that can be condemned."

"But both condemn," the little boy pointed out, his brows puckering.

"It's how it's used," John further explained. "When your Papa storms around Watson Estate mumbling about having to spend the whole damn afternoon with Lady Sinclair, he's being very naughty and deserves punishment for subjecting the rest of us to his foul language—not to mention his disagreeable temperament at the time. But as your mama pointed out, he didn't say damn, he said damnable; which means he thinks it'd be easy to condemn my actions based on the accusation that I abducted your Aunt Carolina."

Carolina's heart didn't know whether to flutter at his styling her as "Aunt Carolina" or melt at the way he interacted with the boy.

"I still think he needs to apologize for saying damn," the little boy declared.

"Oh, all right," Edward blustered, shaking his head. "I apologize if I've offended anyone."

"It's of no account, Mr. Banks," Mother said crisply. "Your word selection was not nearly as unforgivable as your son's free use of such a vulgar word. Perhaps you ought to spend a little more time instructing your son as to what's acceptable to say in public —"

"Would he be taking these lessons from you, Mother?" Gabriel asked.

Mother whipped her head around to pin Gabriel with a sharp stare.

He seemed unaffected. "It would seem to me that you're not exactly an expert in this particular subject, given that your only son cannot abide you and stayed away an additional five years after the war was over just to avoid you; and your daughter ran off in the middle of the night with someone you disapprove of. It seems to me, you're in no position to be giving any sort of parenting advice."

The room grew eerily quiet. Nobody could argue the truth in his words—as unpleasant as it might be.

But that wasn't enough to stop Mother. She might be embarrassed, but she wasn't the type to be so easily deterred. For as annoying as it was that Mother was argumentative and oozed spiteful condemnation, she didn't let what people said or did cow her, and that was one trait Carolina *did* respect. "As truthful, yet tactless, as your words might be, at least *my* children were taught the importance of a proper introduction."

Carolina nearly sputtered with laughter. Mother could be proven a fool again if Carolina were to mention to the room the details of her belated introduction to John.

"Well then, allow me to correct your misconception that the Banks family is so ill-bred we do not bother with introductions," Edward said. He erected himself to full height. "My name is Edward Christopher Banks, the seventeenth Baron of Watson." He removed his gray hat and gave a low bow, then put it back on and motioned to his wife. "This is my wife, Regina, Lady Watson and my son, the honorable Alexander Banks. And of course, you've already met my brother the honorable John Banks."

Mother's face went whiter than any sheet Carolina had ever seen. "Y-you're nobility?" she stammered, her mouth opening and closing like a fish.

Carolina didn't know a thing about English nobility, but if they could reduce her tart-tongued, shrew of a mother into a bumbling idiot, they were a good thing, indeed.

"No, madam, I *was* born of noble blood; these days I'm more commonly styled as an English vagrant." John's voice lacked any hint of emotion, belying the storm of rage Carolina glimpsed in his eyes.

Mother waved her hand in the air, favoring him with a coy smile. "Oh, do be serious. You've become part of our little family. We just didn't know you brought such noble relations with you."

"Part of your family?" John echoed.

A sound akin to an owl's screech—but was actually just Mother's obnoxious, forced laughter—filled the room. "Of course you're part of our family. You married our Carolina, didn't you?" As if suddenly remembering that Carolina and John weren't really married, she blushed. "About that; I'm thinking we should have the wedding here on the plantation." She turned to John's brother and sister-in-law. "You will be in attendance, won't you?"

"No," John said before either of them could answer, his voice hard and abrupt. He squeezed Carolina's hand, as a silent assurance of something, but she didn't know what, then abruptly let go and crossed his arms. "They won't be here. As you've already said, I am an unsuitable choice for your daughter. As such, I regret to inform you of this, but there won't be a wedding to plan because Carolina and I won't be getting married."

~Chapter Twenty-Five~

"What the devil are you doing?" Edward called after John just before he reached the barn.

"Looking for the horse you rode in on." John didn't know why Edward had come across the ocean to see him, but whatever the reason, he was glad as it created the perfect opportunity for him.

Edward grabbed his arm and spun him around. "Damn. That's not as easy as it was the last time I saw you."

John chuckled. "Hard work will add weight to a man."

"At least, it's the good kind," Edward said, taking in John's solid frame. "You're not the boy I remember."

"No. I'm not. I've callused my hands and tired my body doing the work of a man."

"That might be," Edward conceded. "But you're still acting like a boy."

John crossed his arms and leaned against the doorjamb of the barn. "How so?"

Edward raked a hand through his hair. "How can you ask that? You know as well as I do that you must marry her in truth. As a young man who once studied diligently to be a Man of God, you should know that having slept with her you are as good as married to her in a moral sense."

"I know," John said with an overdone frown. "But legally, we're not."

Edward's shrewd eyes narrowed on him and then he sighed. "Are you planning to haul her off in the night?"

"No," John said, shaking his head. "I've already done that."

"So then, you plan to rob that poor girl of a future?"

John snorted. "I doubt anyone could rob Carolina of anything she thinks she deserves."

"Are you saying she doesn't deserve a life of being chained to you? Because I have to agree. Nobody should be made to suffer that torment," he said with a grin.

"She might not find it such torment."

Edward laughed. "Does she enjoy suffering, then?"

"More than most," John muttered. "For weeks she chased after me.... The woman has no shame." He laughed. "Even you couldn't embarrass her."

"Don't challenge me," Edward warned.

John waved him off. "That's a challenge I encourage you to accept, but I doubt that even you could find something that could rattle her."

"And you married her? Willingly?"

John shook his head ruefully. "Yes; willingly."

"I must say that I'm not surprised."

"Not surprised?" John scoffed. "She's everything I once said I didn't wish to marry."

"Then why did you?"

John flashed his brother a grin. "I didn't."

"But you thought you did," Edward pointed out. "For all of your schemes and nonsense, I know better than to believe you knowingly didn't marry her."

"No. I didn't." John used his thumbnail to idly pick at the splintering wood of the barn. "She might not be meek and quiet, and she's certainly not always proper. But she is true."

"True?"

John nodded. "Carolina has the ability to be the most annoying creature I've ever encountered with her constant talking and pressing need to be in the middle of everything; but unlike any other lady who does that, Carolina's being genuine."

"And little Rebecca Klammer wasn't?" Edward teased.

John scowled. "We were six. That doesn't count."

"She seemed to be quite taken with you—even if you were only six."

"And catching bugs," John added. "That's the difference. Rebecca acted like a monkey inhaling nitrous oxide *because* she was six and starved for attention. Carolina does it because that's who she is. She might overdo some things—" like bringing him water while he was outside working— "just to put herself in a position to be noticed. But her words and emotions, they're real."

Edward didn't look convinced.

"It's difficult to explain in words, Edward. But I know when she does those things, it's not meant to annoy someone into paying attention to her. It's because she's being genuine. She's genuinely happy or distraught. She's not just looking for someone to pay her mind, she wants to help. There's a difference."

"If you say so," Edward said with a frown. "I don't see it, but if you do, then who am I to pass judgement?"

John clenched his hands into fists. There was a difference; he just couldn't find the right words to explain it. No matter. Edward's words had nothing to do with Carolina, he was merely poking fun at John for his long ago vow never to marry a young lady who enjoyed being heard in addition to being seen.

"She has this intense loyalty like I've never seen before," he tried again.

"Regina's loyal," Edward defended.

"Of course she is," John allowed, "to you. And you're loyal to her. But Carolina's loyalty is different."

"You mean, because it's to you?"

"Of course; but it's not just that." He sighed. He wasn't doing any better explaining her loyalty to all of those she loved than he'd explained why Carolina's dramatic personality didn't bother him. "Yes, she's loyal to me. But she's loyal to everyone she cares about."

A shadow crossed Edward's face. "I don't know what your

plan is here, but I pray that you do because if what you say about her is true and she's genuine and loyal and all that, then you need her far more than you know."

"I have everything well-in-hand, thank you," John said stiffly, annoyed at the way his brother still seemed to think him incapable of making good decisions. "Why is it that you're here anyway?"

"Because you weren't in Boston," Edward said, his voice devoid of its usual softness.

"You know what I mean."

Edward closed his eyes for an extended blink. When he opened them again, the mirth and laughter that usually filled Edward's blue eyes were gone, replaced with uncertainty. A fist formed in John's gut in anticipation of what his brother would say.

"The archbishop came to see me the month before last," Edward said.

"Is he requesting I return and begin my tenure?"

"Not exactly."

John's gut clenched tighter. Had he been away so long that the archbishop gave his position to someone else? "Then what did he say?"

Edward took a deep breath. "He regrets to inform you that he will no longer be able to find placement for you. Ever."

The blood thundered in John's ears. This could only be the result of one thing. "Who told him?"

"I don't know. A story surfaced in London at the start of the Season."

"Was I mentioned?"

Edward shoved his hands into his pockets. "Not by name. But there were enough hints given to leave no doubt of your involvement."

"All of my involvement?" John asked hopefully.

"I don't think so."

"You don't think so? How do you not know?"

"You know that I don't read scandal sheets," Edward said with a frown. "I didn't even know the story had gotten out until I started asking around after my visit with the archbishop."

John shut his eyes and leaned his head against the doorframe. "I suppose it won't change his mind if I explain everything?"

"I don't think so."

John rubbed the bridge of his nose. Once more, the thoughtless actions of his fourteen-year-old self were coming back to haunt him and ruin his life—and now Carolina's, too. "I suppose I'll just have to stay on this side of the ocean, then."

"You don't have to," Edward offered. "There are many younger sons who have no occupation."

"Absolutely not. I will not live on your generosity, Edward," John burst out. "I am perfectly capable of providing for myself. Or have I not proved that to you already?"

"You have. Your open refusal of the money I put into an account for you was quite enough to convince me that you are able to take care of yourself. But John, this isn't just about you anymore. Soon, you'll be married, and I don't think I need to tell you what follows a happy marriage in a matter of months."

John scowled. "I'm well aware of what my responsibilities will be, but I have no desire to allow my older brother to provide for my family when I'm perfectly capable of doing so."

"All right," Edward said slowly. "Do you have an idea of how you'll do that?"

"Join the military."

Edward's lips thinned into a line. "I hope that's not your idea of a jest, because it wasn't the slightest bit humorous."

John shrugged. "I wasn't trying to be. At least as a widow of a member of the military, she'd have a pension."

"She's about to be a widow of a thickheaded, unemployed younger son of a baron if you're not careful."

"Actually, if that happens too soon, she won't be anybody's widow," John pointed out.

"John, you are intending to do something about that, aren't

you?"

John drummed his fingers on the wood at his side. "You know me, Edward. I'm always planning *something*."

"May the Lord have mercy on us all."

Chapter Twenty-Six

"Might I have a word with you, sir?" John asked as Mr. Ellis wheeled himself into his room.

Mr. Ellis looked startled at first but nodded his consent. "Is this about Lina?"

Now it was John's turn to nod. "It's about our getting married."

"Don't you think that considering the situation this conversation is irrelevant?" Carolina's father asked with a sadness in his eyes John couldn't begin to understand.

"Perhaps a tad belated, but not entirely irrelevant," John said easily.

Mr. Ellis sighed. "I think you'd better speak to her mother, then. She seems to be the one who's taken a keen interest in Carolina's marriage prospects."

"I don't want to speak to her mother. I want to speak to you."

"I can't fault you there," he said with a smile. "She wasn't always so bad, you know."

No, he didn't know. Nor did he care to. Whatever happiness Mr. Ellis thought was buried deep, deep inside Mrs. Ellis was of no account to John. "About Carolina; I'd like to marry her if you're agreeable."

"You would, would you?"

John pressed his lips together and nodded.

"All right, then, for what it's worth, you have my permission."

John sneered at his offhanded tone. "Do you not care more for your daughter than to marry her off to the first bounder who asks?"

Mr. Ellis roared with laughter. "Do you think I have a choice?"

"Yes. You are still the head of this family, are you not? Is your name not on the deed of this plantation? Is it not you who owns every piece of property on this land?"

Mr. Ellis waved his remaining hand through the air. "What I meant is that my daughter has a mind of her own and a will made of iron. I learned long ago that it wouldn't matter if I gave my permission or not, she'd do as she pleased. And I do believe she'd do whatever you ask her to do."

"I'm pleased to hear that, but I haven't asked her yet."

"She's in her room. I trust you know the way there," he said with a slight twist to his lips.

John's cheeks flushed. "I apologize for not doing this the right way the first time."

"No need to apologize, Mr. Banks. God willing, one day, you too shall have children and you'll understand my position better."

"Your position?"

"A man will always love his children; no matter what they do. However, just because he loves them, it doesn't make accepting their choices any easier."

"You don't approve of me." It was more a statement than a question.

"No. It's not that I don't approve of you. I just don't approve of how you handled your courtship with my daughter." He sighed. "But that's irrelevant now. You've both made your choices; whether I approve of how the two of you decided to do things or not, I can learn to accept it." He grinned. "Though I do hope I'm around to see your children give you the same fits. I do believe that shall work miracles in wiping away the heartache I've suffered."

John stared straight ahead as a vision of what life would be like for him in twenty years formed in his mind. He swallowed; then again. With a mother like Carolina, he might need all that money Edward had been depositing for him as a dowry if they have a girl.

Mr. Ellis' laughter brought John back to present. "Has something in that mind of yours frightened you, my boy?"

"I must start praying tonight that she bears only sons," he said half-heartedly. Honestly, he didn't care if she had a dozen girls who were just like her. He'd love her—and them—all the same.

"You haven't changed your mind about marrying her, have you?"

"No. I'd still like to marry her, but my asking depends on you."

"I've already given you my permission. What more are you waiting for?"

"Your promise."

"My promise?'

John nodded. "I want you to promise me that the day I marry Carolina you'll free Bethel."

Mr. Ellis' smile vanished and a blank expression took his face. "Pardon me?"

"Bethel's freedom in exchange for me marrying Carolina."

Mr. Ellis' cold grey eyes penetrated his. "And why would I do this?"

"Because it's what I'm asking."

"Son, you have to understand; a woman like Bethel costs a lot of money. I cannot just free her. It'll cost me half of a harvest's profits to replace her."

John ignored the uneasy feeling in his stomach at the way Mr. Ellis talked of Bethel as if she were a piece of furniture and not a person. "Consider it a wedding present."

Mr. Ellis sighed. "I know Carolina is fond of her, but I cannot free her."

"And why not?"

"Mrs. Ellis would be most displeased. She's come to be quite dependent upon Bethel."

"She can become dependent upon someone else," John bit off.

Mr. Ellis shifted in his chair as best he could. "Isn't there something else I can do?"

"No. You either free Bethel and have the respectable youngest son of an English baron marry your daughter or don't free her and have an exiled vagrant make your daughter his mistress."

"You wouldn't dare," Mr. Ellis thundered.

It was the first time John had heard the man raise his voice. John fisted his hands and willed himself not to cough and give himself away. He had to do this. He had to be strong and put up an impenetrable front, or his only chance at getting Bethel's freedom would be lost.

He clamped his jaw closed to keep a hard, impassive expression on his face and strolled to the door. Stopping, he said, "Sir, you're the one who said Carolina would do whatever I asked of her. Do you truly mean to find out if that's true?"

Leaving Mr. Ellis and his floundering jaw in the room, John left, intent to see if her father's theory was still true after everything he had to tell her.

~Chapter Twenty-Seven~

Carolina's cheeks had never hurt so much from laughing; or pretending to, at least.

Edward meant well by trying to entertain her with stories of John as a boy, but if he meant to distract her, it wasn't working.

And judging by the worry lines on his face that seemed to get deeper by the minute, he wasn't any more able to put John's earlier actions out of his mind than she was.

"I hate to be impolite, but I think it's best if we all go to bed," Carolina said, offering the entire room her best smile.

"I quite agree," Regina, Lady Watson agreed with a smile of understanding. "Come along, Alex."

"But I want to hear more about when Papa had to save Uncle John from drowning in the creek because he'd tied himself to the boat," Alex protested, looking up at his papa with the widest eyes Carolina had ever seen.

Edward sighed. "How about I tell you the story of how your mama broke that very boat when we get upstairs?"

Alex blinked up at his father, clearly weighing his options. He scrambled down off his father's lap and ran across the room to his mother. "You didn't really break the boat, did you?"

Her face grew pink. "I'm afraid I did. But if you want your papa to tell you of my shame, you'll have to come upstairs."

"All right," he said at last. "I've heard the story of Uncle John enough. I've never heard this one." The adorable boy turned around and waved for his father to accompany them.

Carolina stood up, too, and led them up the stairs to Gabriel's old room. "You must forgive the lack of space. Father built the house right after he and Mother married and could only afford to build three bedrooms. This was Gabriel's before the war, and unfortunately there is only one bed."

Regina's gentle hand landed on Carolina's shoulder. "There is no need for you to explain anything. We are accustomed to sharing the same bed, so anything you can offer will be quite sufficient, I assure you."

Carolina accepted the older woman's reassurance and opened the door for them.

"See, just as I said, it's perfect," Regina said, gliding into the room that had been cleared of almost everything save the bed and armoire. Regina immediately started to unpack their luggage, which Dalton had brought up earlier.

"Have a good night," Carolina said, stepping out of the room.

"Carolina," Edward said, joining her in the hall.

"Yes?"

He sighed and combed his fingers through his blond hair the same way she'd seen John do when he was frustrated or uncertain. "Don't give up on him. I have no idea what goes on in that brain of his, but I do know he didn't mean those words he said earlier."

"I know," she said simply. "I might not have known him as long as you have, but I think I know him just as well."

At least, she hoped she did.

The John she knew wouldn't have made that declaration and disappeared for the rest of the day. There had to be more than what she knew. Of course, it'd be a little easier to convince herself of this had he thought to inform her of anything before he vanished.

Blinking back the tears pricking her eyes, brought on by yet another emotionally difficult day, she opened the door to her room and froze.

"John?"

His smile didn't quite meet his eyes. "Is now a good time to talk?" he asked, extending her a glass of water.

"I suppose so," she said laughingly as she closed her door, but didn't take his glass of water. "Although I do wonder why you've waited so long to speak to me when you've had all evening to do so, and yet, you seemed to have made yourself scarce instead."

He swallowed and set the glass down on the little end table next to him. "I know. And I'm sorry."

"Oh? Was your evening as charming as mine?"

He frowned. "Are you angry with me?"

"Can you blame me? I spent the evening with both of our families while you were relaxing in solitude."

"No, I suppose not," he said quietly. "But you must know my evening wasn't any more enjoyable than yours."

She doubted that. "Unless you think to convince me that you had to sit idle and hear tales of your past as a means to attempt to ease the suffocating tension, then I think I might have you beat. It was so awful, even my father excused himself early."

"I have no plan to convince you of such," he said quietly, his face grim. "However, while you merely had to listen to tales of my past, I had to spend the evening standing in dark corners reliving them and thinking of what I'd say to you when this moment arrived."

Carolina cocked her head to the side. There was a rare look in his eye. Not uncertainty necessarily, but he was clearly uneasy and upset. "What's happened?"

"Why don't you come sit down?"

Her stomach lurched at his quiet tone and solemn expression, and she forced herself to walk to the bed and sit on the edge. "All right."

John clasped his hands together behind his back and took a deep breath. "I want you to know that whatever decision you make regarding me once I'm finished, I'll respect."

Bile rose in her throat. "Just tell me," she croaked.

"I won't be able to return to England," he said matter-of-factly.

"H-how come?"

His throat worked and his eyes grew shuttered and dim. "Because of a mistake I made in the past, I will have no future

181

there if I do."

"I—I don't understand."

"I know," he said; his voice terribly uneven. He grabbed the chair that was under her writing desk and moved it so he could sit in front of her. "When I was sixteen, I was sent down from school for the last time, and with the help of Edward, I began training to become a vicar."

"John, there's no shame that you didn't finish school," she said, reaching up to smooth back the hair that had fallen in his eyes.

He pulled away. "That's not the problem. I'd planned to go back to England and take my place as a vicar. But now I can't."

"Because you got into trouble at school?"

He nodded.

"What could a sixteen-year-old boy have possibly done that was so bad his entire future has been tainted?" she asked, unable to hide the disbelief in her voice.

"Actually, I was fourteen when this particular incident happened," he said without much emotion. "It was just never forgotten. In the following two years, I was sent home so often that Edward gave me the option to go to Harrow—the only other school suitable for a young man of my station—or to persuade the archbishop to allow me to start seminary early. I chose the latter. I didn't want to make new friends, or explain why I was joining in the middle of the academic term. I spent the following two years under the instruction of the archbishop and had just finished when I decided to leave for America."

"Because he found out you'd been expelled from school?"

He shook his head. "No. I never told him. I was too ashamed to and believed Edward, when he told me not to worry, one mistake at fourteen wouldn't ruin my life." He idly rubbed his jaw. "He meant well. He couldn't have predicted this."

"Predicted what?" she burst out. For all his sudden interest in talking, he sure wasn't saying much.

"That I'll not be granted a vicarage because of it."

"Because you were asked to leave school at sixteen or what happened when you were fourteen?" she asked, confused.

"The latter." He closed his eyes and rubbed his long fingers up and down his face. When he spoke again, his voice was quiet and uneven. "When I was thirteen, my father died and Edward took his place as baron. Being a baron demanded a lot more of his time than I was able to understand at thirteen. My entire life, he'd been there. Taking me on wild adventures down the creek or racing horses in the pasture. He always answered any question I could possibly think to ask." A slim smile took his lips. "When I was ten and he sixteen, I asked why grapes tasted so good and raisins were horrid. He just smiled and said, 'God had to make some fruit so awful that when threatened to be made to eat it, you'd stay on your best behavior.'.

"But then, when Father died, it seemed that my closeness with Edward died right along with it. He made time for me, of course. But it wasn't every day of the summer like before, because he had a wealth of new responsibility to which he now had to attend. His answers to my questions went from being thought out and fun to clipped and rushed. We were both adapting to the changes that were filling our lives—his with new responsibility and mine, the awkwardness of becoming a young man—and I suddenly couldn't bring myself to ask the things I wanted to know. So when an opportunity to have my curiosity satisfied, without involving Edward, presented itself, I took it."

Carolina had a feeling she already knew what he'd been curious about, but *her* curiosity demanded she ask, "What did you want to know about?"

"Ladies," he said, unable to meet her eyes. "I know for those of your sex, interest in the opposite sex doesn't happen at such an early age, but for mine, it does; and I had no idea what to do or who to ask."

Dread washed over her for the second time that day, sending

every drop of her blood straight to her toes. She thought she knew him. She'd trusted him, not only with *her* body, but her heart, too. How could she have possibly been wrong?

Either oblivious to her distress or under the belief that if he confessed everything, his own conscience would be cleared, he continued. "Not long after Edward married Regina, one of my friends got a girl from a nearby tavern to agree to meet a little group of five of us out in a field south of the school one night."

Carolina's stomach lurched, and that bile she'd swallowed earlier returned as horrible images of what she imagined he was about to tell her cycled through her mind.

"We all brought money to pay her, only things didn't go as planned." He swallowed and took a deep breath. "She arrived as agreed, and we stared at her as if she were the most beautiful creature in existence—though to be blunt, she wasn't. But she was there and willing to give us the answers we sought but were afraid to ask our brothers."

"And did she?" Carolina hated the way her voice wavered and her lip quivered.

"Not all of them."

"Then...What happened?"

John gripped his knees with his palms and his jaw ticked. "We decided on an order. I was to be last." His lips formed a thin line that made little white lines appear around his mouth. "She'd brought us each a pint of ale with her, and despite my not drinking a drop, in a matter of minutes after Matthew Finch began taking his turn, I was just as sick as Oliver Vine, who'd consumed his pint and mine as if it were water.

"I tried to hold an impassive face and convince myself nothing was wrong. She'd come willingly. Besides, it was her profession. This wasn't anything she hadn't done before. They weren't hurting her. In fact, she acted as if she enjoyed their enthusiasm. But no matter what I told myself as I tried to find anything else to look at to distract myself from what was going on, I couldn't quell my unease. Then, my turn came."

Without thought or hesitation, Carolina reached her trembling hand to his. Though this was a story no new bride would love to hear, it seemed it was just as hard for him to tell as it was for her to hear.

He turned his hand over and wrapped his fingers around her hand, giving her an affectionate squeeze. "I couldn't do it, Carolina." His voice and her heart cracked simultaneously. "I couldn't shame her and my family that way. My brother didn't deserve to bear the shame for my actions. And, for as absurd as it might seem, considering she'd just entertained four of my friends, I didn't think that woman deserved to be shamed that way, either."

"What of you?" She heard herself ask.

His cloudy blue eyes met hers. "For a boy of fourteen, it would seem that it was more shameful *not* to take my turn. My friends openly questioned my ability and taunted me as I helped her to her feet and gave her my shirt and breeches to replace the now filthy and torn garments she'd worn to meet us," he said thickly. "I don't know what happened to her after that. I made sure she had all the money I'd carried with me and rode my horse back to Eton clad in only my smalls. That's when I was caught."

"I see," she said, commanding her numb fingers to squeeze his for reassurance. "You were sent home the next day?"

He nodded.

"Why didn't you explain your part?"

He shook his head. "It wouldn't have mattered. It wasn't that I was in trouble for hiring a prostitute, but for sneaking out."

"Oh. And the other boys?"

"I didn't turn them in, if that's what you're wondering. But a few days after I'd been sent home, the story spread, and we were all called back to discuss the matter again," he said almost off-handedly. "There wasn't an actual rule that said anything about what boys did in their personal time; however, the schoolmaster was a prig and took every excuse to send me home that he could."

He twisted his lips. "Not that I didn't sometimes deserve it. This particular incident wasn't the first time I'd gotten in trouble, but it was by far the worst and was never forgotten.

"And it seems six years later, it still hasn't been. That's why I can't go back, Carolina. The archbishop has somehow been informed of what happened that night, and he no longer believes I am fit to lead the lost souls of England to redemption."

She gave a wobbly smile at his attempt at a jest. "Can you not explain to him the extent of your involvement and that you did the right thing?"

"It won't matter. According to Edward the story has circulated around London already. If I had a title like Edward or pursuing a profession in the military, this wouldn't matter, but likely the rumors and exaggerations will make it impossible to weather as a vicar."

"But isn't that what the Bible is all about? Love, redemption and forgiveness?"

"Yes. And even if those who fill the pews each Sunday don't believe it, the Bible is also full of immoral sinners in need of those things. But sometimes it's hard to see your own mistakes, when someone else's are so blatantly obvious. I think that's the archbishop's real motive. I might have been innocent that night, but nobody except those who were there knows that." He gave his head a shake. "But it matters naught, because until some machine is invented that can wipe clean the mind of anyone who's ever heard the story, one version or another will always be remembered. This isn't one that goes away."

"So what does all of this mean?"

"Besides that I cannot return to England and live the life of a respectable vicar?" he asked with a hint of his usual crooked smile.

She nodded.

"That depends on you, Carolina," he said, the humor once again gone from his voice and face. "Since we are not legally married, you have a decision to make."

~ Chapter Twenty-Eight ~

John could barely hear his own words over the sound of his blood roaring in his ears. What would she say? Would she agree to marry him now that she knew the truth of his past, or would she not want to tether herself to a man who truly would live out the rest of his life in exile?

"May I ask you something?"

"I would have told you," he blurted. "Perhaps when you were giving birth to our first child and were already angry with me. But I would have. There just wasn't a good time to tell you before we married." He snorted. "I didn't even think I'd marry you until just hours before I did, and for some reason, our ride to the city didn't seem the most appropriate time. But I swear I would have told you."

She pressed the tips of her delicate fingers to his lips to stop his sudden flow of immaterial explanations. "As charming as it is that you thought to tell me of this while I'm delivering our first child and not wanting to ruin our elopement with this, I hadn't planned to ask if or when you planned to tell me. I might be a bit...er...lively at times, but I'm not completely silly. This isn't one of those things you just blurt out. Even I understand that. But that wasn't my question, anyway. I already know you would have told me."

He knit his brow. What else could she think to ask? Surely, she had to know by listening that he hadn't found enjoyment in what he'd seen. She should also understand now why he was so coarse with her the first time. A lump formed in his throat. He hadn't meant to hurt her; he just didn't know that he would.

"John?"

He started. "Sorry. I was..."

"Thinking of the same thing I was, I suppose," she said with a telling blush. "It's all right, John. I couldn't possibly hold *that* against you. Besides, you certainly made up for it soon after."

"Then what was it you wanted to ask me?"

"Why would you think I'd have changed my mind?"

His mouth opened and closed, but no words came out. "I—I don't know," he said at last. "I thought you might think less of me and decide I wasn't the man you wanted to spend your life with."

"How could I possibly feel that way? You did the right thing."

"But I didn't go out there intending to do the right thing. I went out there just as set on bedding her as my friends."

She waved her hand through the air. "That may be. But I don't think you'd be the same man that you are today if you hadn't gone. And he's the one I love..."

John's heart soared, and elation at her admission of love cut off whatever else she was saying. She loved him. Of course, he already thought she might, but to her hear say it— "Wait. What did you just say?" he asked, as the words she'd said following her confession of love started filtering into his mind.

"I said that I don't understand why you'd think so little of me as to think I'd throw you over now that I know the truth." That usual light in her eyes was gone now, replaced with a stony hardness he hadn't seen before. "Do you think so little of me that you believe I'd leave you now that your future is uncertain?"

He pressed his lips together. "No. But I wanted you to know that you have a choice. That you do not have to be condemned to be the wife of a depraved warehouse laborer, if you don't want it."

She lowered her lashes and shook her head. "I know better than to think you're trying to talk me out of the commitment I made to you."

John reached forward and tipped her chin up, so she couldn't look away unless she really tried. "It won't be easy, Carolina. There's a man I met in Boston who said he was looking for someone to start a church somewhere in New York. I refused him at the time, and I don't know if it's still available. But I'll go to Charleston tomorrow and send him a letter explaining the situation. If he doesn't see fit to hire me or doesn't need me, then all that's left is a mill, or warehouse, or some other equally laborious job. You do understand what that will mean, don't you?"

She nodded and threw her arms around him. "I don't need money, John. I just need you."

John wrapped his arms around her and pulled her to him. "You do know we won't be able to hire someone to help around the house or help you with the children?"

"I don't care about that. I don't want anyone raising my children, but me. And you, of course," she added, almost as an afterthought.

"Well, I should hope so," he added with a chuckle. He scattered kisses along her cheek on his way to her mouth. "We should probably get to sleep," he murmured against her lips.

"Of course," she murmured back, not taking her lips from his.

He pressed a chaste kiss on her lips. "I should go. Now that my chances of ministering to the lost souls of England have evaporated, I need to be more mindful of what I do while here in America, or we might have to leave this country as well to escape my tarnished reputation."

She grinned at him. "You don't actually have to leave."

"I think I do," he said, desire thick in his voice. "A few more minutes in this room with a bed and your sultry smile, and I might be tempted to knowingly dishonor you."

That brazen minx had the nerve to peer down at his lap. "Oh, I see."

"Yes, and now you know why I must bid you a good night," he said, brushing another kiss across her soft lips.

"You can stay if you want," she said.

Honor and desire began a battle that would have no victor in his mind. He *wanted* to stay. They wouldn't do anything they hadn't already done. But still, he shouldn't. "Carolina, you know that I want to stay more than anything. But I can't. I can't share your bed again until we're properly married."

"Sure you can," she argued, reaching for something on her nightstand. She straightened, showing him a needle she held between her fingers.

Instinctively, he closed his legs together. "What exactly do you plan to do with that?"

She laughed in that carefree way she always did that made his innards flip. "Not what you're thinking." She took to her feet and pulled back the coverlet. "Take off your boots and shirt and lie down."

He stared at her. Was she cracked? "Carolina, I don't think this is a good idea."

"If you'd prefer not to share my bed, I'm sure my mother's is comfortable."

He scowled. "There's nothing wrong with the barn."

"Are you saying you'd rather sleep with the animals than me?" she asked lifting her dark brows.

"No," he said slowly, still eying the needle in her hand.

"Take 'em off," she encouraged with a gesture to his feet.

He obliged, then removed his shirt and climbed into her bed. "Nothing will happen, Carolina."

"Oh, something's about to happen," she muttered, covering him with a sheet.

He shut his eyes and willed the vivid memories of the last time they were in a bed together to leave his mind. "What are you doing?" he demanded as her soft breasts pressed against his chest.

"Making a bundling bag," she said as if that meant anything. She moved farther down his body, her soft body pressing against his and making him hard. "Hold still or I might prick you."

He groaned at her unintended reminder of what he'd like to be doing with her tonight. "You must stop this madness."

"Not until I'm done."

"And what, pray tell, is it that you're doing?"

"Sewing the sheets together."

He caught her eye. "And you think that will stop me?"

A slow smile spread her lips. "Yes. And if you get tempted, just remember, I'll be sleeping with the needle by my side."

~Chapter Twenty-Nine~

Carolina wasn't sure who got less sleep: her or John. Between the two of them fidgeting or trying to get closer to the other and being stopped by the barrier she'd sewn between them, it was pure torture.

"This is ridiculous," John said, attempting to tear the row of seams between them just as the first ray of sunshine filtered in through the window next to her bed.

Carolina laughed at his attempt to free himself from the bag she'd sewn him into, starting at the top of his left collarbone then going all the way around his body to stop at the right, sealing all of him except his neck in a pocket of sheets, just the way Marjorie had described.

"Carolina, please, have mercy on a man and come help me," he said, scowling.

Carolina smiled and climbed on top of him. "I rather like you this way."

"You mean, at your mercy," he said, craning his neck just enough to give her a quick peck on her cheek. He looked so helpless trapped in his bag; it was adorable.

"Just so." She bent to give him another quick kiss and was taken by surprise when two bare hands came up and took hold of her.

"Got you," John growled, rolling her onto her back and showering her with kisses.

"You tricked me."

"Just a preview of what life will be like as my wife," he said between kisses.

"The kisses or the trick?" she asked, pretending to push him away.

He gently nipped her jaw. "Both."

Good, because there was no way she'd want one without the other.

He nipped her again and she squealed.

"Shh."

"Don't worry," she said, running her knuckles over the coarse stubble on his cheek. "The worst they can do is demand we marry, and we've already decided to do that anyway."

His smile vanished, and he rolled off to the side. "About that."

"Yes?" She ignored the way her voice hitched on the word. Surely he wasn't about to insist they wait to get married until he secured a job. Though, it wouldn't surprise her since he was such a serious sort at times. "John?"

He brought his hand up to idly scratch his cheek. "Do you remember what I did just a minute ago?"

"Yes. I also remember agreeing to remarry you last night," she said pointedly.

"I remember that, too." He flashed a smile at her. "But I meant, do you remember when I pretended I was trapped?"

"Yes." Was he addled? His kisses were drugging, but not *that* drugging.

"Right. Well, I might have played a similar trick on someone else," he said with a slight cough; his face turning an unusual shade of red.

"What have you done?"

"I might have played a trick on your—" *cough, cough, cough.*

"You what?" she asked, trying not to laugh at the way he was struggling to keep a straight face, despite his body's reaction to his obvious discomfort.

He took a deep breath; then another. "I told your father that I didn't plan to marry you—"

"Yes, I do believe I was in the room when you made that pleasant announcement," she said sarcastically. "I was the one who entered the room as your wife, stood beside you when it was explained that we weren't legally married, then remained frozen in place as you announced to our families you had no intention of making me your wife and left."

He knit his brows, twisted his lips, and cocked his head to the side. "That was *you*?"

She playfully swatted at his arm. "Yes, and I already know you told my family you wouldn't marry me—" she frowned— "though I still don't know why. You didn't talk to Edward about your trouble from England until after you'd said that."

"Yes," he agreed. "And I also talked to your father privately, later."

"And you told him again that you had no intention of marrying me?" she asked, to clarify.

He nodded. "I want something from him, and he wants something from me." He came up on his knees and pushed a tendril of her dark hair behind her ear. "No matter what, I intend to marry you, but I don't want him to know that until he agrees to give me what I want."

"What is it you want? Employment?" She sorely hoped not. It had been hard enough living in this madhouse for nineteen years. Any longer and she might need to be locked away.

His rich chuckle brought her from her thoughts. "Do you think my prospects are so dim I'd have to accept work here?"

"No," she said quickly. "I just didn't know if you'd planned to work here until you hear back from your friend in Boston."

"Carolina, I mean this as no offense to you, but there isn't enough gold in England that would make me want to work here another day. The only reason I worked here as long as I did was because of you."

She started. "You did?"

"Yes. I had enough to pay the passage before my sunburn."

"You'd planned to marry me even then?"

"No," he corrected. "I didn't plan to marry you. I just—" his cheeks reddened— "I wasn't quite ready to leave yet."

"I knew it, you rascal. I knew you felt the same way I did the night we met."

He tipped one shoulder up. "I don't know if I'd go that far. But you seem to think my eyes were speaking to you that night, so I can't deny it completely." He straightened. "But regardless of how I felt for you then, I do love you now, and I plan to make you my wife as soon as I can. But I need your help."

"You mean you need me to pretend we haven't decided to marry," she said flatly.

"Exactly. Just until I get what I want."

"And is this how a future Man of God should be acting? Playing tricks and being deceptive?"

"Ah, but you forget, we don't even know if I will be a Man of God or a coal miner."

"Nobody will get hurt by this, will they?"

"No."

"Well..." She tilted her head to the side and tapped her index finger against her cheek. "If nobody will be hurt by it, and it's for the greater good—" she queried him with her eyes, waiting for him to nod— "then I suppose I'll play along."

"Good. I thought with your flare for dramatics you'd enjoy this."

He was right, of course. As long as nobody would get hurt by his scheme, she saw no reason not to join him.

He dressed and went to the window. "How did you get down from here the night I came to your window?" he asked, poking his head outside.

"I climbed down the tree that's in front of the other window." She pulled on her stockings and slipped her feet into her shoes. "Why?"

"I don't think it's wise we go down to breakfast together."

"So you'd planned to avoid that by jumping out the window?" she asked flatly. When he nodded, she laughed. "And you thought *I* had a flare for dramatics. You can just take the backstairs down to the kitchen and then wait there a few minutes before joining us for breakfast." She finished dressing then stepped into the hall and motioned for John to join her when she saw that it was clear. "Go through that door and go slowly down the stairs; they're steep."

John placed a chaste kiss on her temple and then walked very carefully to the door she'd indicated.

Carolina took a deep breath and made her way to the dining room, hoping it was still too early for anyone else to be up yet.

No such luck.

Gabriel and Father were already seated at the table, and the thunderous footfalls of a four-year-old descending the stairs echoed throughout the house.

"I see we'll all have a pleasant breakfast together," Mother said a moment later, gliding into the room just as Carolina was taking her seat.

"Not quite all of us," Father said with a pointed look at the empty chair beside Carolina.

Carolina shifted in her seat. Father was clearly unhappy and likely it was because of whatever John had asked him for. "I'm sure he'll be along soon."

"He'd better be. We have things to discuss," Mother said, placing her napkin in her lap.

Just then, to Carolina's great relief, John walked in and wordlessly took the vacant seat Carolina had saved him.

"Where have you been, Uncle John?" Alex asked before anyone else could.

"Taking care of things I hope you never have to worry about," he told the boy.

"Well, I hope he does," Edward said, frowning. "I would like to have grandchildren one day."

Beside him, his wife nudged him and John shook his head. "You'll have to excuse Edward. He often speaks first and thinks second."

"Then he and Lina shall get along quite well," Gabriel teased.

John shook his head again, slower and with a hint of sadness on his face this time. "I don't know..." he said without much emotion, staring at Gabriel who winked then turned back to his breakfast.

Carolina's heart skipped a beat. Gabriel knew what John was doing, and he seemed to be willing to playact with them.

"They may not spend much time together," John continued with a casual shrug. "There will be an ocean dividing them, after all."

Father's dark eyes locked with John's, a silent message passing from one to the other. All movement and noise in the room evaporated, giving way to amazement at the intensity in John's blue and Father's gray eyes. Neither man seeming to back down. Thank goodness John wasn't fibbing about the ocean separating her and Edward, or he'd give himself away with one of those coughing fits he was prone to have when he was found out.

The silent tension filling the air made it too thick to so much as breathe. Even little Alex seemed transfixed on the stare-down going on between John and Father.

A muscle in Father's cheek ticked, and Carolina was sure she'd find John's hands clenched into fists in his lap if she could tear her gaze away long enough to look. But she couldn't. Like everyone else in the room, she didn't want to miss a second of what she might forever remember as the true final battle of the Revolutionary War.

"Whatever it is the man wants, just give it to him, Calvin," Mrs. Ellis snapped, only adding to the tension.

"Is that what you want, Hazel?" Father asked, his eyes not leaving John's.

"Yes," she said. "Lina and I have a wedding to plan."

Carolina twisted her lips and fought the urge to look down at the end of the table to confirm that was her mother speaking with that nauseating, sweeter-than-sugar tone and not a being from another planet that had taken over her body.

"All right, John, you win" Father said slowly. "I'll free Bethel the day you marry Carolina."

~ *Chapter Thirty* ~

Relief coursed though John and all the constricting tension drained from his body. To swiftly be replaced by two arms wrapping around his neck and pulling him close.

"Thank you! Thank you! Thank you!" Carolina cried, scattering kisses on his cheeks. Only a few short weeks ago, he'd have cringed at her unbelievably bold behavior, but now he welcomed it. Partially, because it drowned out Mrs. Ellis' shrill protests about freeing Bethel; but mostly, because he'd come to love this woman more than anyone, and her happiness was what he valued above all else.

From the corner of his eye, John caught sight of Edward whose eyes were shimmering with amusement and shoulders shaking with mirth. John shook his head. Edward had once predicted he'd marry a woman as spirited as Carolina—and like it. There was no use in denying it, that's exactly what he'd done, but he didn't like it. He loved it.

"Don't be thanking him yet," her mother said. "He hasn't actually married you yet, and until he does, Bethel will continue her duties."

"Of course," Carolina agreed automatically, taking her time about releasing John.

"Very well, I think we could host the wedding four weeks from this Saturday," Mrs. Ellis continued, turning to Edward and Regina. "Will that be all right with you?"

"It won't be all right with me," John said through clenched teeth.

"And why not? You do want it to be proper, do you not? She does only get one chance at a wedding, you know."

"She may very well be carrying my child already. I won't allow speculation about why she's giving birth not even eight months after we're married." Not to mention, he didn't think he'd survive four more days without having her again, let alone four more weeks.

"He's right," Edward agreed, picking up his fork and stabbing at his eggs. He brought his fork up close to his mouth and looked straight at John and Carolina. "Better to have it believed they married so they could start a family, not married because they'd already started one."

John grinned at his brother. He could say whatever he wanted. Carolina was not one to be scandalized. "As Edward so eloquently put it, I wouldn't like Carolina's virtue to be speculated on."

"Well, it's not like it's untrue," her mother argued.

John reached for Carolina's hand under the table. "Carolina, what do you want?"

"You're right, someone will surmise—"

"Forget I said anything about that. Nobody but us will know the truth unless you tell them when we married," he cut in, chastising himself for being so careless in what he said and how it might make her feel. "When do *you* wish to marry?"

"I—I don't know. As soon as we can?"

"Is that what you want or are you saying that because you think it's what I want to hear?"

"What do you think?"

He chuckled. "Will this Saturday be soon enough?"

"This Saturday?" Mrs. Ellis shrieked. "That's in four days! That's not enough time to plan a proper wedding and replace Bethel."

"It had better be," John said, eliciting a wide grin from Carolina.

"But—but—but—" Mrs. Ellis started.

"Stop your protesting, woman," Mr. Ellis said with a scowl. "It's not as if we have a lot of guests to invite."

Mrs. Ellis moved to protest again, but John had no intention of listening and motioned for Carolina to join him outside.

"Thank you again, John," she said, as soon as they were outside; tears filling her eyes.

He wrapped her in a hug. "I told you I'd find a way to help Bethel."

"I know and I never doubted you."

That made one of them at least. "I need to leave for Charleston now."

"To post your letter?"

"And find a job."

"Do you have an idea of where you'll find one?"

He poked his bottom lip out in an overdone frown and nodded. "I think so, yes. I plan to ask Mr. Morrison for my old job back."

"You want to work for him again? I thought Gabriel said he cheated you?"

"He did," John acknowledged, pushing a lock of her silky hair from her eyes. "But I think he did it so I'd be forced to come back to see him, and he could try to talk me into taking a job from him again."

"Do you really think that was his reason?"

John thought back to the day when Mr. Morrison had stuffed his wages into his pocket. "I think so. He'd asked me to stay on, no less than four times, and had never cheated me before. It had to have been on purpose."

"That, or fate," Carolina added, smoothing his lapels. "The Lord does work in mysterious ways, does he not?"

He dropped a kiss on her forehead. He'd been so wrong in his original assessment of her. She'd make a great vicar's wife. If only he was certain he'd be a vicar. He pulled back. "If I don't come back tonight, then I'll be back by Saturday."

She blinked her eyes rapidly and the gesture tore at his heart.

Pulling her close to him, he whispered. "It'll be all right. Gabriel will be here to make sure nothing happens to her while I'm away. He loves her as much as you do. He'll keep her safe. Now, give me a kiss. I'll be back by Saturday."

***

"That boy won't be back, and you're about to lose your only chance at a somewhat respectable future," Mother said, for what had to be the hundredth time since John had left on Tuesday.

Carolina ignored her and pulled her white lace stocking up. John might not always use the most respectable tactics for accomplishing his goals, but he wasn't the kind who'd make bad on a promise. He'd promised her he'd come back, and he would. She knew he would.

"You do realize your wedding is to start in an hour, and nobody has heard a word from your groom since he left?" Mother asked, likely just to be annoying.

Praise the Lord that after today, Carolina wouldn't have to spend another moment alone with her mother. A pang of guilt settled in her chest at how cruel that sounded. But that guilt was quickly extinguished when her mother spoke again.

"Charlie is already downstairs waiting. I'll go speak to his mother to see if he can stand in as the groom."

Carolina whipped around to face this heartless creature she had to claim as her mother. "You have got to be the most selfish, faithless person I've ever met."

"No. I am rational. A characteristic you seem to be sorely lacking."

Carolina recoiled at her mother's words. "Don't," she hissed. "I might not be the meek, demure miss you wanted your daughter to become, but I am not the imbecile you believe me to be, either."

"Are you sure? It would seem the man to whom you've pledged your love has given me no choice but to believe he won't be coming back for you. Even that lofty lord of a brother of his disappeared with his wife and child, after claiming to have to go on some sort of an adventure." She twisted her lips in disgust as she said the words. "I had believed that at least he being a baron would mean there was some honor in the family. But frankly, I'm not sure those weren't paid actors."

Carolina shook her head as a red haze clouded her vision. Her mother's stupidity didn't even deserve an answer. John would not abandon her. She slid her feet into her slippers and grabbed her parasol, then walked from the room, her mother trailing right behind her.

"Lina, I am just trying to protect you. I won't have it spread around the countryside that my daughter was abandoned at the altar by some English bounder."

"After everything that's happened, you're still trying to push me to marry Charlie," she said in disbelief.

"He's a nice boy," Mother argued.

Carolina stopped on the stairs and turned to face her mother, then in a low voice said, "Yes, he is exactly that: a boy. I know you and Mrs. Fields would rather live your lives denying it, and I hate to be so cruel as to be the one to point it out, but it's the truth."

Mother pinched her lips together. "A boy he may be, but he might be your only choice. So I'd suggest you start speaking better of him."

"And I'd suggest you start speaking better of John."

"Yes, love?" said the object of her affection as he rounded the corner. "Did you want me for something?"

"Only to make me your wife," she said, grinning.

He returned her grin and extended his hand toward where she was standing on the stairs. "I think I can manage that."

~Chapter Thirty-One~

John couldn't contain the grin splitting his face. But no matter how besotted he must appear, he had no intention of hiding the joy he felt at seeing his bride walk down the aisle toward him, clad in a dark blue, white lace-trimmed gown with tears shining in her eyes.

He was rewarded most sweetly when a grin took her lips and stayed there throughout their vows.

"'Lations, Lina," Charlie said, coming up to them as they made their way to where a long buffet table of food had been set out for the guests.

Carolina released John's hand and gave Charlie a hug. "Thank you, Charlie."

"Congratulations, Lina, Mr. Banks," Charlie's mother said with a surprisingly congenial smile.

"Thank you, Mrs. Fields," Carolina said uneasily, her gloved fingers making idle movements on the handle of her parasol. "I thought to come see you. I just couldn't think of what to say." Was it just John, or did she seem slightly uncomfortable? She had no reason to be.

He was about to come to Carolina's defense and explain, as nicely as he could, why Carolina couldn't possibly have made a good wife to Charlie, but was spared when Mrs. Fields spoke again.

"I know." She sighed. "It's best this way, I think. It might have pleased Charlie to no end to spend each day in your company, but I doubt that would have been quite as enjoyable for you."

Carolina swallowed. "I'm sorry," she said quietly. "I don't think I'm who he needs."

"No, you're not," she agreed, not unkindly. "Perhaps he'll find her one day. But it's most clear the two of you belong together."

"Isn't it though?" Mrs. Ellis intoned. "I knew these two would make a match of it all along."

John and Carolina shared a secret smile and then walked away without bothering to respond.

"May I have this dance?" he asked as the musicians strummed the first note of what would be the first song they'd dance to as a married couple.

"You remembered," she marveled as the first song they'd danced to in Charleston began to play.

He squeezed her hand. "Of course I did. How could I possibly forget? A man always remembers what's going on around him during those life-altering moments."

"Like when he realizes he's just fallen in love," she teased as he spun her around to the music.

He cocked his head to the side. "I don't believe so, no." He remembered music was involved when he first realized he was in love, but it certainly wasn't this song.

She swatted at his shoulder. "Say what you want, but you were in love long before the melody."

"Let me guess; my eyes told you this in that stuffy Charleston ballroom."

"Of course they did. When I could see them, anyway," she amended. "Your long hair kept falling in your eyes, blocking my view."

He shook his head. No matter what he said, he'd never get her to give up on her belief, nor would he want her to. That was just another thing about her that made her unique.

After the first song, a few of the neighbors joined them on the yard. "Who's that?" he whispered, spinning Carolina enough so she could see the young lady dressed in a faded purple dress, standing on the far end of the lawn.

She smiled. "Oh, that's my friend, Marjorie. She's the one who suggested I bring you lemon water for your sunburn."

"I'll have to be sure to thank her," John said.

"If you'd like, I can introduce you so that you can."

The eagerness in her voice caught him unaware. "I'd be honored."

Because she was Carolina and did not have a worry in the world of what others would think, she stopped dancing mid-step and tugged him by the hand toward the young lady in question. "John, I'd like you to meet my friend, Marjorie Reynolds."

"It's a pleasure to meet you, and I must thank you for the brilliant advice you gave Carolina. I appreciated it very much."

The young lady's eyes went wide and her cheeks turned crimson.

He turned toward Carolina who was on the verge of laughter. "Is something amusing?"

"He's not thanking you for *that* suggestion," Carolina said, waving her hand through the air. "Although he should be; he enjoyed being sewn up in a bundling bag just as much as the lemon water. He'd just never admit it."

John looked at the girl in amusement. Carolina was right, he'd never admit to enjoying the bundling bag—mainly while she was sewing it and right after it came off. But he had enjoyed it.

"I must be getting back before they notice I'm gone," Marjorie said.

Carolina reached for her hand. "Thank you for coming. It means a lot to me that you came, even if it was just for a few minutes."

Tears welled up in the girl's gray eyes. "I wouldn't have missed saying my goodbyes for anything."

"Goodbye, Marjorie," Caroline said, hugging her friend for what might very well be the last time.

"Goodbye, Carolina." She wiped her eyes and turned toward John. "It was nice to meet you, John, and I wish you both the best of luck."

John stood frozen as the young girl ran off. "Why is she in

such a hurry?"

"Mother terrifies her."

"Lina's not jesting, either," Gabriel said from behind them.

John and Carolina turned around. "Do you lack the manners to know not to creep up on someone like that?" John asked, scowling.

"No," Gabriel said without hesitation, an unusually blank expression on his face. "Mother asked me to come and collect you two. For some reason, all the neighbors gathered here today to see the two of you."

"Mother doesn't like Marjorie, and I daresay the feeling is reciprocated," Carolina confided as they made their way back to the small crowd of thirty neighbors who'd come out to witness their wedding.

"John," Edward said, walking up to John and Carolina after they'd rejoined the crowd and were surrounded by their little group of guests. "We need to be leaving soon if we're to get a good night's rest before our ship leaves tomorrow."

John nearly laughed at Edward's blatant lie. When they'd come by John's lodgings last night, he'd said they planned to stay in Charleston another week, at the least, while Mr. Rivet stuffed an opossum they'd trapped while exploring the lowlands. Another trophy to adorn their awkwardly decorated townhouse to symbolize their love and remember their adventures together, he supposed. Likely Edward's excuse was because he was ready to be away from Carolina's mother. He understood that.

"As I was saying, where would you like Regina to put it?" Edward asked, jerking John from his wandering thoughts.

"I can take it," Carolina offered, extending her hand toward a very quiet Regina.

Edward stood back and gave a pointed look to Regina, who blushed a little, then handed Carolina a little parcel wrapped with brown paper and white twine.

"You might wish to read the note before you open it," Regina said quietly.

Carolina plucked the note off the top and held the parcel in one hand as she lifted the note closer to her eyes with the other. Color rose in her cheeks. How unusual. He glanced to a seemingly disinterested Regina and Edward and then leaned over her shoulder to read what they could have possibly written to make Carolina's face grow redder by the second.

Dearest Carolina,

He'd recognize Regina's writing, full of soft swoops and gentle curves, anywhere, and his body relaxed considerably. She was one of the most respectable ladies he'd ever met, but that still didn't explain Carolina's reaction, so he continued.

Having not known you very long, we weren't sure what we should get you for a wedding present. But having been a new, inexperienced bride myself, I realized what I needed most wasn't dishes or silver, but some <u>instruction</u> when it came to certain matters...such as that of the duties of a wife.

Now, I know you're entering into this marriage a little better prepared than I was when I married Edward; however, a lady can never have too much knowledge when it comes to certain aspects of her marriage. So yesterday, when I was at a bookshop in Charleston and found a copy of the very book I found so....shall we say...<u>enlightening</u> that Edward keeps a copy in his study and I keep a copy by my bedside, I knew exactly what a blushing bride, such as you, needed more than anything else.

I hope you enjoy the book and the wonders it will do for a certain aspect of your marriage.

Regina

John had barely reached the end, when Carolina's startled cry rent the air. John snapped his head up and caught a glimpse of his brother's broad grin just before narrowly missing the opportunity to take hold of his wife as she darted toward four-year-old Alex who had managed to take the book from Carolina's grasp and was now running through the yard, ripping the paper off and hollering, "A present! A present!"

~Chapter Thirty-Two~

"Now I have you all to myself," John whispered as he carried Carolina over the threshold to the little room he'd rented in Charleston until he could afford something better.

"Yes, and we can use the present from your brother and sister-in-law to help us decide how we should spend our first evening together," she teased.

John set her down and plucked the book from her hand. "As long as the ideas come from Song of Solomon, I'm agreeable."

She laughed. "You're incorrigible."

"I know." He moved his lips to the crook of her neck and between kisses said, "That's why you love me."

"Indeed it is," she agreed.

"You're not angry with me about that are you?"

Carolina shook her head and ran her fingers through his blond locks. "Why would I be angry with you because Edward and Regina gave me a Bible?

"Because it's my fault there was a scene," he said sheepishly.

"You mean you told them to buy it and then bribed Alex to take it from me and start running around unwrapping it?"

"No. But I might have issued a challenge from which Edward had no intention of walking away."

Ah, that explained it. "No. I'm not upset; nor was I embarrassed. I actually thought it was quite comical once I realized what it was; clever, too."

"Clever? Edward?"

"Actually, it was from Regina," Carolina corrected, pushing his coat off his shoulders. "The note only *implied* the book was inappropriate. But once I learned what it was, I realized her wording fit perfectly to lead me to think one thing, when it was actually something else. As I said, it was very clever on their part."

John shook his head at her logic. "I have no idea what I did to deserve a woman like you, but I sure do love you."

"I do believe I shall never tire of hearing you say that," she said, pulling his shirt free from his breeches.

"Oh? And how do you feel about me showing you?" he asked, making quick work of the row of buttons that went down the back of her gown.

She shivered. "It's been a while. I might need to be reminded."

His eyes darkened, and he pressed his lips to hers, his hands moving at a harried pace to remove her gown and untie her corset.

She sighed his name against his mouth, curling her fingers into his hair and pushing her body against his.

"Carolina," he rasped. He pulled back long enough to undress her and then himself. Then his lips were back on hers, and his hands were gliding up and down her body.

She felt boneless in his hold and offered no protest as he carried her to the bed. He kissed a path down her neck and across her collarbone, his hands freely roaming her naked body. Her skin, which was already warm, heated to new heights when he bent his head and drew one of her nipples into his mouth.

She arched her back, offering him more.

But he didn't greedily take more of her breast into his mouth; instead, he went slowly, driving her mad with want. "You wicked man," she said on a sigh.

He flicked his tongue across her nipple as if to acknowledge he understood her meaning perfectly, and he hadn't forgotten what it took to send her into a frenzy of need.

"Oh, you think to torment me?" she breathed, moving her knee to rub ever-so-lightly against the inside of his thigh and all the way to his—

"You minx," he growled, leaving behind her right breast and turning his attention to the other. This time, his wicked ministrations were not so soft and gentle, as he sucked the crest of her breast fully into his mouth and began plying its budded peak with his tongue.

She cried out, and his only response was to bring his hand up to her right breast and cover it with his large palm.

Carolina's body reeled with excitement under his touches, and she tightened her grip on his hair when his mouth released her swollen breast and he pressed open-mouthed kisses down the bottom curve and to the top of her ribs, then down her abdomen. He guided her body down to the edge of the bed, leaving her legs to hang off the side, and then moved to stand between her parted thighs.

She watched him as he straightened and let his eyes linger slowly down her body, taking a measure of pride at the way his throat worked and his body reacted to the sight of hers. She loved that she could be the one to do this to him.

A slow, wolfish smile bent his lips. "Most people don't get a second wedding night. I'll have to be mindful to take full advantage of this rare opportunity."

Carolina wrapped her legs around his waist and drew him closer to her, then reached up and pulled him down to her. "I'm sure you will. But have you forgotten that your bride isn't a missish virgin, and she might end up being the one to take advantage of you?"

"Don't make a promise you don't mean to keep, love," he said, his voice raw and his eyes full of challenge.

Carolina tightened her legs around his waist and made a rolling motion with her hips, a silent acknowledgement that she'd accept his challenge.

He groaned and followed her lead, rolling onto his back and bringing her to sit on top of him.

She placed her hands on his shoulders and leaned forward, pressing kisses all over his hard, muscled chest.

"Carolina," he breathed, bringing his callused hands up to

glide along her back.

Her skin tingled and she continued to kiss his chest and then his neck. She nipped his shoulder in the way he'd done to her so many times when they'd first married.

He groaned and she pressed her bare breasts flush against his abdomen. "You temptress."

She slid farther up his body until her lips were on his and her breasts were pressed against his chest.

He moved his hands up to her shoulder blades and used his thumbs to gently rub the sides of her breasts while she kissed and nipped his soft lips. He kissed her back, startling her. His hands stilled and he brought his right hand up to her cheek, digging his fingers into her hair.

She sighed his name against his lips and then broke their kiss, forcing herself to sit up. "Do you suppose..."

"I do," he rasped.

She grinned and moved her hips down his body until she was straddling his erection. Using her left hand on his shoulder for leverage, she lifted up on her knees and moved him into position, then slowly sank down.

"Carolina," he grunted, moving his hands to her hips.

She covered his hands with hers and pulled them away. "I said I planned to take advantage of you, and that is exactly what I'm doing."

"No, you're torturing me," he corrected, bucking his hips to push himself further inside.

She rose up on her knees just enough to almost separate them, but not quite. "That'll be enough of that, Mr. Banks," she warned with a shake of her head.

He groaned again and threw his arms over his head.

Slowly, she sank back down, taking every delicious inch of him inside her, then rose back up on her knees again, repeating her movements. She had no idea who was tormented more by this and frankly didn't care. She leaned forward and placed her hands on his shoulders, her hair now falling down to drag across his abdomen and chest with each of her movements.

She locked her eyes on his face as she continued to move over top of him. She increased her pace and his face hardened, his eyes traveling back and forth from hers to her breasts, that bounced with every movement she made.

She bit her lower lip and sped her pace again, that familiar fluttering in her abdomen forming. John lifted his hands and cupped her breasts, shaping and caressing them in time with her movements. He moved the pads of his thumbs across her hardened nipples, and she cried out his name.

Carolina lowered her upper body closer to his, her energy waning but her desire still strong. As if he knew what she wanted but realized she might not be able to achieve it on her own, he slowly moved his hands to her hips and held her tightly as he began meeting her movement, pushing himself further into her than she'd been able take him on her own.

His shoulders grew tight under her hands, and his face contorted in what she might think was pain if she didn't know any better. "Now, Carolina."

His ragged command was her tipping point and suddenly wave after wave of delicious euphoria came over her as she continued to move her hips in time with his. Somewhere through the fog, she heard herself give her husband the same raw command he'd given her, followed only a second later by a savage shout filling the air as John slowed his movements to a stop.

Breathlessly, Carolina collapsed on his broad chest and pressed her ear against his heart that was beating as rapidly as her own. "Perhaps next time my plan for torture will work," she whispered.

John's big hand came up and pulled her hair away from her damp face. "You always have a plan, don't you?" he teased.

"Yes, and it always goes the opposite way I want it to," she confided, repositioning herself to be more comfortable.

He idly ran his knuckles against her cheek. "How so?"

"I wanted to drive you mad with need, but it was me who ended up mad and you had to help...you know..."

He lifted one shoulder up in a lopsided shrug. "I don't see a problem with that. In fact, I think it's a good thing we both need the other's help in order to find our own satisfaction."

"Perhaps so," she acknowledged, seeing the logic behind his words. "But that still doesn't make me feel better about all my failed attempts to gain your attention."

He laughed. "Do you mean bringing me the water while I was working or having me find you swimming naked?"

She sat straight up. "W-what? You saw *me* swimming naked?" The memory of the day her mother had hosted that wretched supper and how she'd gone swimming earlier that day to forget about her anger over her mother's wish for her to marry Charlie flashed in her mind. "Is that why you decided to marry me? Because you'd seen me naked?"

"No. I've already told you. I didn't decide to marry you until just hours before I came to your room that night. But—" he rolled her off of him and turned on his side to face her— "my decision had nothing to do with seeing you naked. I'll admit it didn't deter me, but I was already in love with you before then—I just hadn't realized it yet."

"Oh? And when did you realize it?"

He grimaced. "You don't want to know."

"Yes, I do. I want to know if my plans worked."

"This wasn't planned, believe me."

Now she was more curious than before. "How do you know?"

"Because even you wouldn't stoop so low as to ask Charlie to play awful music just so you could show off your musical abilities."

"How do you know?" she demanded, trying in vain not to laugh. He was absolutely right though, she'd have never done that to poor Charlie.

"Because that's not like you, Carolina," he said, idly stroking her hair. "You might be a bit overly flirtatious at times and perhaps a little too spirited at others, but under it all, you have a pure and tender heart like I've never seen before. You open yourself up to be mocked by protecting someone else who doesn't know the difference, and you offer to be punished in the stead of someone you love." He snorted. "You even rubbed salve on a sunburned man who'd been unnecessarily nasty and even brought him cool water and a picnic—"

"That wasn't my idea, it was Bethel's."

He frowned. "What, tending to me while I was in bed?"

"No, I did that on my own. But before you were sick, she told me to bring you the water...and the picnic."

"She did, did she? And what did your brother think?"

Her face heated. "He told me to stop annoying you and let you come after me," she mumbled, still as unimpressed by his advice now as she was then.

"And did you ask anyone else for ideas?"

"Marjorie. But she was no help, either. When I told her what Bethel and Gabriel had said, she got this strange expression on her face but didn't tell me anything."

"That's because there was nothing to tell," John said, grinning. "Don't you see? What Gabriel told you to do, and Bethel helped you do, and Marjorie didn't tell you to do is exactly what you needed to do: just be yourself. Carolina, I won't lie. I don't like theatrics and openly expressing feelings. My mother and father did both of those things, for different reasons, of course, but their reasons weren't genuine. With you, it is. When you giggle or grin, it's because you're truly happy. When you cry, it's because you're genuinely upset. When you say something, no matter how blunt, it's because you mean it. Those are the things I love about you, Carolina."

"I love you, too, John," she said, bringing her lips to his.

"Good. How about if you show me at least once more, then

we'll go to sleep so you'll be able to appreciate the surprise I've arranged for you for tomorrow."

"Surprise?"

He nodded, taking her right breast into his hand and rolling her nipple until it hardened. "Didn't you wonder why I was a little late this morning?"

She shook her head and bit her lip, too distracted by what he was doing to her to respond.

No more words were spoken as John made love to her again, going slowly and showing no sign of the urgency they'd both had before.

When they were done, she laid her head on his chest and twirled his chest hair between her fingers. "I never doubted you were coming today, John," she said a while later when their breathing had returned to normal.

"I know," he said. "But I think you've already forgotten who you've married."

"No, I haven't."

"Good. Then you should know, your ploy to extract the details from me about your surprise tomorrow is futile."

She groaned. "You do know me well."

"Indeed. But I look forward to getting to know you even better over the course of the rest of our lives."

"And I look forward to discovering all of your tricks and schemes."

"That's not going to work, Carolina. Go to sleep."

Sighing, she said, "Just as I said before, none of *my* plans ever work."

He chuckled and dropped a kiss on the top of her head. "Don't worry. A few years in my company and you shall be a grand schemer, indeed."

Grand schemer apprentice or not, she couldn't hardly wait to spend every day for the rest of her life in his company.

~ Chapter Thirty-Three ~

John could hardly sleep in anticipation of what he had planned for Carolina today. This, of course, was a scheme he'd been unable to make work without help and was pleased when Edward agreed to provide it. His chest constricted for a moment. After Edward returned to England next week, he might never get to see him again.

He shoved the thought from his mind. As Carolina had said the other day, the Lord works in mysterious ways, and perhaps one day they'd reunite.

But that wasn't important because today was for Carolina.

And Bethel.

"Wake up," he whispered. "It's time for your surprise."

Her eyes snapped open and he chuckled. "Is it here? Do you have it?"

"No. We have to go out to get it."

She sighed and leaned her head back against the pillows. "Can it wait?"

He picked up his pocket watch. "No. We only have an hour."

"All right," she said with a wide yawn.

He helped her out of bed and into her gown. "You don't mind if a few others join us, do you?"

She eyed him curiously. "No."

"Good," he murmured. "I didn't think you'd mind seeing Bethel on her first day as a free woman."

"Thank you," she whispered, planting a kiss on his cheek. "I know you used your brother's title as leverage for her freedom, but to me, it was still you who made it possible for her to be free."

"Even if I used ungentlemanly methods?" he teased, pulling

his shirt over his head.

She flicked her wrist. "I wouldn't consider it ungentlemanly if it was for the greater good."

"You're so forgiving it's frightening," he said, not even half-jesting. "Come on, let's go."

"Where are we going?"

"You'll see."

"Why are we at Reynolds Ridge?" she asked flatly when they arrived, by way of a rented team and wagon. "And why is Bethel dressed like a queen?"

He didn't answer her right away; he just pointed to where Silas was standing by a tall oak tree, dressed in one of Edward's nicest costumes."

"What's going on?" she repeated.

"I's ta git married," Bethel said, leaning in to give her a hug.

"Bethel, you don't have to. If you need a place to stay until you can find employment, I'm sure we can find something." She looked to John for agreement.

"But I's wants ta," Bethel argued, shooting her a big smile. "Rem'ber I's told yous if I's e'er free, I marry Silas?"

"Yes," Carolina said, nodding. "But you don't *have* to if you're not ready."

"Oh, I's ready, Miss Lina. I's been ready s'nce I first met him. Jist like you," she added with a giggle. "'Sides, af'er wes marry, wes both be werkin' here at Reyn'lds Ridge. For pay."

Tears filled Carolina's eyes. "I'm honored to be a witness, Bethel."

"Excellent," Edward said. "Now, we just have to wait for the judge."

"Thank you," Carolina said with a slight hitch in her voice.

Edward obviously knew she was thanking him for the trouble he'd gone through to find someone who'd actually marry the pair, because he bowed and said, "It was no trouble. I was glad to do it." He frowned. "I just hope he didn't change his mind."

"He didn't," said a masculine voice.

"Mr. Murphy?" John and Carolina said in unison, snapping their heads in the direction of the new voice.

Mr. Murphy removed his hat. "Mr. Thaddeus Murphy, at your service."

"But we thought..."

"You were an impostor," Carolina finished for him.

Mr. Murphy laughed. "No. The impostor is right where he belongs: in a holding cell awaiting trial. I am the real Mr. Murphy."

Neither John nor Carolina spoke. Nor did they move. Just stood there, staring at the man as if they had no idea what to believe.

Wordlessly, Mr. Murphy pulled a thick piece of vellum from his pocket and handed it to John.

John scowled and opened the thick paper. He blinked at the scrolled text. "We've been married this whole time," he breathed, handing the paper to Carolina.

"But you never gave us a certificate," she protested after she'd finished reading it for herself.

"I was playin' cards," he argued with a scowl. "And winnin', too. I didn't have time to fill out all the papers just then. I had to get back to my cards.

Carolina stared blankly at the man, much the same way John imagined he was doing, too.

"I went to deliver it the next day, but you weren't at the inn I suggested. I didn't know how else to reach you," Mr. Murphy continued.

"That place wasn't fit for a man to take his new bride," John said through clenched teeth.

The older man shrugged. "By the looks of you two that night, I thought it was the best you could afford. Besides, all you really needed was a b—"

John quelled the man's words with an icy stare he'd perfected from years of seeing his father give it to anyone who dared cross him. "If we were married this entire time, then..." He trailed off and looked to Bethel.

"She's still free," Gabriel said, coming up behind them; Mr. Ellis rolling along next to him. "Even *you* couldn't have been so devilish to have planned this."

"No," John agreed. "I sincerely thought we weren't married." He frowned. "Well, not originally, but later. After you showed me the newspaper article about the man who'd been jailed for impersonating a judge and marrying couples, that is." And now that he knew they *had* been married that whole time, he'd be lying if he didn't admit he was a little disgruntled at not being able to spend those four grueling nights in Carolina's bed instead of alone in his.

He glanced at a laughing Carolina and the thought was gone. Giving up four nights of passion was an easy price to pay for the smile on her face at seeing Bethel granted freedom and marrying a man who loved her as much as John loved Carolina.

"Just think," Edward said, grinning. "Not only did you get to enjoy two wedding nights, but each year you'll also get to have two anniversary celebrations."

John liked the man's logic. "Or, if I forget one, I'll get a second chance to redeem myself," he mused.

"Oh, if you plan to celebrate twice, you'd better remember a gift for each occasion," Carolina said, wagging her finger playfully at him.

~Epilogue~

April 1812
London

"And just where do you think you're going?" Carolina asked, as her gentle hands fell on John's shoulders.

He tried to push her hands off. "Did you see who your daughter just left with to go to the gardens?"

"*My* daughter?" Carolina asked, grinning; her hands still firmly in place on his shoulders.

"Yes, she's your daughter when she does something scandalous, such as leave the ballroom with a man who has somehow earned himself the nickname of the Dangerous Duke."

Carolina rolled her laughing brown eyes. "I wouldn't worry overmuch about them. Neither of them have that look about them when they see the other."

He groaned. "Carolina, please. I cannot have her outside with that man. Eyes speaking or not, she *cannot* marry him." He grimaced. "I won't allow any of my daughters to marry a gentleman like him. They all need quiet country vicars."

Carolina's throaty laughter filled the air. "You'd have to pay such a gentleman a hefty price to take one of our daughters; and I daresay, even the amount of money you saved from when Edward was still trying to give you money, won't be enough to buy all three of them quiet country vicar husbands."

He scowled. "How unfortunate." He pulled his wife close to

him and led her into the first steps of a waltz.

"You can't blame that on me."

He looked down to where their bodies were closer than was proper, even for a waltz. "No? I do believe it is their scandalous American behavior that will present the most challenge in their quest to find husbands."

She lifted her brows. "Oh, do you now? I think it's their stubbornness."

"That's another trait they get from you, too," he protested.

A grin took her lips. "Perhaps, but they also get their scandalizing tongue from your brother."

He heaved an exaggerated sigh. "That seals it. They're destined to lives of spinsterhood. Scandalous behavior and stubbornness on both sides, they're hopeless."

That sweet smile he'd spent the last twenty-four years adoring spread her lips. "You never know. There might be hope for them after all. There was for both of us."

He nodded as a movement along the back wall caught his attention. He frowned. "What do you make of that?"

Carolina craned her neck to see. "Hmm, he doesn't look very pleased, does he?"

"No; and neither does she," John commented about the stony look on their eldest daughter Brooke's face as she entered the ballroom and went to stand with her youngest sister Liberty. John pulled his wife closer to him as he sought out his forlorn middle daughter Madison, who was turning down yet another gentleman's request for a dance. "I do wish things had worked out for Madison and that Leo fellow."

"I know you do," Carolina said, sadness for her daughter's lost chance at love lacing her voice. She offered him a watery grin. "And so do I."

"Is that because his eyes spoke of love or you wanted your daughter to have the same experience as you and forever love an English bounder?"

"Both," she admitted. "But mainly because the love was mutual, and for as much as she might deny it, I think she still loves him and always will."

Silence engulfed them. Carolina was likely right, as she always was where their girls were concerned. She might not have the most genteel and eloquent way about her, but even after all these years, she was still genuine. And that's what he loved most about her.

"Not to worry, love," he said softly. "We'll stay here as long as we need to in order for her heart to mend."

"Of course," she agreed with a swallow.

"Just think," he said, trying to lighten the unease that had settled over them at the mention of Madison and the string of misfortunes she'd suffered. "With three daughters as...er....spirited as ours, I doubt there'll be an unexciting moment."

"Including this one," Carolina said, her eyes flaring wide as their oldest daughter's voice drifted to them from across the ballroom.

"Just so," he agreed, letting her go.

He walked over to a nearby column and leaned against it, shamelessly watching his wife walk away. Ironic that when he was younger, he'd have never been able to imagine his life with a woman like her; and now, he couldn't imagine what his life would have been like without her.

Author Note

One chilly December afternoon when I was eighteen, my best friend and I decided to marry. Instead of having a large church wedding with me in a flowing white gown and him in a tuxedo surrounded by hundreds of our closest friends and family, we thought it would be better to go to the courthouse in a neighboring city.

We were not, however, married at the courthouse by a judge but rather were lured across the street and married in this "quaint", if you will, building. Following the quick wedding, where I wore a see-through dress sans slip and he wore a nice suit with borrowed (and dirty) shoes and socks, we were assured our wedding license would be mailed to the courthouse to be put on record.

Being the diligent worrier that I am, I needed to ensure it was received and insisted I'd bring it to the courthouse myself. When I brought it in to have it stamped and recorded, the lady behind the counter puckered her brow and declared that she'd never heard of such a man performing weddings, but that didn't mean he wasn't licensed to do so...

That was a few years ago, and to this day, I still find myself checking court records on occasion, waiting to discover that this fellow has been imprisoned for fraud and I'm not really married.

If you enjoyed *His Yankee Bride*, I would appreciate it if you would help others enjoy this book, too.

Lend it. This e-book is lending-enabled, so please, share it with a friend.

Recommend it. Please help other readers find this book by recommending it to friends, readers' groups and discussion boards.

Review it. Please tell other readers why you liked this book by reviewing it at one of the following websites: Amazon, Barnes and Noble, or Goodreads.

Other Books by Rose Gordon

BANKS BROTHERS' BRIDES

His Contract Bride—Lord Watson has always known that one day he'd marry Regina Harris. Unfortunately nobody thought to inform her of this; and when she finds that her "love match" was actually arranged by her father long ago in an effort to further his social standing, it falls to a science-loving, blunt-speaking baron to win her trust.

His Yankee Bride—John Banks has no idea what—or who—waits for him on the other side of the ocean... Carolina Ellis has longed to meet a man whom she can love, so when she glimpses such a man, she's determined to do whatever it takes to have him—Southern aristocracy be damned.

His Jilted Bride—Elijah Banks *cannot* sit still a moment longer as the gossip continues to fly about one of his childhood playmates, who just so happens to still be in her bridal chamber, waiting for her groom to arrive. Thinking to save her the public humiliation of being jilted at the altar, Elijah convinces her to run away with him, replacing one scandal with one far more forgiving. But when a secret she keeps is threatened to be exposed, it falls to Elijah to save her again by revealing a few of his own...

His Brothers's Bride—Henry Banks had no idea his brother agreed to marry a fetching young lady until the day she shows up on his doorstep and presents the proof. To protect the Banks name and his new sister-in-law's feelings, Henry agrees to marry her only to discover this young lady's intentions were not so honorable and it wasn't really marriage she sought, but revenge on a member of the Banks family...

Coming 2014
Gentlemen of Honor Series (Regency)

Secrets of a Viscount—One summer night, Sebastian Gentry, Lord Belgrave hauled the wrong young lady to Gretna Green. When her identity is exposed, the only obvious solution is to get an annulment. Only, just like his elopement plans, things didn't go as planned and while she has reason to believe they are no longer married, he knows better. Wanting to make things right for her, he offers to help her find a husband —what neither counts on is it just might be the one she's still secretly married to.

Desires of a Baron—Giles Goddard, Lord Norcourt is odd. Odder still, he has suddenly taken a fancy to his brother's love interest, the fallen Lucy Whitaker. Lucy was once thrown over by a lord and she has little desire to let it happen again, but she's about to learn that his desires just might be enough for the both of them.

Passions of a Gentleman—Having been thrown over twice already, Simon Appleton has given up his pursuit for a wife—especially if his only choice is the elusive Miss Henrietta Hughes. But when he discovers a secret about her, he's not above helping to protect her...

Already Available:

SCANDALOUS SISTERS SERIES

Intentions of the Earl—A penniless earl makes a pact to ruin an American hoyden, never suspecting for a moment he'll lose his heart along the way.

Liberty for Paul—A vicar's daughter who loves propriety almost as much as she hates the man her father is mentoring will go to any length she sees fit to see that improper man out the door and out of her life. But when she's forced to marry him, she'll learn there's a lot more to life, love and this man than she originally thought.

To Win His Wayward Wife —A gentleman who's spent the last five years pining for the love of his life will get his second chance. The only problem? She has no interest in him.

GROOM SERIES

Four men are about to have their bachelor freedom snatched away as they become grooms...but finding the perfect woman may prove a bit more difficult than they originally thought.

Her Sudden Groom—The overly scientific, always respectable and socially awkward Alexander Banks has just been informed his name resides on a betrothal agreement right above the name of the worst chit in all of England. With a loophole that allows him to marry another without consequence before the thirtieth anniversary of his birth, he has only four weeks to find another woman and make her his wife.

Her Reluctant Groom—For the past thirteen years Marcus Sinclair, Earl Sinclair, has lived his life as a heavily scarred recluse, never dreaming the only woman he's ever wanted would love him back. But when it slips out that she does, he doubts her love for his scarred body and past can be real. For truly, how can a woman love a man whose injuries were caused when he once tried to declare himself to her sister?

Her Secondhand Groom—Widower Patrick Ramsey, Viscount Drakely, fell in love and married at eighteen only to be devastated by losing her as she bore his third daughter. Now, as his girls are getting older he realizes they need a mother—and a governess. Not able to decide between the two which they need more, he marries an ordinary young lady from the local village in hopes she can suit both roles. But this ordinary young lady isn't so ordinary after all, and he'll either have to take a chance and risk his heart once more or wind up alone forever.

Her Imperfect Groom —Sir Wallace Benedict has never been good with the fairer sex and in the bottom drawer of his bureau he has the scandal sheet clippings to prove it. But this thrice-jilted baronet has just discovered the right lady for him was well-worth waiting for. The only trouble is, with multiple former love interests plaguing him at every chance possible, he must find clever ways to avoid them and simultaneously steal the attention—and affections—of the the one lady he's sure is a perfect match for him and his imperfections.

FORT GIBSON OFFICERS SERIES
American Historicals based in Indian Territory mid-1800s)

The Officer and the Bostoner—A well-to-do lady traveling by stagecoach from her home in Boston to meet her fiance in Santa Fe finds herself stranded in a military fort when her stagecoach leaves without her. Given the choice to either temporarily marry an officer until her fiance can come rescue her or take her chances with the Indians, she marries the glib Captain Wes Tucker, who, unbeknownst to her, grew up in a wealthy Charleston family and despises everything she represents. But when it's time for her fiance to reclaim her and annul their marriage, will she still want to go with him, and more importantly, will Wes let her?

The Officer and the Southerner—Second Lt. Jack Walker doesn't always think ahead and when he decides to defy logic and send off for a mail-order bride, he might have left out only a few details about his life. When she arrives and realizes she's been fooled (again), this woman who's never really belonged, sees no other choice but to marry him anyway—however, she makes it perfectly clear: she'll be his lawfully wed, but she will *not* share his bed. Now Jack has to find a way to show his always skeptical bride that he is indeed trustworthy and that she does belong somewhere in the world: right here, with him.

The Officer and the Traveler—Captain Grayson Montgomery's mouth has landed him in trouble again! And this time it's not something a cleverly worded sentence and a handsome smile can fix. Having been informed he'll either have to marry or be demoted and sentenced to hard labor for the remainder of his tour, he proposes, only to discover those years of hard labor may have been the easier choice for his heart.

About the Author

USA Today Bestselling and Award Winning Author Rose Gordon has written eight unusually unusual historical romances that have been known to include scarred heroes, feisty heroines, marriage-producing scandals, far too much scheming, naughty literature and always a sweet happily-ever-after. When not escaping to another world via reading or writing a book, she spends her time chasing two young boys around the house, being hunted by wild animals, or sitting on the swing in the backyard where she has to use her arms as shields to deflect projectiles AKA: balls, water balloons, sticks, pinecones, and anything else one of her boys picks up to hurl at his brother who just happens to be hiding behind her.

She can be found on somewhere in cyberspace at:

http://www.rosegordon.net

or blogging about *something* inappropriate at:

http://rosesromanceramblings.wordpress.com

Rose would love to hear from her readers and you can e-mail her at rose.gordon@hotmail.com

You can also find her on Facebook, Goodreads, and Twitter.

If you never want to miss a new release, visit her website to sign up to be notified and you'll be sent an email each time a new book becomes available.